I0823652

Ruby Falls

Also by Gin Phillips

The Well and the Mine

Come In and Cover Me

Fierce Kingdom

Family Law

Ruby Falls

GIN PHILLIPS

Atlantic Crime
New York

FIRST EDITION

Printed in the United States of America

This book is set in 11.5-pt. Scala Pro by Alpha Design and Composition of Pittsfield, NH.

First Grove Atlantic hardcover edition: March 2026

Library of Congress Cataloging-in-Publication data is available for this title.

ISBN 978-0-8021-6692-0
eISBN 978-0-8021-6693-7

Atlantic Crime
an imprint of Grove Atlantic
154 West 14th Street
New York, NY 10011

Distributed by Publishers Group West

groveatlantic.com

26 27 28 29 10 9 8 7 6 5 4 3 2 1

To Mary Ella Marshall, who never stopped going full throttle on rope swings, hunting for snakes, and playing in the mud. She taught me that grown women can have as much fun as they want.

And to all the women throughout the centuries whose lives were one long series of gifts given—meals cooked, homes created, loved ones cared for—whose names weren't recorded by waterfalls or billboards or history books.

The gray bat skims along the cave floor, missing the man's forehead by millimeters. The way bats maneuver is sorcery, like much of what happens down here, and if he were alive, his heart would be racing.

The room is pitch-black. The floor is damp and wet, not that any of that matters now.

His clothes have gone stiff as his limbs. He is turning to mineral, maybe, a thought that would have struck him as funny once.

Continents collided to form this mountain. At some stage it was the floor of an ocean, and ancient sea animals are frozen in the rock, long-term residents. The walls around him are encyclopedias of eras and species and deaths, but he will not be joining the fossils. Someone is bound to come for him, eventually.

He is not alone. All the animals are welcoming him, bats and newts and a spider, near translucent. Ants have found the bare skin of his neck, drawn by the gaping hole. The millipedes, slower but bigger, are cutting in line. He is a banquet, and if he were alive, he would be equally disturbed and pleased. He dislikes—disliked—wastefulness, so it's appropriate that at least the bugs are getting something out of his murder.

December 1928

He's likely dead, although the children have no idea: Frances is shelling peas in her nightgown, aluminum pan wedged between her knees, and Justin keeps jabbing at logs and stirring up ash as if he's accomplishing something. Eunice has miraculously kept track of the peel from her Christmas orange, and she's arranging pieces of it along the floorboards.

Ruby, though, is wound so tight that she's run into the doorjamb twice. Her face is smooth as a pond, but the rest of her is off-kilter. Her dark hair is falling from its bun as she takes the poker from Justin; she props it against the brick and bashes her shoulder into the mantel as she stands. She'll be covered in bruises tomorrow.

"Time for bed," she says to her children, cheerfully.

Ada watches them all from the armchair, her hands still pink from finishing up the supper dishes. She's sat in this same spot many other nights, watching her closest friend's family go through their nighttime routine. At eleven, Justin is past his mother's shoulders. His body is sloughing off childhood, and he's all sharp angles.

"Already?" he asks.

Ruby nods and presses her cheek against her son's head. He leans against her briefly and disappears toward the back bedroom, but Frances doesn't slow down with her peas. She shakes a shell loose from her finger, and it teeters on the edge of her pan.

"I don't know where Cannonball is," she says.

"In your bed as usual, I imagine," Ruby says. She rubs at her shoulder and looks toward the front door. She's been looking toward it all day.

"I might have left him on the porch," Frances says, still shelling.

"You never take Cannonball on the porch," Ruby says. "He's by your pillow. Go on and check, and I'll finish up the peas."

"I'll be done in a minute, Mama."

Frances is being pigheaded enough that Ada wonders if she's more aware than they've suspected. It was Frances who answered the phone yesterday afternoon, after all. *A happening in the elevator shaft,* one of Leo's men had said. *He needs to come as soon as possible.* Why any fool would leave that message with an eight-year-old girl, Ada still doesn't understand, but when Leo came home his daughter met him at the front door to tell him there'd been an accident, and he didn't even take his hat off before he drove to the excavation site.

No tragedy, his men told him. The opposite. They'd been jackhammering and found an opening in the rock. The rush of air meant the passage might lead somewhere, which is the sort of thing Leo has never been able to pass up. The man can't resist a leap in the dark. When Ruby's family picked up and left Indiana, he followed her here to Chattanooga. She married him a year later. When he heard the old tales about sealed-off caves at the bottom of Lookout Mountain, he got the lunatic idea to stick an elevator in the middle of the mountain. And, lo and behold, he raised a couple hundred thousand dollars to do it. So when the workmen drilling the shaft for that elevator found a passage to some unknown world, of course, Leo had to crawl into the void. He's always been so sure that good things will happen.

Ada could have told him that his luck wouldn't hold. No one gets everything they want.

Seventeen hours ago, Leo and his men went into that crevice with nothing but flashlights, and they vanished completely. Ada's been here since midafternoon, entertaining the children and helping with chores, but mostly making sure Ruby isn't alone with her thoughts.

The clock on the mantel chimes, an off-key jangle that makes Ada think of loose springs.

"Bring her to bed while I herd the other two?" Ruby asks, nodding at Eunice.

The room still vibrates with the tinny echo of the clock. Ada realizes she's missed part of the conversation. Frances has finally put down her pan of peas, and she's tugging at the hem of her nightgown.

"Sure," Ada says. "I'll get her."

For a moment, Ruby's face ripples and the fear breaks through, but she puts her smile on again as she turns to Frances. The two of them slip away to the back of the house, and Ada turns her attention to little Eunice. The girl is completely absorbed in her orange, flipping pieces of peel and spinning them. She's sitting on her knees, and the soles of her feet are black with dirt.

"What are you doing, baby?" Ada asks.

"Making a new orange," Eunice says.

"You heard your mama say it's time for bed?"

Standing, Eunice lets the orange bits in her hand fall to the floor, shaking her head. Ada holds out her arms. She's afraid the girl will dart away—this would be a bad evening for a game of chase—but instead she comes closer, her wristless baby hands landing on Ada's thigh, bunching up her skirt. Ada wants to jerk away, and she wants to never move. She freezes like when she sees a deer, as if even blinking might break the spell, and she tries to soak up the feeling of the small hand on her, even though she knows she can't. She's learned that well enough. She held her son after he was cold, tried to memorize the weight of his head against the hinge of her elbow and the look of his fingers and toes, as if they were words on a page and she'd be able to picture the letters later and compose the whole of him again.

She can't.

It's unbelievable, still, that she knew the feel of him against her ribs and lungs and bladder for all those months and she waited so long and then he was gone in a matter of days. It could be that way with Leo, too. It can be that way with anyone. The difference in *here* and *gone* is only a breath.

"Come on, sweet," she says to Eunice.

She knows these children well, and sometimes she's forced to sing "Home on the Range" a dozen times before Eunice goes still in her miniature bed, but tonight the girl's breathing slows after the first verse. When Ada comes back to the sitting room, Ruby is sitting in the rocking chair, her hands hanging limp over its arms.

"Thank you," Ruby says. "You didn't have to throw out the water, too."

So she noticed that Ada finished up the dishes. She's always appreciative, Ruby. Quick to notice a kindness and quick to do a kindness herself. Competent, too, even though she's pretty.

"What can I do?" Ada asks. "You need to tell me because I don't know if I'll guess right. You can go down to the site and wait, if you want, and I'll stay with the children. We can try a hand of rummy. We can talk. Do you want to talk?"

"He's always said some of those passages could be filled with water," Ruby says. "He said there could be flooding."

"If there was flooding, he'd turn around," Ada answers, which is true.

She could say more, of course. She could promise that Leo will be fine. She could say that all manner of possibilities might have kept him in the caves for this long, but neither one of them would believe it. They are both women who get frustrated with stupidity, which is one reason they're friends.

"He's good at climbing," Ruby says. "I trust that. He knows what he's doing."

"He does. Everyone knows he's good at it. Smart and safe."

She wishes she hadn't said "safe." The word is hanging in the air, and she struggles to think of something else to say that will knock it loose as Ruby kicks off her house slippers, tucking her bare feet under her.

The air has a hint of orange in it.

"I don't want to talk," Ruby says.

"You're not doing a good job of convincing me."

Ruby laughs, louder than the joke deserves, and Ada would like to believe it lets some pressure out. The bad kind of feelings swell up like blisters inside you. They need to be popped one way or the other, but Ruby's not the sort to cry in front of an audience.

They've always made each other laugh. It's another good reason for friendship, but it's turned out that pain is a better one. The ties that bind start to unravel when your measure of joy is too different: Ada learned that with her neighbor Joyce Springer, happy as a clam with her four boys and her tall husband who still has all his teeth. She and Joyce used to make a point to hang out the wash together, but after the baby died, Joyce started going silent, always dipping her hand into her pocket for a clothespin and sticking it in her mouth, as if Ada didn't know she was well able to talk around a clothespin. But Ada was glad enough for the silence. She didn't want to hear about those four boys any more than Joyce wanted to tell her about them. It's hard when one person has a full pitcher and another has an empty one. Joy is like money that way—Rockefeller could never be friends with a beggar.

She and Ruby were big-bellied together, and they had their babies the same month and they lost them within a month of each other, too. They never talk about it, but their pitchers are always next to them.

"You should head home," Ruby says. "I'll be fine. And Gerald will miss you."

"He'll make do," Ada answers. "He's likely out there on the porch, watching for that old fox."

She has no idea if Gerald might be missing her. It's not the way they talk with each other. But she suspects that if her husband had the choice of picking her or a fox to walk toward him through the glow of the streetlamp, he'd pick the fox.

Someone knocks at the door, and both she and Ruby jerk in their chairs.

"Thank God," Ruby says, on her feet in one motion, running to the door and throwing it open even as Ada winces, knowing Leo would never knock on his own door.

She's right. It's Ruby's mother and sister, both of them attractive and dark-eyed like Ruby, only shorter and finer-boned. Ada doubts either of these women could have hefted the basin of dirty dishwater into the backyard, and if sometime tonight a man comes to the door to announce that Leo is dead, surely neither of these women will be able to catch Ruby if she keels over.

The last time Gerald had one of his spells, Ada caught his full weight, all two hundred pounds of it, and she eased him down so he didn't have so much as a bruise.

She should go home, though. There's nothing to do here but keep Ruby company, and family has first rights to that. Ada will go on home and sit with Gerald on the porch and maybe they'll see that fox or maybe they'll listen to the owls, and if there's any word about Leo, news will spread quickly enough.

She stands, going through the niceties with the women at the door—it's so good to see them—oh, it's an easy walk home—she only lives three doors down—yes, the house with the crepe myrtle—when the front door opens. No knock at all, only the turn of the knob, and a man is standing there.

She's not sure, in that first second, whether he's Black or white. Every inch of his skin is muddied, and his shirtsleeves are stiff on his arms. His face is like charcoal, and the whites of his eyes shine too bright.

Leo.

He's back, and he doesn't seem to be hurt, although she can smell him from here. He's wide-eyed and vibrating like a dog spotting a squirrel.

Ruby pushes past them all, wrapping her arms around her husband's shoulders, her forehead pressed against his filthy neck. He locks his arms around her as well, his helmet in his hand, dipping his head down in what is maybe a hello but possibly an apology.

"We found something," he says. "We found something I can hardly even—"

"You couldn't send a message?" Ruby says, pulling back. Her voice is wet, not angry. "We thought—"

He tosses his helmet through the still-open door, and it lands with a clatter on the porch. He nods a quick hello at all the women who are not his wife, running a hand over his face. It doesn't make a dent in the dirt.

"They told me when we got back up top that everyone was worried," he says. "I'm sorry. The time got away from me and I—listen to me, honey. You won't believe it. That passage—no one had any idea it was there. Two hundred and sixty feet down on the west side of the shaft, maybe twenty inches high. We shimmy in and we go on like that for six hours before we can stand up. We come out into muck and a foot of water, but eventually we come to a room like an auditorium. Maybe a hundred feet high. And, listen, there's a waterfall—a big one—underground."

"People talk all the time about going in those caves before the railroad sealed them off," Ruby says. "No one ever mentioned a waterfall."

Leo shuffles toward her, even though she's only inches away from him.

"Not in the old caves," he says. "This is another level. A middle level that no one even knew about. Maybe no one ever. And we've found it. Ruby, it was like discovering God."

When he smiles, his teeth are as white as his eyeballs. He takes another step and sways slightly. Ruby frowns.

"You're limping," she says.

He runs a hand down her shoulder, and somehow she doesn't object, even though Ada's breathing through her mouth to avoid the stench rising off him.

"I fell in a lake," he says. "At the base of the falls. Are the children asleep?"

He's peering toward the back of the house, and Ada can see eagerness and love even through the muck. This last one was the third baby they buried up at Forest Hills, him and Ruby. Aside from her baby boy, Ada has also lost two others who were only small shapes in a wash of blood. But Ruby still has three little ones and Ada has none, so their pitchers are not identical.

"You can wake them," Ruby says. She still hasn't let go of him.

Leo looks down at himself. "Nah. I want to lay eyes on them, is all. And, if you're lucky, I might even go wash off."

"You might burn these clothes," Ruby says, starting to sound more like herself. "If I'm lucky."

There is no *if*, Ada thinks.

One Week Later
1929

Ada spots Ruby fastening her purse at the bottom of the post office steps. She's been keeping an eye out for her ever since Hilda Delano ran up with a fistful of yams at the grocery store, practically shouting.

"You went into the mountain with him?" Ada calls.

Ruby's breath smokes in the cold air, and her eyes are hidden in the shadow of her hat. "I had to see for myself, didn't I?" she says, grinning.

Ada has heard the story a dozen times since yesterday. Three days after he was given up for dead, Leo Lambert launched himself into the rock again, only this time he took his wife with him.

Ruby ducks her chin into her woolen collar. "He was right. That waterfall was like seeing God. Like when the burning bush talked to Moses—that's what I expected. For God to say something."

Ada finds the answer frustrating. It doesn't help her to picture it in the slightest.

"Was it frightening?" she asks.

They pause at the curb, waiting for a streetcar to pass. A paper bag blows across the asphalt and under the rails; it's smashed by the car and resurrected, floating away over the opposite curb.

"I'd never have done it without Leo next to me," Ruby says. "I'd never even have stuck my head into that first crevice. You look behind you, and it's pure nothingness, like all your strings have been cut. Like a coffin. But when I felt it closing in around me, I'd see his boots kicking along in front of me, and he'd be rambling on about limestone, and I'd settle."

This is more helpful. Ada understands darkness and crawling and coffins.

"So you didn't feel what he feels?" she asks, stepping onto the crosswalk.

Ruby shakes her head. "What do you think he feels?"

"You know very well," Ada says. "It's like he's got electricity running through him."

Last week wasn't the first time Ada has seen Leo vibrate while he talks about shafts and sea level. It reminds her of how her mother talked about four-part harmony and how her grandfather talked about Wordsworth. She has never loved anything so much that her body cannot contain it.

"I felt some of that, I suppose?" Ruby says, in a way that tells Ada she did not. "I could have done without wading through water—oh, and when we got to the end of that tunnel, we had to climb down a rope. My shoulders still ache."

One of the new school buses turns the corner, exhaust streaming behind it. Ada catches the eye of a redheaded boy blowing like a pufferfish against the window.

"Do you want to see?" Ruby asks.

Ada turns away from the pufferfish. She feels sure she's misunderstood.

"Not the falls," Ruby says quickly. "But I could show you the passageway. Leo's put a stop to the drilling until they work out what comes next. The site should be empty, so—"

Most of the time, Ruby Lambert is who everyone expects her to be: She keeps her windows clean and her floors swept and her hair is never stringy and her caramel cake is coveted. When she plays tennis, she expects Leo to hit the ball straight to her so that she won't be forced to perspire. But she is this woman, too, and this is the version Ada likes best.

"Yes," Ada says.

"You want to see?"

"Hush. You know I do."

She wants it desperately, all of a sudden, and she wonders if this is what Leo feels every single moment of the day.

At the hacked-up excavation site on top of Lookout Mountain, piles of limestone stretch in every direction, tall enough that Ada can't see over them. In the middle of the discarded rock, a tower of wooden scaffolding rises over a square crater that looks like it might go to the center of the earth. A bucket bigger than a bathtub sits on the ground next to the scaffolding, attached by ropes and pulleys, and Ada remembers hearing that workers are lowered down the shaft in a bucket, carrying their drills and dynamite with them. She has no idea how she and Ruby are supposed to maneuver this bucket, but Ruby does not pause before slipping under the scaffolding, nerve-rackingly close to the edge of the hole. Beyond her, Ada spots a wooden ladder sunk into the rock itself, even as Ruby is already starting down it into the darkness, pulling an Eveready flashlight from the large bag slung over her shoulder.

Ada follows, holding tight to the sides of the ladder. Ruby insisted she wear a pair of Gerald's work boots, which slide back and forth on her feet so much that she worries she'll miss a rung. She's more grateful for the pair of Leo's pants that Ruby foisted on her—he's a smaller man than Gerald—which don't get tangled the way a skirt would.

At the base of the ladder, they step onto a platform—the shaft goes no further. The sunlight is only a sliver along the base of one wall, and the entire space can't be more than eight feet in either direction. The air is colder than it was up top.

"Gloves," Ruby says, handing them over. She pulls a caver's helmet out of her bag, a lamp already clamped onto the front. "I didn't refill the carbide, but you'll only need a few minutes. In and out, Ada. Just far enough to see what it's like."

Tucking her flashlight in the waistband on her pants, Ruby steps toward a crack in the wall no more than two feet across. She pulls a matchbook from her pocket, strikes a match, and lights the lamp on the helmet in Ada's hands.

When Ada peers into the crevice, she loses track of whatever Ruby is still saying. Her lamp turns the darkness into a landscape as she eases in, headfirst, elbows inching along the rock. There's no way to move forward other than by inches; her light zigs and zags, picking up the angles and curves of the rock. She thought she might be afraid, but the deeper she pushes into the tunnel, the more giddy she feels. She learns to keep her chin down so she doesn't bang her helmet on the ceiling. It takes a full minute to work herself entirely inside the passageway, and then her shoulders and hips start to find a rhythm. Every push and slide reminds her that she has a body, and she hadn't even known she needed reminding.

"He says he's naming them after me," Ruby calls.

When Ada looks back, she's surprised that she hasn't gone more than ten feet. "Naming what?"

"The falls." Ruby sounds almost embarrassed. "He's calling them Ruby Falls."

"That's perfect," Ada says.

And it is. She flattens herself, resting her jaw against the rock, splaying her gloved hands on it. Imagine, having a man give you a waterfall as a present. She thinks of how Gerald brought her tulips, always yellow, that first spring they started going together, and she never worked her way up to telling him that purple ones were her favorite, and then by the second spring he stopped bringing flowers at all. He is a man who only thinks of giving at Christmas. But sometimes when her feet are cold, he warms them in his lap.

They are not unhappy.

She pushes forward again, wanting to feel the rock close around her tighter. She thought the dark would be overwhelming, but she doesn't see it. She sees only the light.

"You can back on out whenever you want," Ruby says.

"Not yet."

Ada does not want to go back. She wants to go deeper and darker and further, and she wants to save up this feeling that her body can take her to someplace she's never seen. There are so many places she's never seen, and this tunnel might lead to all of them.

Two Years Later
1931

She enjoys the precision of peeling tomatoes, the shavings of red and the slap of slices on saucer. In grammar school she watched, horrified, as Lucy Millstone bit into a tomato that still had its peel, and it was like watching someone eat the rind of a watermelon. Now—sunlight hitting the countertop, a mockingbird gulping hackberries outside her window—her fingers have become her mother's as she holds the tomato in one hand and works the paring knife with the other. The peel falls to the counter and sticks.

You taste the dirt when you leave it on, her mother always said.

Ada spins the naked tomato, giving it a good shake of salt. There's no need to slice it. No one to share it with. She may never need a serving dish again. She bites into it like an apple, licking the juice from her chin.

Whatever happened to her mother's platter with the pink roses? It was always filled with tomato and onion, and she can see her mother standing in the kitchen—all the women in her family were always standing in the kitchen—slicing away, and she can see her grandmother next to her, sifting flour like snow, housedress buttoned to her chin.

She buries her mouth in the tomato again. She has her own communion every time she lays out the tomatoes and onion and field peas and corn. All the women before her pull up a chair at the table, tucking their napkins in their laps and going heavy with the salt. *Do this in remembrance of me,* they tell her, and she does.

She's heard that in Africa they worship ancestors. She might, too.

The wind rattles the glass of the window, which never quite shuts all the way. A train whistle blows, as it does dozens of times a day, but she doesn't hear it much anymore. For years after the baby died, she'd wake up thinking she heard his snuffling cries, and she doesn't hear those anymore, either. You can stop hearing anything after a while.

The tomato is gone.

She has no idea how long she's been standing here, but so what? If she stood here eating tomatoes all day long, who would notice? She takes off toward the den, rounding past the fireplace, taking her usual route along the edge of the rug back toward the kitchen table. She likes to move as she thinks, and her feet sometimes start this loop between kitchen and den without her mind's consent. *You're wearing a trail,* Gerald used to say.

Some days when the clock strikes 5:30, she still expects him to walk through the door. For months, she kept seeing him cold in that hospital bed, when she tried to close his mouth but couldn't make his jaw move, and she'll never understand why the men at the bottling plant waited so long to call her after he hit the floor. It doesn't matter now. These days she mostly pictures him coming through the doorway, stomping mud from his shoes.

She stops at the basin, where her breakfast cup and saucer are still unwashed. She gives the dishrag a slosh in the cold water, and a few soap bubbles resurrect themselves. A glimpse of herself in the window captures the threads of gray at her temple, and Gerald once said her hair was like a cord of mahogany, but it is turning into birch.

A single pulled-cotton cloud hovers in the sky: "*I wandered lonely as a cloud,*" her grandfather loved to announce whenever he spotted one of them on its own, and Ada would aways smile even though she'd heard the same line a hundred times.

She was twelve when he moved into their house, long after he'd lost his taste for Wordsworth. He spent his days in a rocking chair and stared at nothing for hours. He'd get up for meals, where he drank black coffee and ate every bite on his plate, and then he'd go back to facing the wall. She thought he'd gone crazy, and maybe he had, but she knows now that he wasn't staring at nothing. He was moving through the rooms inside his head. She wanders them herself now, peeping through doorways carved of memory and bone. She can step into the kitchen on Thanksgiving morning to watch her mother and aunts laughing—*I swanee,* they say—handing each other spoons and holding out beaters for her to lick clean. She can nestle next to her still-healthy grandfather as he reads to her on his porch swing. She can watch her father lift a calf and she can stand up in front of the schoolroom and win the spelling bee in seventh grade and she can go to the ocean with her friend Nellie English, where they saw a thousand shining jellyfish on the sand. She can fling open her bedroom door to see Gerald in the early days, back when they had a contest to see who could catch a lizard faster—she could—and she can see him when they first got married and he would come up behind her and put his hands on her hips when she was cooking, until once she spattered grease on herself and told him *stop that* and he did.

She can watch the light through the window in her childhood bedroom, falling on the yellow sheets. She can watch herself and Nellie picking out patterns for their graduation dresses, poring over lace trim. She is beginning to like these rooms more than any real rooms filled with real people.

It worries her. Her great-aunt—tobacco on her breath—said there comes a time when the past is more interesting than the future. She said there comes a time when all your choices have been made.

Ada is not a toothless old man in a chair. She's forty-six. When Babe Ruth came to town last month, she sat in the bleachers as the Yankees played the Lookouts. They had a girl pitcher as part of the exhibition, and when the girl struck out the Babe and Lou Gehrig, too, the crowd went crazy, applauding and laughing, and Ada realized she was crying. No one seemed to be able to tell the difference, and she wasn't sure she could, either.

If this is grief, she's not sure what she's grieving. It doesn't seem to be Gerald.

The wind is picking up. The air outside is a swirl of dust and leaves and crepe myrtle petals. The phone rings, jarring her to a stop when she didn't even know that she was moving again. She's been circling the dining room table.

"Hello," she says, grabbing the phone from the nook in the wall, and only as she speaks does she realize she shouldn't have picked up the phone because it'll be Ruby.

These days it's always Ruby.

"Ada," says the voice, crackling with static.

Yes. Ruby.

"I know I never got back to you about supper tomorrow," Ada says, looping the cord around her finger.

She's tired of the constant invitations: The charity makes her uncomfortable. While she's well aware of her friends' concerns—they are not subtle people, her friends—Gerald's grandfather built this house, and she owns it free and clear. She has the garden out back, and a woman on her own can eat squash and tomatoes for every meal if need be. She's better off than most people these days. She can always sell the car.

"It's not about that," Ruby says. "I'm up at the restaurant and I need a favor."

This is better: Ada would much rather help than be helped. In the summer months, the restaurant at Ruby Falls hosts dances on the rooftop, and Ruby lends a hand on nights they're short-staffed.

"My heel caught the edge of my skirt when I was coming down the stairs," Ruby is saying. "It ripped nearly to my hip. Could you bring me your black taffeta?"

"It'll be too long on you."

"It'll be fine. If you don't mind the drive. I'm so sorry to ask, but I—"

"I don't mind."

Ruby keeps right on going. "I can't walk around like this. You're a godsend, I swear, and you should at least stay and have dinner."

Ada considers the phone in her hand, wondering if Ruby has only gotten trickier with her charity. But, no. She would never sacrifice her best skirt in the name of kindness.

"It's no trouble, Ruby," she says.

She talks over a thank-you and another apology—she suspects she does this same thing, apologize a dozen times when once would be sufficient—and sets the receiver back in the cradle. The receiver's still rattling as she turns to hunt for the keys. Gerald always kept them in his jacket, and now they float loose around the house. She finds them in the silverware drawer next to the ring of measuring spoons, which makes a kind of sense.

The wind blows her dress so tight against her legs that it's indecent, and a swathe of her hair pulls loose from its pins. She can smell the rain coming as she walks from the parking lot to the honest-to-God castle that Leo had built from limestone left over from the elevator excavation. The whole structure looks like it's out of the Middle Ages, and Ada half expects a drawbridge to swing down as she makes her way up the stairs to the entrance.

Below her, Chattanooga shimmers at the base of the mountain, and, overhead, strings of lights sway along the roof. Bits of waltz and laughter drift over her, and it's a relief to hear evidence of paying visitors. As much as it seemed like Leo was steered to Ruby Falls by the hand of God, it's turned out that God had terrible timing. The stock market crashed while they were excavating the path to the falls. He and Ruby opened the restaurant two days after a mother out in Harriman drowned her three children and hung herself rather than let the whole family starve to death. The tours got started as the banks fell like dominoes, and now the whole world is a row of dominoes: too few jobs and too many bread lines, and no one has twenty cents for eggs, much less a dollar fifty to go stare at a waterfall.

But somehow—in the middle of all the worry and want—the weekend dances here have caught fire. Either the city somehow holds a shocking number of people who can afford dancing shoes or people need an escape badly enough that they don't mind skipping a meal or two to pay for it.

Ada pauses at the base of the front steps as a man shoves through the lobby doors, hat pulled low. He jogs down the steps close enough that she'd swear her skirt whips against his trousers. He doesn't slow or look up when she offers a "good evening." She stops, watching him go. She knows her dress isn't nice enough for these dances—could he tell so quickly that she doesn't belong here? But, no, he's not a fancy type, either. No suit. Not even a tie. As he passes under the streetlight, she realizes it's Talmadge Cunningham, the best of the cave guides, even though he's not thirty yet. The boy needs to learn some manners.

She picks up her pace, relieved to step into the stillness of the lobby. She spots Ruby immediately behind the brass cash register, an empty dance floor and mostly empty tables behind her. If the weather were colder and the roof was off-limits, the band would be playing on the mezzanine and dancers would be packed between the rows of tables and the stone fireplace. For now, though, it's only one white-haired couple finishing up a meal.

"Bless you," Ruby says, holding out her hands for the skirt draped over Ada's arm. She steps from behind the stone desk and offers Ada a flash of leg and garter. Her skirt has nearly split in two.

"You look like a harem girl," Ada says.

"I told you. I'm going to run in the back and change, and then we can order your supper."

"I'm not staying. I didn't dress for it."

She couldn't dress for it. The skirt she's handing Ruby is the only one in her closet suited to this sort of affair, not that she would come to a dance anyway. The world is like Noah's ark—everyone two by two, like the couple at the table.

"What you're wearing is fine," Ruby says.

"It's not. I've seen the pictures in the newspaper. Anyway, I already ate. Was that Talmadge Cunningham who just passed me on the stairs?"

Ruby nods. "Just got off his shift. We can argue about supper when I'm decent. You go sit down and look at the menu."

Ada considers and, after a moment, shrugs. "You need me to watch the ticket desk?" she asks.

Ruby's backing toward the closest hallway, holding the taffeta skirt as a shield. She'll have to restitch her torn one—she has three decent skirts compared to Ada's one, not exactly an abundance. She and Leo may own this place, but they spend their time working, not dancing. "I was only standing here to have something to hide behind," she says. "The party goes until eleven—midnight, if everyone's having fun—but tours stop at nine. No one'll need a ticket."

That's what Ada was hoping. She has no intention of staying. She waits until Ruby disappears down the hall and then turns to head home: She'll make her apologies later. She stops, though, when she notices the sign over the doorway behind the old couple at the table.

TO TOURS, it reads.

She's clicking across the hardwoods before she makes up her mind to do it, striding through the doorway and around the corner. She realizes she's heading to the elevator at the same time she sees its accordion metal door, wide-open. It's famous in its own right as the longest elevator ride in the city, and she rode down it once on the official Ruby Falls tour. She'd hoped being inside the mountain would bring back the feeling of crawling down that narrow passage with nothing but the light of her lamp, but instead the electricity and labels and crowd only pushed the memory further away. She can hardly remember the feel of the rock anymore, which is likely for the best.

Surely, it's for the best.

She glances down the empty hallway. She should not do this. But she can, if she chooses—no one can stop her—and the thrill of that is so much greater than the fear.

She's still looking over her shoulder as she steps into the elevator, and when no one comes, she moves faster. She turns to what looks like a tambourine attached to the side of the wall—a simple-enough throttle. She grips the lever just as the guide did, pulling it even with the red bar—*red for Ruby,* she remembers thinking—and the elevator judders to life. The floor drops beneath her, and the limestone flashes past her through the glass wall.

She didn't expect it to be so easy.

The long drop happens quickly. The elevator slows and stops just as she's getting used to the feeling of falling. As soon as the door opens, she sees that they've turned off the lights on this level. She steps onto the rock floor, and the single bulb from the elevator illuminates the few feet in front of her, leaving everything else in darkness.

Close your eyes, her father used to tell her when he blew out the lamp at night. *Everything will be brighter when you open them.*

She closes her eyes. When her parents had company, sometimes her father would look at her mother and say, "I love that woman more now than when I married her." He would say, "I'm a happy man." She's not sure either of those things were true, but she understands why he liked to say the words. A story gives you shape. She wants to believe she and Gerald were happy, too. One day, though, as he crumbled his cornbread into milk, he said to her, *They'll be planting the squash now,* and it came to her: He wished he'd stayed on his family farm in Clayton. She knew it more surely than if he'd announced it. She knew it from a place truer than words.

The thing was that before they married, he asked what was important to her when it came to setting up house, and she said they shouldn't live near either of their families. She meant it as a gift to him. She wanted the two of them to have something all their own, and she believed he wanted that, too, but instead he'd wanted that same dirt he'd grown up plowing, only he never said. Maybe he never forgave her for it or maybe he never blamed her at all, but he had a sadness about him by the end, and maybe that was about the babies but maybe it was about the farm, and if she had daughters she'd tell them that before you marry you should talk to the man about what he wants and what you want, and also after you're married, you should keep talking.

No one ever said.

Now she's not sure how much either one of them talked or listened, and yet she does miss how he ran a hand over her head every morning. She laid out his clothes and laughed at his crow calls and never cooked carrots because he hated them, and it's stupid to wonder about love—isn't it?—when the proof of it was right there every day.

She opens her eyes, and nothing seems brighter. She expected to be able to hear the falls, but there's no sound at all. She stares into the dark: The path leads to the largest underground falls in the entire United States, the brochures say. A hundred-and-forty-five feet tall. The route is nothing like Leo's original tunnel: The pathways have been blasted with dynamite, widened and straightened and paved so that it's an easy half-mile stroll. She does not like it this way.

If she chose, she could take the elevator down to the lower level of caves where everyone of a certain age in this town wandered until the railroad closed them off decades ago. Leo added bridges and electric lights down there, too, but only so far. They say the wild passages go for miles.

She keeps facing the darkness, though. She has a sense that if she reached past the cone of light from the elevator, her hand would evaporate. Everything in the world that exists is contained in this patch of light.

She takes another few steps. Her toes are in the darkness, barely solid.

She likes how the world shrinks here, and it turns out she has not, after all, forgotten the feel of the rock, the tightness and coolness of it. She thought she buried her longing, but it might have been more seed than corpse.

She makes herself turn around. She pushes the throttle and lifts herself back up to real life. She was barely gone five minutes. The husband and wife in the restaurant are still leaning over their tablecloth and Ruby is walking across the empty dance floor, searching but unworried. Ada makes her excuses, hugs a still-sputtering Ruby, and takes her time strolling back to the parking lot. She passes under the streetlamp and hears the soft thudding of moths. She feels for them, ugly little things, bashing their heads against the glass. They don't even know what they want, and yet they want it badly.

The restaurant is open for dances only on Friday and Saturday, and Ada doesn't want to wait another full week. In less than twenty-four hours, she's passing the empty ticket booth again. No sign of Ruby. It's a little after nine p.m., and a few diners are at the white-clothed tables, but Ada walks quickly and confidently. No one speaks to her.

The elevator is open and abandoned, as she'd hoped. She pulls the throttle to yellow this time because she doesn't want smooth walkways. She wants to slide and crawl and she wants to wonder whether her next step will be onto rock or open air and isn't it odd that with a husband dead and tomatoes for most meals, what she craves is uncertainty?

Labyrinths, Leo once said about the lower caverns. She likes the word.

When she steps onto the bottom level, she's relieved that the lights are off here, too. She's brought a flashlight and a candle. In the light of the elevator, she drops the tote bag from her shoulder and pulls out a pair of Gerald's old pants and boots, which she slides on under her skirt. She rolls up the pants and belts them, then unbuttons her blouse and trades it for his old work shirt. She leaves her bag of discarded women's clothes by the elevator and heads into the dark.

She's been on this tour, too, but it's different with only her flashlight. Her shoulders brush against rock as she walks forward, turning sideways at times to squeeze through a narrow pass. She skims her light over the walls, which are dark gray, unlike the sand-colored ones of the top level. When she rubs a hand over them, her fingers come away black, and she remembers hearing something about soot from train engines.

She should have brought gloves.

When she comes to a spiral staircase cut into rock, she keeps a tight grip on both the railing and the flashlight as she heads down to an even lower level. At the bottom of the stairs, she ducks under a low overhang, and her light catches writing on the wall. Signatures, at least a dozen of them: *George Cowarden, 1911. Tom Wallace, Jackson, Miss., 1842. Eben McAllister.* The words must have been carved by blades. She's lifting a finger toward the letters when her light catches an opening in the rock to her left, long and narrow, like a giant slot in a mailbox. It might be a little over two feet high.

She drops to her knees, considering. She slides her hands in first, watching for anything slithering. She ducks her head inside, and the path in front of her swims in the light. It's awkward figuring how to move herself forward with froggish kicks of her bent legs, and she bangs both her head and her flashlight against the ceiling. In the moment that her feet kick against rock instead of open air, she thinks she cannot do this. She inches forward, though, and the firmness under her hands becomes a comfort instead of a threat. It anchors her.

The route in front of her narrows, too tight, and she veers around it with a kick of her foot. The slab of rock on her left is closing in on her, so she snakes right. The rock is so clean, no mud or moss or crawling things. She maps the possibilities in front of her, and when she finds a taller space where she can raise onto her elbows, she moves faster. She is only a body, and if her mind exists at all, its only purpose is navigation. She has no thoughts other than left and right and forward and push and flatten and bend.

She has no idea how many minutes have passed when she pulls herself into a larger chamber, shoving her head and shoulders free and then pulling her legs to her chest. She shines her light on what might be a millipede embedded in the smooth rock, fossilized. The ceiling ripples like a lake.

She has found something in this dead end. Her house is still silent and the chairs at the dinner table are still empty, but she has found this.

When she gets home, she washes her hands in the sink basin, and the water looks like peanut butter as it runs down the drain.

She dips her head under the faucet, and as she scrubs, she can hear pebbles hitting the basin like the lightest of hailstorms.

She has always known the library holds lifetimes. When she was little, her grandfather would take her to fill up a satchel, but that did not prepare Ada for how she could live a life in the caves by turning pages. She learns that water carved the passageways through Lookout Mountain millions of years ago. She learns about calcite draperies and flowstone and columns. She learns a caver should carry at least three sources of light, and a carbide lamp will last four hours. She learns about Charles Harvey, who was lost in Mammoth Cave for nearly two days after his lantern went out; and Mary Bliss, killed by a rockfall on her wedding trip; and Floyd Collins, who died of exposure after more than two weeks of being stuck underground in Kentucky when a boulder pinned him by the ankle.

She confines herself to the books for a week, and then she makes a stop at W. K. Garmany's for a helmet and rope and carbide. She buys two pairs of men's pants, and no one questions any of it.

Two Months Later
1931

She's at least a mile from the authorized passages: She's ventured deeper ever since she realized that the staff at the castle cleans for at least an hour after the dancing stops. But no one cleans near the elevator, so no one notices a woman hurrying back to the parking lot in the middle of the night. Ada has other time constraints, though: This cartridge of carbide will run out in less than two hours. The two flashlights in her pockets are less predictable. The batteries could last several hours or they might sputter out after a few minutes.

Her sleeve rips, and her elbow stings. She suspects she's bleeding, but she doesn't stop to check. If she bleeds on this rock, will the blood ever come out? In a thousand years, will it still be here?

She sees a widening ahead and lunges forward into a small chamber. A draft is coming from an opening in the floor, and she angles her light to get a view of the uneven ground below. She lets herself down slowly through the hole, dropping the final few inches.

Her ankle turns slightly, but it's hard to care. The corner of the ceiling above her has partially fallen, cracking open to show dark crystals shining like fresh-poured chocolate. The rest of the room glitters as if it's sprinkled with diamonds, every surface sparking in the light as she turns her head.

Like discovering God, she thinks.

She wonders if any human has ever seen this place. She does not want it all to herself. She's heard the caves have been a hideout for outlaws and Civil War soldiers and Cherokees fleeing the Trail of Tears, and she likes to think some of them stood on this same patch of ground, as dry-mouthed as she is.

She pulls off a glove and runs her bare hand down the crystals. She sinks to the balls of her feet, staring: She wants to come back here as she lies in bed tonight, to shut her eyes and take her time.

A chunk of white crystal drips from the ceiling like an old man's beard.

She shakes herself free, mindful of the limits of her lamp, and she has a moment of true panic when she can't boost herself through the ceiling. The opening she dropped through is nearly at eye level, but even with a jump, she can't lift her body weight. She tries a second time—a third—her hands scrabbling on the rock above her before she falls back, staggering. Her ankle throbs.

She takes a breath and jumps again, grabbing at the edge of the opening with both hands, swinging herself toward the wall. She fails a few times until, finally, she lands her feet solidly against the wall, pushing off with enough force that she works one elbow and then the next through the opening overhead. She wriggles the rest of the way, rolling onto her back until she catches her breath.

It feels like more than blood is pumping through her. It feels like she's full of light.

She launches herself back into the tight passageway toward the main cavern. Her headlamp flickers, and she freezes, but the flame surges again. It's a warning. She speeds up, glancing up every now and again at the twine she's tied to guide her way. Time stretches into taffy down here, unreliable, and she thinks she's been fast as she tumbles into a larger passageway, but her lamp goes out entirely.

She has her flashlight in her hand in seconds, shoving back the darkness before she's forced to acknowledge it. The batteries clank against the casing of the Eveready, and in two heartbeats the beam of light lands on the knob of rock where she knotted her twine. She unloops it, relieved. She's on familiar ground now. She checks Gerald's old wristwatch, which has lodged halfway up her arm, and it's midnight, but that's alright. The way to the elevator is almost entirely walkable from here, much faster than crawling.

She's just reached the domesticated part of the cave when she sees the dimmest of lights ahead, soft as a glowworm. She presses against the wall without conscious thought. She's had to delay her descent twice because of customers standing in view of the elevator, and once she ran into Ruby in the restaurant. But in the six times she's made it underground, she's always been alone. Leo has an army of electricians and mechanics and janitors working on the passageways, but they don't seem to work at night.

She unpeels herself from the wall and starts forward again. She doesn't know how long she has before her flashlight dies. Whoever this is, she's going to have to make it past them, although she's not sure how, considering that she can't straighten her arms without touching limestone on each side.

The glow brightens as she comes closer, and she strains to hear anything but her own footsteps. Usually, workers come down here in teams, and she doesn't hear voices or the banging of tools. Maybe this isn't a worker. She flashes back to the old stories of bootleggers and escaped convicts.

She has no choice, though, so she keeps creeping forward. When she rounds the bend, at first she doesn't see anyone at all. A lit lantern has been abandoned a few steps in front of her. She considers it for a moment before her light catches a pair of boots and trousers and the broad back of a man facing the wall. The muscles of his shoulders shift, and his groan echoes off the rock. It's a sound of pleasure, and Ada's first half-formed, horrified thought is that he's with a woman, but she sees no skirts behind him, and her mind stutters to a stop as she hears a steady stream of liquid splashing onto the ground.

She's caught someone relieving himself. She's standing here while a stranger takes himself in hand—even if she can't see it, she knows it's happening—and she has never seen—never heard—a man do this. He's less than ten feet away from her, pants undone, and she is still standing here, still standing here.

He's still going. Embarrassment heats up her face, spreading down her neck, and finally she jerks her flashlight away so that it comes back to heel at her feet, but it's too late.

"Hello?" the man calls, head twisting.

"Sorry," Ada says, turning her back to him, sidestepping along the opposite wall as fast as she can move. "I didn't mean to—"

She's afraid he will reach out and grab her—she's within a step—but he's laughing softly. Laughing. She lunges, full speed, praying her ankle holds, and she puts more distance between them with every breath.

"Who the hell—?" he says, but she's out of sight and he's only a voice again.

Her embarrassment is tipping over into annoyance because she's lost the light inside her that she took from the crystal room and she doesn't know if she'll ever get it back and what was he doing there, urinating in a public place when it's nearly midnight? No, it was not exactly public, but close enough. He was right out in the open. He should have been the one to apologize.

By the time she gets to the elevator, annoyance is all that's left.

She ducks behind a low overhang, turning off her light. She wants a better look at him, and he doesn't take long. By the time he reaches the elevator, she can make him out clearly. He's got more gray in his dark hair than she has. He's square-headed and thick-necked, at least six feet tall. He's wearing coveralls, which leads her to believe he does work here, although it's not the typical body for a man in the caves. They're usually slender, like Leo. This fellow would have a tough time squeezing through the narrow spots.

He does not look the least bit sheepish or angry or anything else. He looks as if he's headed home after a normal day's work of having women come across him doing his business. He pauses at the elevator and turns, a slow 180 degrees, and she ducks her head as he looks her way.

She waits, tense, for footsteps headed through the gravel toward her, but all she hears is the sound of the elevator door closing. In a moment, she stands, watching the bottom of the elevator as it climbs the shaft, her mind full of men who think the entire world belongs to them. They are like dogs, marking everything in sight, and the minute a woman claims something for herself, they piss on it, too.

One Month Later
1931

She's gotten her confidence back after a couple of trips without seeing another soul underground. Tonight, she's stopping at the falls level, all wide paths and smooth surfaces, so no need to shuck her dress or bother with a helmet. She only has to slip on her boots after she steps out of the elevator, and she's midway through the laces when she realizes the obvious: It's not dark. Lights are gleaming all the way down the passageway.

Before she can make sense of it, a man steps out of the rock and shadow not twenty feet in front of her.

"Ma'am," he calls.

She has a wild moment where she hopes to pretend he's talking to someone else. He's tromping toward her, though, and she stands, the open door to the elevator tantalizingly close.

It's the same man she saw relieving himself. She recognizes the shape of him, the broad shoulders and the boulder of a head. She's not sure what he's doing here, but it doesn't really matter. He has some official role, and she can only wait for him to throw her out.

"I've seen you," he says instead.

She's not sure what he means. Hopefully, he's seen her aboveground visiting Ruby or strolling down the street. He couldn't have gotten a clear look at her all those nights ago.

"I've seen you, too," she answers.

He doesn't react to that. She's having trouble looking straight at him, remembering the splash of urine on rock and the way he groaned. Such an unwanted intimacy, knowing a man's private sounds.

"How is it that you're down here?" he says.

"I'm friends with Ruby and Leo." She's not sure whether this will ultimately make the situation better or worse. "I was exploring a little."

He hums something like agreement. She thinks he glances at her bag, slumped and half-open on the other side of the elevator.

"I'm Quinton," he says. "They've got me laying out a stone rim around the pool at the base of the falls, and I've been trying to sort out a drainage issue without visitors running around. I can't think of what they've got you doing."

She's almost sure he's teasing her, and, for the first time, she thinks it's possible that she won't pay a price for this.

"You know they don't have me doing anything," she tries, crooking her neck back to look him in the eye.

He steps back. "I had an inkling. You're not supposed to come down here alone—"

He waits long enough that she has to fill in the gap.

"Ada," she says. "Ada Smith."

"It's not safe," he says. "There's no way Leo knows you're down here by yourself."

She fights back a surge of what might be rage that he would tell her what she can or can't do, even though she knows he's right. She doesn't have permission to be here. More than that, caving alone is a cardinal sin. She's read the terrible stories and she's heard Leo talk more than once about incompetent men getting themselves lost or hurt—flashlights or legs broken—and she remembers her own panic in the crystal room. If she'd been trapped, she could have died there. She knows it.

She's breaking the rule, though, because she has no choice. This man has a right to be here, and she does not, and it's not his fault but the anger doesn't have to make sense for her to feel it.

"I do know," she tells him, keeping her smile in place. It's easier to look him in the eye now. "But I'm careful. I'm never far from the main path."

If she guessed a thousand sentences that might come out of his mouth next, she would not have guessed the correct one.

"Where you headed?" he asks.

A stream of water winds its way over the pathway, pooling near her boots. She can't see any reason she shouldn't tell him the truth. He'll likely escort her back aboveground regardless.

"I've been reading about minerals," she says.

He gives a nod, finally pulling off his helmet. He waits.

"I believe there's a good deposit of iron oxide on this level," she says.

"More than one. The paths have flooded, though." He glances toward her feet. "I'll show you, but you'll get your shoes wet."

"They've gotten wet plenty, but you don't have to do that. I can manage just fine," she says, and she thinks maybe she can manage it better. His head alone would barely fit in some of the crevices she's slithered through.

She's about to tell him how she doesn't want to interrupt his work, but he turns and walks away. This is the most effective argument he could have made: Without him pushing, she finds that she wants to see what he will show her.

So she follows him through the blasted passages where the ceiling is smooth as concrete and the wall is pockmarked by slots where they wedged the dynamite. The overhead lighting is helpful for speed, she has to admit. When they pass into the natural caves, the blankness of the ceiling gives way to stalactites, some long enough to threaten impaling, some short as thumbtacks, and many broken with only stumps left behind. Ruby's mentioned that people are breaking off pieces of the cave and selling them, and Ada's not sure where she stands on it. The cave is a wonder, yes, but people are starving. It's hard to begrudge them a piece of rock.

Quinton doesn't chatter, which she appreciates until she starts to feel the weight of the silence.

"Cave flower," he announces finally, pointing to a crystal formation small enough to hold in her hand. "Looks like a thistle, doesn't it? They say in some places they grow in gardens, hundreds of them, but this is the only one I've seen here."

"Is it on the tour?"

"Not so far as I know."

"You don't give tours?"

"I don't like to play schoolteacher."

"Isn't that what you're doing now?"

"Sorry."

"No," she says quickly. "I was joking. I appreciate your pointing things out."

She isn't sure what to make of him. He is not, after all, the kind of man who thinks he owns the entire world. He's being generous. He's accompanying her instead of forcing her to leave, and maybe that has to do with regulations, but, judging by her first glimpse of him, he doesn't seem like the sort who's overly concerned with rule-following. No. He's the sort who roams here at night, unsupervised. Unchecked.

She might have been foolish to come with him, no witnesses in sight. He could do anything to her, and no one would know.

Leo, she tells herself. Leo would not have hired a bad man.

"You don't have to be a guide to see things," Quinton says, starting forward again. "You walk through here, and there's always another revelation. You know that, though."

That sentence has the feel of a trap, and Ada takes her time about answering.

"Do I?" she says.

He pulls a flashlight from his pocket, which surprises her, since the bulbs overhead are bright enough that there's no need. But he presses the light against a column of white rock, and the light turns it translucent as an ice cube.

"Onyx," he says. "Since you're interested in minerals. There'll be more up ahead."

"I thought onyx was black."

He gives a nod, and for all his talk about not wanting to be a schoolteacher, she feels like she's raised her hand in class and given the right answer.

"That's right," he says, ducking low under an overhang. "But you'll see it in white, too. Sometimes brown."

These paths are so much wider than the ones in the lower caverns. She could walk side by side with him, if she wanted, which she doesn't. She weaves around a stalactite thicker than her head and notices white rock like melting snowballs overflowing a shelf to her right.

"Calcite?" she asks.

"Yeah. Not translucent like the onyx."

She closes the distance between them slightly. She can't work up any fear of him.

"So what have you seen?" he asks.

"Where?"

"Anywhere. You wouldn't keep coming down if something hadn't snagged you."

Keep coming down. They've come to a short bridge over a pool that disappears under the rocks on her left. She can't make out anything past the sheen of its surface, and now this man has dropped enough hints that if she doesn't acknowledge them, she'll seem either cowardly or obtuse.

"I saw you on the lower level," she admits. "Last month."

"Yes. I recall."

Well, that's clear enough. She's thankful he doesn't slow down or turn around: She has no interest in further discussions about that night.

"That same night I found a room," she says. "It glittered all over, a million flecks, but it also had a pocket of crystals big as rock candy."

"What color?"

She expected him to lecture her, about both the caves and her behavior, but she never considered that he would listen. She hasn't spoken about the room to anyone, and the words fall out of her without any effort at all.

"The big crystals were like brown topaz," she says. "Or chocolate."

"The flecks were gypsum, I imagine," he says. "Satin spar, maybe, for the brown ones? I've never seen any here. Was the opening off the Serpentine Trail?"

"I don't know the names you use," she says.

She's told herself a hundred times to pay for another ticket and listen to what the guides have to say, but she can't make herself do it. She's afraid she'll lose more than she gains. She has a sense, every time she lets herself into the darkness, that she belongs here. If she pays her money and pushes along shoulder to shoulder with all the gasping women and joking men and nose-picking children, she'll be the tourist she once was, the old Ada.

"I'd like to see it," he says. "This room of yours. Do you think you could find it again?"

"You'd never fit."

She spots another spray of calcite just above her head, and then he's vaulting off the path and onto the slope of a rock wall. He drops one hand to the ground, and the back of his shirt pulls loose from his pants. She can barely see the strip of skin exposed, but it's shocking. She has not seen a man's bare back up close in years—she thinks of Gerald pulling a shirt over his head or dragging a washcloth over himself on the back porch when the dirt and dust had formed a second skin—and now she's staring, and Quinton doesn't notice because he's focused on something ahead.

"Come on," he says to her.

He doesn't offer her a hand. She steps up beside him, hunching so she doesn't hit her head, and she kneels to get a clearer look at the low expanse in front of her. She could go at least twenty feet if she were flat on her belly, and she wonders how far the crevice extends.

"They act like this is an in-and-out cavern, no offshoots," he says, "but you can get places. No shortage of secret passages. If you crawl back far enough, you can work your way to an underground stream about twenty feet below us, but you'd need a rope."

He jumps back to the asphalt path, landing two-footed. She does the same, and he's already moving by the time she lands.

She hopes he's not planning on going all the way to the waterfall. She hasn't been to Ruby Falls itself since her time on the tour, and she doesn't like to think about why. She hopes it's not jealousy—she'd hate to think she begrudges Ruby her massive valentine of a tourist attraction. No, it's only that she doesn't care for the way they've tried to tame this place, like jamming a lion into a cage.

"I'm serious about the gypsum," Quinton says over his shoulder. "You think you could show me?"

She hears a train in the distance, a long lowing.

"I was serious when I said you wouldn't fit," she says. "It was more than an hour past the marked trail, and, yes, I know I shouldn't have been there."

"You weren't nervous?" he asks, and it sounds like curiosity, not judgment.

"I tied twine to my entry point."

"My father taught me that same thing," he says. "Sometimes you run out of twine, though."

"It makes me think of the Minotaur's maze. How Ariadne gave Theseus the thread to find his way?"

"I might have said Hansel and Gretel," he says, and she can't tell whether he knows the Greek myth or not.

He stops, and Ada spots the mix of white calcite and rust-colored iron oxide flowing down the wall even before his flashlight beam hits it. She read that it would be blood colored, but it's dried blood, not fresh.

"This is the biggest deposit," he says, "but if you start looking for it, you'll see it all along the path."

"You know a lot about this."

He's moving again, not waiting. He treats her like a man, and she tells herself it's a compliment.

"We had caverns on our land in Jasper," he says. "You could stand in front of the rock and feel the cold air blowing in summer. My dad used to take all four of us down there—us kids could fit into more places than he could. We had a code—two taps and then three taps meant we'd found a new room. One tap, three taps, one tap meant we'd gotten lost. We had one for if our light went out and another for if we'd gotten hurt."

They pass a series of formations shaped like beehives, rock rising into mounds. She has an urge to crack them open and see what's inside.

"You went in caves as a child?" she says.

"Every one of us. My sister Marnie could fit anywhere—girls are smaller."

If she reminds him of his sister, that might explain his helpfulness. A rock juts out at head level on her left, and another one muscles in at hip level on her right.

"There was a magic to it back then," he says. "Like you'd slipped into a world you invented as you went along."

"I felt that way about our persimmon tree out back," she says. "It was all sorts of things other than a tree."

He tilts toward her, enough that she can see him smile. "Persimmons," he says. "My great-aunt made a syrup for sore throats from them."

Ada remembers hearing about such a syrup from a grade school teacher who also swore by maple bark for pain and wormwood for sores. She thinks back on that teacher, and she considers the darkness of Quinton's hair and eyes.

"Are you part Cherokee?" she asks.

His pace stays steady. "A small part."

Plenty of people around here could say the same. The government tried its best to erase the Cherokee from this place, but it couldn't stamp out the names on the rivers and towns and the state itself, and it couldn't erase fry bread and pine needle baskets and the occasional newborn with coal-colored hair.

The bulb above them burns brightly. It's always nighttime in caves, but here Leo can turn on daylight whenever he chooses. Quinton lifts his hand to duck under an overhang, and he's taken off his gloves. He's got a smear of blood across his knuckles.

"You hurt your hand," she says.

He glances down briefly, shaking his hand like he's jarring loose a mosquito.

"You have to stop it, you know," he says once his hand goes still.

"Pardon?"

"I've been doing this for over forty years," he says, "and I never head down here on my own. If you do, you're stupid, which it's clear you're not."

She speaks with this tone of voice to Frances or Eugenia when they try to tell her that the elves will steal your shoes. She half expects him to pat her on the head, and perhaps he doesn't think of her as a man or his sister, but as a child.

"You were down here alone," she says. "Both times I've seen you."

"And a group of men upstairs know exactly where I am, every time. If I don't come back up, they'll come looking. Can you say the same?"

She tightens her hand around her flashlight. Her own knuckles ache from where she bashed them last weekend, and the scabs keep cracking when she holds a broom. Her knee's slightly swollen from falling after missing a handhold, and she's got a thread-thin slice at the edge of her scalp from standing up too quickly. And yet it seems to her that it should be her choice if she wants to bleed.

Quinton

The woman has gone silent with fury by the time he hustles her into the elevator, and he's glad she's so eager to leave. Leo would not be pleased to find her down here, and he would be less pleased that Quinton's been escorting her.

Quinton stares at the elevator shaft, empty now. A woman looking for oxides. He couldn't have been more surprised if a rhinoceros had appeared on the footpath. He checks his pocket watch—half past eleven—and the cut on his hand is still oozing. It must have happened when he was hauling the stones, although he didn't feel it. Now that he knows it's there, he feels it.

Which doesn't matter, as long as he doesn't have to look at it. The least bit of blood takes him right back to Deer Creek, the mud red-black as the water, seeping into his shoes, and it turns his stomach, still.

Everyone said, *You need money, go bleed the hogs*, but he hadn't wanted to do it. As soon as you got within a few blocks of the slaughterhouses, you started seeing stray dogs with red dripping from their snouts. They'd slink up and nuzzle you, blood-faced and pitiful. But it was 1902, and he was twenty-two years old, and the Cincinnati meat houses paid fifty cents in your palm at the end of the day. After a while he got hungry enough that he walked past those dogs and got the job. Every day was pigs crammed so tight they couldn't turn around, and then a fellow would start swinging a mace and the pigs would fall in piles, snouts still twitching. A hook came up out of the floor and yanked them to a room below, and he would be waiting to slit their throats.

He made it a month before he decided he'd rather go back to being hungry, so that's what he did and he did it well. He roamed the construction yards until the day he was headed down Sycamore and got snagged by a window with gold letters spelling out THE LIBERTY. There were nearly as many taverns as men in that city, but the mounted animals behind the glass caught his eye: a buck with antlers as wide as his arms. A moth-eaten fox with bald spots. A lynx with its teeth pulled back in a hiss.

He was standing there, hypnotized, when a drop of water hit his cheek. He looked up and saw a quarter-sized hole in the eave of the roof, easy enough to patch, and he'd always loved fixing something that was broken. That's what was in his head, and a version of it came out of his mouth when a man came to the doorway.

"Thank you kindly," the man said, in a tone that was not appreciative at all. He was in the shadows, but something about the way he leaned into the doorway made it clear the bar was his. "I've got a bucket. Sits right on the floor for free. Works just fine."

Quinton turned away because he'd argued before and it never got him anywhere. People didn't want arguers working for them. But for some reason the man called him back and told him to come inside. They stepped into a large room of wood and brick, and the man's face wasn't what Quinton had expected. He wore pince-nez glasses, and his cheeks were smooth and round. He looked more like a librarian than a tavern owner.

They stopped in front of a long wooden counter, scuffed and scarred. Liquor bottles were lined up along the shelves, shiny as Christmas ornaments.

"I'm Emory Webster," the man said. "You like beer?"

"Not much," Quinton said, hoping it was the right answer. He didn't want to insult the man's merchandise, but he'd been brought up Baptist and hadn't yet shaken it.

"Good. I've got a job pays twenty cents and all the beer you want." Mr. Webster smiled at his own joke. "Plus lunch, same as the breweries do it. My roof is dandy, but I need someone to take a look at the cellar."

He had to have known what he was saying wasn't true. The breweries let you drink all you wanted, sure, but they paid $1.25 a day, not that Quinton could afford to be picky. Soon enough he was following Mr. Webster into a cellar lined with wooden racks where barrels were piled on top of each other, most of them stamped with a D.R. logo. The smell was sweet and sick and heavy.

"Should it smell like this?" Quinton asked.

"Hell, no," Mr. Webster said. "The last batch Danzy Ross sent over are leaking all over. Bungs popping, maybe, or could be bad staves. The lager seems fine, but the ale's seeping, and there's damned fruit flies everywhere."

"You want me to clean up?" Quinton guessed—smartly, he thought, given that he'd only understood half the words Mr. Webster used.

His new employer looked down his pince-nez. Now, when he pictures the man, it's that look Quinton sees. Pretend sternness.

"I want you to find the leaks and plug them," Mr. Webster said, flopping a hand on the nearest barrel. "I need to get ready for the lunch crowd, and it ain't as if you're building a submarine. Most likely any leaks will be around the seams of the thing. The seam's here where the head meets the staves."

He kept on about sealing gaps with paraffin and hammering a bung. He said to follow the flies and the smell.

"I can clear up the flies faster," Quinton told him, "if you give me a bowl of syrup from your fountain machine. They'll drown in it."

"Two sentences at once," Mr. Webster said. "I call that progress."

Quinton spent the next few hours feeling for wet spots around the seams of each barrel. He picked splinters from his fingertips. He'd find a section of dripping wood and wedge in a toothpick or ten toothpicks or he melted paraffin on top of it, corralling the drips to fall just so. He ran his hands over wood and wax.

He remembers a mouse near the wall, weaving like it was trying to learn a waltz. He remembers Mr. Webster's hand landing on his shoulder, the two of them walking up to the bar packed with platters of brown bread and sausage, mustard and sour pickles, dried herring and paper-thin slices of yellow cheese. He told Mr. Webster about the spinning mouse, and the man laughed and said that every animal liked to go on a bender now and again.

When Quinton left at the end of the day, Mr. Webster clapped a bundled napkin into his hand. It held two cold sausages and a hunk of soda bread, and when Quinton got back to his spot under the hedges in Eden Park, he made himself take a breath between every bite so that it would last longer. He came back to the tavern the next day and the day after that, and for over a year Mr. Webster always had work for him, even if the work didn't really need doing.

Could someone be family when you'd only just met them?

He doesn't see why not. His father barely met his own parents, but they were always there. Or *not* there. His father's mother was Cherokee and his father's father was white, back when they were herding the tribe by the thousands from Fort Cass to Oklahoma, leaving bodies strewn all along the way. Quinton's grandfather stayed with his grandmother when she was forced to leave, but they didn't think their baby boy would survive the journey. So they left Quinton's father with his aunt—his white aunt—and he never saw his parents again. It left a hole of some kind, Quinton thinks, and his father was always looking to fill it. He wanted a different job, a different house, a different city, a different wife. A different son. Maybe he loved the caves because he wanted a different world entirely.

Emory Webster was evidence that a man could be happy with exactly what he had. He went through the day with so much contentment he had enough to pass it around.

Quinton owes him for that. He owes him for the full stomach and for never cheating on a paycheck. He owes him for the suppers at his home, where Mrs. Webster would always put the breadbasket by his plate. He owes him for lessons about floorboards and water pumps and for saying "smart boy." He owes him for ordering him to resurface the cellar ramp after the deliveryman busted a barrel of lager because footpaths wound up being his ticket to Leo Lambert and Ruby Falls. There'd been some raveling along the pathways, the last thing you wanted when solid footing was already an issue. Quinton came to Leo with the idea of a cold asphalt-gravel mixture, and now he's part of this place. It's another kind of family.

It's easy to think of the past as being fixed, as if years work like miles. It feels like Quinton could travel that old route to Cincinnati, and he'd find Emory Webster waiting there. As long as he keeps his distance, his old boss is still attached to his proper place behind the bar, filling glasses and climbing up to the top shelf.

That's where Quinton tries to keep him, anyway. He tries not to think of him that last time in the back room. The slack face. The blood, pooling.

You want to learn how to drain the tap? Mr. Webster would ask, staring down those pince-nez. *You want to learn how to recane a stool?* And Quinton learned plenty, didn't he? He learned about paraffin and wood staves. He learned meat keeps you full longer than bread. He learned if you want to slit a throat, you do it in one deep stroke under the jaw, and if the blood doesn't come right away, you've missed the artery.

The cut across the back of his hand is deeper than he realized—the blood splats on the elevator floor, three drops in a steady rhythm, and somehow, it seems, he's circled back to blood again.

Ten Months Later
1932

Ada has kept her promise about the caves, in a way. After her run-in with Quinton, she stopped exploring the edges of the known world and stayed closer to the labeled paths. And as soon as winter ended the rooftop dances, she rarely tried for the caverns at all. It was too much of a risk trying to slip past the jammed dance floor. But once the weather warmed and the dances moved outdoors again, she couldn't resist heading underground. These days she leaves a note on her kitchen table, knowing if something were to happen, Ruby would eventually find the message.

Sometimes she catches the flicker of a shadow in the caverns, and when she rounds the next curve, she's sure Quinton will be there, accusing, but he never appears.

When she does see him again, he's at her front door. She spots him through the window, and she watches him lift his hand, lower it, and lift it again. He goes through the motions twice before he actually knocks, and he's talking before she's fully opened the door.

"I've got a proposition for you," he says.

"Good afternoon to you, too."

He smiles at that. Behind him, a coal truck jolts over a branch in the road.

"You've heard about the mind reader coming to town?" he asks.

"I have," she says, proud that she sounds perfectly at ease. She's once again having trouble looking him straight in the face. "Ruby told me Leo invited him to the caves to put on an exhibition. It's supposed to be good for publicity. He's impressive, supposedly. A doctor."

She can tell by Quinton's tone that he's not in favor of the exhibition, but Lord knows Leo and Ruby need whatever boost they can get. The food stations are feeding over three thousand a day in Chattanooga alone. The Lookout Mountain Hotel and the Fairytale Inn went bankrupt months ago, and a dozen other hotels and restaurants have shut their doors. Every month the paper includes a roundup of the latest batch of closings.

Ruby's had to take in washing to pay for the elevator's gas.

"Jeremiah Hagathorn is his name," Quinton says, "and he calls himself a professor alright. They say if you're sitting next to him, he can see your thoughts. He's driven around Chicago blindfolded and never hit a thing. If you picture a name in a hotel register, he can drive to that hotel and point to the name. So maybe he can manage to read minds, but I'm not sure how that'll keep him from killing himself if he's wandering around caves blindfolded."

Ada thought, when she saw him on her porch, that he'd found out she was still sneaking into the caverns. She doesn't know yet if this is better or worse.

"Here," he says, holding out a newspaper. "Today's."

She folds the front page in half and scans the first column:

> Professor Jeremiah Hagathorn and his wife, Editha, will arrive at Lookout Mountain this fall as part of an exhibition designed to showcase the power of the human mind and the natural wonders of Chattanooga. The professor has made a name for himself from Cincinnati to Chicago by displaying his

> talent for reading minds. He has been invited to Chattanooga by Leo Lambert, discoverer of Ruby Falls, in hopes that he will perform the most mindbending display of his abilities to date. He will navigate the underground passages of Lookout Mountain using only his psychic energy to locate a hidden hatpin.

When Ada looks up, Quinton is studying her, not making any effort to pretend he's been doing otherwise. She's never loved it when someone watches her read.

"Do you want to come in?" she asks.

She wonders if he, like her, is weighing the repercussions of him staying outside, increasing the chances that the neighbors will see him talking with her, as opposed to the lesser likelihood—but higher risk, rumor-wise—of neighbors catching him coming and going from inside her house. Probably not.

He nods, stomping his boots on the mat before stepping inside. He takes off his hat and starts to sit down in the straight-backed cane chair by the coatrack, and she's glad when he reconsiders. She's not sure it would hold him.

"Tea?" she says, wishing she had sugar. "Or I've got coffee on the burner I can warm up."

He rests a hand on the back of the too-spindly chair. "I'll take the coffee, if it's not too much trouble."

She taps the back of her oak rocking chair, and he drops into it with less jouncing than she expected. She steps to the stove, pulling her matches out of the drawer.

"I'm surprised Ruby hasn't mentioned this to you," he says. "Leo's made it clear he wants someone outside of the usual crew."

She's pleased that he remembers she's friends with Ruby. She's pleased he remembers her at all, and, wait—she gives the aluminum pot a jostle as the flame flares up—he'd have to have done some asking around to figure out where she lives.

"I still don't know what *this* is," she says. "And Ruby doesn't know anything about me going in the caves."

He reaches behind him, adjusting the pillow behind his back. It's flat as a pancake, barely softening the wood, and Ada resists the urge to apologize for it.

"Any reason for that?" he asks.

"For what?"

"For why Ruby doesn't know you let yourself in?"

This tests the limits of her desire to share her secrets. The answer does not reflect well on her. She takes her time fussing over the stove, fooling with knobs that don't need fooling with.

"I don't know that she'd approve," she says. "She'd worry."

"You're still doing it, I assume," he says. "Letting yourself in."

"I leave a note. What's your proposition?"

He rocks back and forth, knees wide and feet flat on the floor. She hands him his cup of coffee, and he nods his thanks.

"They've got a committee set up," he says. "Leo's on it, of course, and some combination of Ruby Falls investors and cave guides. They've planned out what'll happen when the magic man gets to town. Two of them will head into the caverns and hide the pin on Sunday, and on Monday the professor will be set loose to find it. He'll go into the caves with the same two committeemen who hid it, and he'll—supposedly—read their minds. He'll have his manager and a newspaperman along with him, and he's got twelve hours to find the pin. That's what everyone will tell you."

She wishes she'd poured herself a cup of coffee so she'd have something to hold in her hands. She takes a seat in the cane chair.

"What are you telling me?" she asks.

"Leo doesn't want the mind reader to fail. If he finds the hatpin, it'll mean real publicity all over the country that'll bring in paying visitors. Leo's not gonna let the man break his neck. He wants a safety net in place."

"I don't know what that means."

"We'd be the safety net, you and me. The pair of us follow behind the official group and keep an eye on them. We'd have extra food and water and light. We'd be there to lead them back if they got themselves lost or to go for help if there's a need."

She puzzles through that.

"They can't get lost on the way to the waterfall," she says. "There's no breaking your neck walking down that path."

"They aren't limited to the falls. You didn't read that far?"

"These people are allowed to roam through the lower caverns?" she says. "All six miles of them?"

Quinton smiles, and she sees a hint of vibration in him. Maybe he's more like Leo than she's realized.

"Six miles of mapped passages," he says. "No telling how much is unmapped. Those tunnels could twist through the mountain forever, and the mind reader could crawl through all of them if he's so inclined. He can fall down chasms if he likes. He can tumble into a stream and die of hypothermia. He could die of thirst, I suppose, if it stretched out long enough."

Outside, a crepe myrtle branch is trembling in a way that means a bird has just flown off. Ada can understand why the newspapers would like the story Leo is selling. But nothing Quinton has said explains why he's sitting in her den.

"You must know men you could ask to come with you," she says.

"I do," he says. "But they want credit. They want to be the one leading the famous professor around the caves. They want their names in the paper. If you agree to this, you can never mention it. Not to friends, not to family, not to anyone. The newspaper version has to be the only version that exists. I like the men I work with well enough, but I don't trust them to keep quiet."

"Why would you trust me?"

"It's clear you can keep a secret."

The way he's looking at her reminds her of the way he looked at that cave flower, which she found in one of her library books: anthodite. That's the fancy word for it. She suspects that she's one more curiosity Quinton has discovered, and she'd like to think that means she's a revelation but it more likely means she's a Siamese twin or bearded lady.

"I come with you for twelve hours and follow the mind reader around," she says. "I keep quiet. That's the entirety of the job."

"Once we're down, we can't come back up," he says. "Reporters and everyone else will be watching the entrance. We can't be seen by the professor and his people, either. The newspaperman has to think the risks are real, so we only show ourselves if someone's stupider than expected."

A woodpecker is testing its mettle against the neighbor's pines.

"Leo knows you asked me?" she asks.

"Not yet. I told him I would check with someone. He doesn't know who." He sets his empty coffee cup on one knee. "You called it a job, and it is. You'll get paid. The usual guide's rate is forty cents an hour, although paychecks are running a couple of weeks behind. More than that, lately."

She wishes he'd move that cup off his knee because she doesn't have so many that she wouldn't miss a broken one. But it's a wide knee, and the cup sits there steadily enough as he sways forward and back, the chair creaking under him.

She could use the money, but that's not the part that's sticking in her head. *The usual guide's rate.* Quinton is offering her something official. She's to keep it secret, but Leo will know. The other men in the caves might know. She's heard plenty about Abby Milton with her law degree and that woman reporter for the *Chattanooga Times.* She's heard about the colored woman doctor who started the Negro hospital over on Eighth Street. People give those women room.

When all this hullabaloo is finished, she will have room, too, and she doesn't care if anyone thinks she's a bearded lady. She only wants the caves.

Two Months Later
1932

Morris

Morris has a moment of panic that he's lost the hatpins, but it turns out he's only confused his pockets. He feels the sharp points now, stuck solid in the lining of his jacket, two pins instead of the single one Leo requested because, as everyone knows, it's better to be safe than sorry.

Of course, he hasn't lost the pins. He doesn't lose things. He's had his favorite letter opener for three decades. These caves turn back time, which sounds appealing, but it only erases all the years it took to learn who he is and what he's good at. Today is the first day Morris has felt nervous in a long time. The elevator door rattles shut behind him and he makes himself take another step onto the rock. He wishes they were heading down the nice, smooth path to Ruby Falls instead of launching themselves into the lower level of the mountain.

"They wouldn't expect us to hide it behind the falls," he says.

Talmadge stops suddenly, and Morris puts out a gloved hand to keep from running into the younger man's narrow back. He had to buy a pair of gloves special for this trip.

"He'll get to the falls in thirty minutes," Talmadge says, starting forward again. "An hour if he's particular. Even if he doesn't have a bit of psychic ability, the professor could find the pin up there if he's decent at hide-and-seek. We've got to get deeper if we want this to stretch out like Mr. Lambert wants."

"That's what they'll expect," Morris says. "It'd throw them off to hide it on the upper level."

Talmadge doesn't look back. Anyone could tell he's a professional guide just by looking at him, wiry and sure-footed, loose-limbed in the way of men barely into adulthood. Completely relaxed.

"We're not trying to throw them off, Mr. Efrom," Talmadge says mildly. "We head in here at nine a.m. tomorrow morning. The deadline is nine p.m. Twelve hours. Mr. Lambert says it doesn't have to take all of that, but he wants the suspense to build. So we just need to think through the math of it."

Now he does pause, half turning. He has a gentleness to him that's appealing, and Morris likes him. Morris likes most people.

"Let's say we want this thing to go for nine hours," Talmadge says. "All of us back aboveground at six p.m. That'd be nice, right? Reporters are ready for something to happen, excited when we all come through the door, and maybe we still get home in time for dinner."

"Makes sense," Morris concedes.

It's hard for him to accept guidance from someone younger than he is—more than three decades in this case, Lord have mercy—but the truth is that it's getting rare to find someone older than he is.

"So we need to hide the pin at least three hours into the passages," Talmadge says. He must see something on Morris's face. "We're moving faster than the group will be able to move. The more people, the slower you go. It won't take us half that time to go hide it. But I figure three hours for them on the way in, three hours on the way out, and that'd leave three hours to account for rests and wrong turns. Just as an estimate."

He's headed forward again before Morris can respond. It's not as if he can fault the boy for wanting to please Leo. He prefers the Ruby Falls idea, though, and not only because he'd prefer to make this quick. It would work better for advertising: The papers will surely carry photos, and it would be nice to highlight the main attraction. He pictures a shot of a hand reaching through the spray of the falls, just past the footpath so the handrail doesn't show. Plus the falls—Leo's discovery of them, his naming them after his wife—make for a great story, although maybe that's only another word for advertising.

"Gum?" Talmadge asks, rattling a tin of Chiclets.

"No, thanks."

Morris hasn't chewed gum in years: Back when they started dating, Miriam got onto him about smacking, and eventually she wore him down. One of the hatpins in his pocket is hers, and he feels a gnaw of guilt at pulling it out of her jewelry box.

Talmadge is chawing too loudly. Morris tries not to hear it.

The ceilings down here are higher than he remembers, but he knows they'll shrink. This first section has the feel of a storm shelter, and when he's gone through the tour with the people packed shoulder to shoulder and the smell of spearmint and pomade in the air, the passage felt more like a movie theater than a cave. But it's only him and Talmadge now, and he can feel the emptiness around them. A thousand feet below the mountain's surface, Leo says, and the number won't leave Morris's head. He should have poured a splash of whiskey in his coffee this morning.

"I don't know why you volunteered," Talmadge says, although he sounds more sympathetic than condescending. "You didn't have to come. Other men on the committee know the caves."

"Leo asked me," Morris answers.

He appreciates that Talmadge is doing him the courtesy of not mentioning what's obvious to them both. Unlike him, other men on the committee don't hate these caves. Everybody else goes soft-eyed when they talk about the old days of creeping through tunnels with nothing but matches and candles, kicking empty Schweppes bottles in the dark. They were kids, though, and it's that youth that these thick-waisted women and shiny-headed men long for, not the caves. They were all terrified, trying not to show it, and that's what youth was most of the time, but apparently no one remembers that part but him.

He and Harold Box used to crawl through these crannies with their daddies' cigarettes. They'd come in through the old railroad entrance, which is blocked now, and Harold always wanted to go deeper, but Morris wouldn't. He was afraid of the darkness and the rustlings, and, more than that, he was worried hell might be waiting for him if he went too far, which was stupid but he didn't know it then. He'd have sworn he felt the heat ahead of him, and sometimes he could smell burnt skin in the air, like he did the time Preacher Cox called the schoolchildren together and told them to hold their hands over a lighter. The preacher told them that's what hell would feel like, and Louis Maier threw up.

Preacher Cox is right, his mother said when Morris showed her the blisters on his palm, and look at him, a man past his sixth decade with loose skin at his jaw and puffy veins along his hands and this place has turned him back into that boy who flinched at his mother's voice.

He bends nearly in half as the ceiling drops in front of him, smooth and mottled. The soot isn't uniform, the sand-colored rock peeking through in patches. He straightens and lets out a long breath.

"Mr. Lambert knows you hate it down here?" Talmadge asks.

So much for not mentioning the obvious. "No," Morris says on an exhale. "No reason Leo would know. He said the mind reader's people wanted someone who wasn't familiar with the caves. I fit the bill."

He also fits the bill in other ways. Leo trusts him to make sure this venture goes well, and he wants it to go well every bit as much as Leo does. Not because he wants to protect the five hundred dollars he put into this place—he's given up on ever seeing a penny of profit—but because if Ruby Falls collapses, it'll take Leo with it, and Morris has no intention of letting that happen.

I know what sort of caver Talmadge is, Leo told him. *But I know what kind of man you are.*

Leo's right: There's no telling about the rest of the men. Darkness and tight spaces don't always bring out the best in people. Morris is here to be a voice of reason, a role he's used to playing. When Leo was bidding out the elevator shaft and wanted to go with a new engineering firm from Memphis because its president was pleasant to sit with over supper, Morris insisted on Salmon & Cowan from Birmingham because even though those fellows were as humorless as the dirt they were going to dig up, they'd finished projects from Georgia to Kentucky. And what happened?

That pleasant fellow's Memphis firm went belly-up before the shaft was even finished.

He and Talmadge have come to a staircase, and Morris remembers the trail turning snakier on the lower level. The walls around him have the ripples of a dry riverbed, and even if he didn't know that rushing water carved these passageways, he thinks he could guess.

The image does not leave him feeling more settled.

"You think the mind reader can do it?" he asks, because the ceiling hangs heavier when they keep silent.

"I think it's possible," Talmadge says. "There's a world beyond this one. Isn't that what the Bible tells us?"

Morris doesn't love talking about the Bible down here.

"I don't know that the Bible is big on mind reading," he says.

"I don't see how it's any different," Talmadge says. "You believe in spirits or you don't. If you do, why couldn't a person talk to them?"

He speeds up, and Morris realizes that the guide has been taking it easy on him. He hopes his slowness hasn't put them off schedule: He hates to be late.

"You truly think an hour for us will add up to three hours for them?" he asks, lengthening his stride.

"Maybe," Talmadge says. "Just trying to map out a route that'll make a good show."

Nothing that happens down here fits Morris's idea of a good show. He'd prefer a nice fiddle or a ventriloquist. He and Miriam used to love to go to musicals at the Tivoli.

The beam from Talmadge's headlamp skims over a cluster of small, dark shapes that Morris suspects are bats. He hopes they're sleeping.

"So far as I understand, Hagathorn isn't a medium," Morris says. "I don't think he communes with the dead."

"But reading minds is similar, isn't it?"

"I suppose," Morris says. "A world beyond this one, like you say."

"You have to have faith. That's our job in all this, isn't it?"

Morris is still unclear about his part, which seems to primarily involve picturing the location of the hatpin in his head. He would rather host a fundraiser or organize a dinner.

"Faith in what?" he asks.

"Don't know that it has to be specific," Talmadge says, smacking away at his gum. Miriam would never have made it this long without losing her temper. "A sense of something more. You can't feel it down here? How there's something bigger than you are?"

Morris laughs, and he's glad for it. He always feels better when he laughs. "Oh, I know it's bigger than I am. That's the problem."

Talmadge cuts him a look over his shoulder. They're at the end of the lighted pathway, and the way ahead is black. Past the final post of the handrail—in the crossover between electric light and natural dark—a small pool shines silver. A shallow shelf of formations juts above the pool like a row of flower bulbs. Onions, possibly. Morris had forgotten how the mind works down here, always trying to translate rocks into some known language.

They trudge along. The ceiling is covered in nipples of stalactite, and as it swoops down, Morris hunches over. As it rises, he straightens. The light on his helmet catches the guide's arm and shoulder, casting the shadow of a tentacled monster.

Time passes. It would be easier if he could close his eyes.

Talmadge drops to his hands and knees, and a dim pool of light spreads around his boots as he crawls forward.

"Don't you get afraid of your lights going out?" Morris asks, lowering himself to the ground. His knee pops.

He's not used to following. He'd rather get back aboveground, where people ask him what to do instead of telling him.

"Nah," Talmadge says. "I always have extra."

Morris has always assumed the men who choose to spend time down here thrive on the undercurrent of fear. It's never occurred to him that they might not feel it in the first place.

"You're never afraid?" he asks.

"It's no harder than following a recipe," Talmadge says, rising halfway as the ceiling lifts again, his back still bent.

"Sure."

"I'm dead serious. If a light goes out, I have backups. If I do wind up in the dark, I stay put and wait for someone to come for me. I keep track of my rights and my lefts. It's a good measure simpler than your job."

"I don't think that's true."

"How many people work for you?" Talmadge asks.

"Fifty-three."

Morris wishes he was with them now, dealing with the shipment of boxes that got soaked in the rain or working out the schedule for next week that everyone will complain about regardless because everybody wants more hours. He could be figuring out how to give Doug Varner time off with pay while his boy is up in the hospital in Knoxville, or he could be solving how the women's watches are still walking off the shelves. When people get hungry, they get clever with their stealing.

The path forks and Talmadge heads right. Morris wishes desperately for the ceiling to lift enough for him to straighten entirely and give his back a rest, but he's forced to stay folded. His knees are bent as well, and he thinks he's heard of some medieval torture device that smashed a man in half. The iron shackle or the iron scavenger or something along those lines.

He makes the mistake of glancing behind him, and it's nothingness. The darkness is right on his heels.

"We've got a squeeze coming up," Talmadge says. "Not a long one, though."

A squeeze. Morris has never heard the term, but he knows what it means. It's when the rock closes around you like a Chinese finger trap. Sure enough, what looks like a wall ahead is not a dead end after all. The rock stops at about the height of his knees, and the opening below spreads for several feet.

Talmadge drops to the ground, peering inside. His headlamp lights up smooth rock in every direction.

"We'll push through here for maybe ten feet," he says, the sound muffled. "Then it opens up."

Morris kneels himself, and his knees complain but his back is better. He lowers his cheek to the ground, feeling the coolness of it even though his helmet clanks on the rock and keeps his skin from actually touching.

He's staring into a tomb. An iron maiden. His mind is stuck on torture devices. The rock will crush him as soon as he slides inside, and he can already feel his lungs collapsing as his mind winds back to the store. He's gotten a dozen complaints about the Anderson boy in footwear, and he needs to sit down and talk to him.

The watches. Maybe one of the fitting rooms could be turned into a room for trying on jewelry. A closed door and an employee playing chaperone. When he focuses hard enough, he can make himself gulp down air.

"No," he says.

Talmadge already has his arms and head inside the tomb. He crooks his head, and his light whips across the chamber. "What's that?"

"I'm not going any further."

"You're serious?"

"I am," Morris says, pleased to hear the firmness in his voice. This is the version of himself he needs down here.

Talmadge slides out and spins around. His face is concerned, not angry. "You alright?"

Morris nods, although "alright" is not the word he would choose. "I can't be closed in all the way like that. I can't do it."

"That's fine," Talmadge says slowly. "That's fine. You don't have to do anything you don't want to do."

He's likely said this same thing to plenty of people who lost their heads underground, but it's effective anyway. Morris turns away from the tomb of rock, but rock is the only view in every direction. He tips his head to his muddy knees.

They both breathe. The air is damp and leaves the taste of metal in his throat.

"I'm sorry," he says.

"It's alright," Talmadge says, flopping onto his backside. His boots are nearly touching Morris's.

They breathe for a while longer. Morris closes his eyes.

"I can hide the pin," Talmadge says. "I don't mind. You can wait here."

He's a good man, Morris thinks.

"I think that's best," he says.

He becomes aware that he's rocking back and forth slightly, and he makes himself mostly come to a stop. He concentrates on taking slow breaths, and his mind goes quiet after a while. When he opens his eyes and lifts his head, Talmadge is watching him. It looks like he's finally spit out the gum.

"Better?" Talmadge asks.

"Yeah," Morris says.

"No hurry."

Somewhere out of sight, a drop of water plinks against stone. Talmadge runs his thumb over the top of his boot, streaking a path through the dust. Something about the tone of his voice registers.

"Is there?" Morris asks. "A hurry? Are we off schedule?"

"They can wait."

Morris clamps his hands around his knees. He's gone back to rocking, he realizes, and it's possible they have been sitting on the cold ground longer than he realizes. Half an hour? And Talmadge had already been slowing the pace, hadn't he?

"My apologies," he says.

"None needed."

"How have we been sitting here?"

"About an hour, maybe."

"I do think I'm fine," Morris says, after more minutes have passed. "I'll be alright. Here, I mean. I'll stay here while you go hide the thing."

"Sure," Talmadge says, unmoving still. He's more solicitous than Morris would have expected. "If you're steady enough. The only issue is that—"

Ah. It's something other than solicitude.

"Leo promised the professor that both of us would hide it," Morris finishes.

"He said it was part of the deal," Talmadge says. "The mind reader said two of us had to know the location for the—I don't know . . . something—to be right."

Morris runs a finger under his helmet, which is starting to bite into his scalp. The damp material of his trousers shows the ridges of his kneecaps. They are a landscape all their own, and he studies them.

He's turning back into a self he recognizes, and his thoughts are clearer, thank God. As long as he doesn't look into that slit of rock, he's alright. This is no problem at all. A kindergartener could solve it.

"You'll tell me where you hide it," he says. "You'll tell me what to picture, and I will. The professor will get exactly what he was promised—two minds primed to be read. It won't be any different than if I stood there next to you hiding it."

He yanks off his glove and reaches into his pocket, fumbling to find the pins. He pulls one out, and the pearly head of it catches the light as it drops it into Talmadge's glove.

Talmadge closes his fingers around it. "You're saying we don't mention this to Mr. Lambert?"

"You don't have to do anything you don't want to do," Morris volleys back to him.

"I can't lose my job, Mr. Efrom. I can't. I can't lie to my boss."

"I would never lie to Leo," Morris says, and he wouldn't. "He's the only reason I'm down here. If you like, we can tell him everything, and I'll make it clear that the problem was entirely mine. We can reschedule the whole event—you can come back down here with someone else some other time, and that would be fine, too."

He is maneuvering things, he knows. He can't help it. He's well aware that Talmadge is not a man who wants to waste his time, which is a fine quality. Morris himself does not want to redo this whole damn thing, not after all the flyers and newspaper copy. He does not want his weakness to cost them all. Not when there's no need.

"If we keep quiet about this," Talmadge says, tucking the hatpin into his own pocket, "you'll have to come back down here tomorrow, you know."

"Let me ask you this," Morris says. "You think you'll bring this bunch of people down here who have never set foot in a cave, and every one of them will be ready to launch themselves into a crack? You think I'll be the only one with limits?"

Talmadge considers the narrow gap behind them. "That's a fair point."

"I thought it was."

"I could pick a different route tomorrow, I suppose," Talmadge says. "Less direct."

"If you avoid the crazy squeezes, I'll be fine," Morris says. "As fine as any of the others. You do your part and I'll do mine."

He keeps his eyes on his knees but he thinks of Miriam, always Miriam. She fretted over that electric iron from the moment they bought it, perpetually afraid she'd left it plugged in and the house would burn down. They'd be headed down the highway to visit one of the boys or to catch a show and she'd say, *Morris, turn around. We have to check the iron.* It must've happened a dozen times, and he always turned around and she'd never once left the iron on. That last time she said it, he'd pulled over on the side of the road, walked around to the trunk, pulled out her iron, and handed it to her. *You schemer,* she'd said, laughing. *You take care of everything, don't you?*

Her laugh! Like she'd smoked a thousand cigarettes, when she'd never tasted one.

"There's a waterfall in a mile or so," Talmadge says. "Not nearly as big as Ruby Falls, but it'll catch their attention, and the timing should work out right. That's the spot I'm leaning toward."

"Head on, then," Morris says.

"Yeah?"

"Yeah."

Talmadge pushes to his feet, as much as he can. He shuffles and circles until his palms are sliding inside the squeeze again. He pauses there, arms and legs splayed, facing into the darkness.

"You sure?" he asks, voice muffled by rock.

"I am," Morris says. "Don't worry, Talmadge. I'll be here when you get back. It'll all work out—I'll make sure of it."

And he will. He knows too well that he cannot fix everything, but he comes closer than most people, and here is the proof: He's covered in muck, shaky, near paralyzed, and yet this young man is obeying him, slithering into the rock with his heels kicking behind him. He's nodding even as he dives headfirst into the abyss, confident that Morris will manage whatever comes next.

Tom

Jeremiah slams a hand onto the sofa cushion, nearly knocking a jack of spades from Tom's hand. The two men in the armchairs across from them flinch.

They've been stuck in this hotel room since breakfast seven hours ago, and while Tom's been side by side with Jeremiah for much longer, they've never been caged inside a single room. Jeremiah has never done well with constraints, and the way he's stewing bodes poorly for how he'll do trapped underground.

It bodes poorly, too, for Tom being able to handle him. Over the years, he's fine-tuned his methods: First, he takes a stab at reasoning, which Jeremiah responds to every now and then. If that doesn't pay off, Tom tries distraction, and, if that doesn't work, he has no choice but to compromise. It's not so different from how his wife deals with the children when they cause a commotion on the train: She talks to them calmly, then she offers up a lollipop or a butterscotch, but if the fuss goes on long enough, she'll agree to about anything to make them shut their mouths.

Jeremiah slams his hand down again, but Tom has moved his cards a safe distance away. It's not ideal, playing a round of Tonk on a coffee table. The way they've arranged the armchairs means they're all hunched and bent-kneed and playing footsie with each other.

"Where the hell are they?" Jeremiah says.

He's been asking that for the past hour, as if anyone in this room knows more than he does. The Tonk game is Tom's version of a lollipop. He's already tried reasoning, but it won't hurt to try it again.

"You heard Lambert explain," he says, taking a card from the pile and then immediately discarding it. "It's just taking them longer than expected."

The two other men study their cards as if no one has spoken, which is fair enough since it isn't their job to deal with Jeremiah. Their job is to bide their time in this room, just as the newspaper men are biding their time in the lobby, and all of them are charged with the single function of making sure Jeremiah Hagathorn doesn't set foot outside. There can't be any chance of him crossing paths with the men who hid the hatpin until the newspaper reporter is around to play chaperone. *Sequestered in his private quarters, physically incapable of receiving any information regarding the location of the hatpin,* the contract said.

"Draw, Professor," says the blond-headed committee member, Ed. He owns a grocery, and he's drunk at least a dozen cups of coffee.

"How hard can it be?" Jeremiah says, drawing. "They walk in the cave and set down a hatpin."

He has a point, but Tom does not want to admit it, because if you concede a point with Jeremiah, it only builds his momentum. Still, the guide and the Woolworth's owner walked out of the lobby this morning insisting they had plenty of time to be back for a round of photos at three p.m. It's nearly two hours past that, and instead of the drinks and early dinner they should be enjoying, they're still imprisoned in this room. Barring injury, Tom isn't sure why two men who've lived here their entire lives haven't managed to find their way in and out of a cave by now.

He does not want to mention the possibility of injury to Jeremiah. Blood or broken bones would only delay the demonstration further.

"Are you going to be this stir-crazy tomorrow?" Tom asks.

Jeremiah flicks a card with his too-long fingernail. "I'm not stir-crazy."

"Plain crazy, then."

"We'll be moving in the caves," Jeremiah says. "It's the stillness I can't stand."

No, it's the boredom he can't stand. He's fanning himself with his cards, and Tom tries not to look at what's in his hand.

"It's not a bad turn of events, Jeremiah," he says. "Maybe they got lost. The newspapermen would love that. It'll only highlight how unpredictable the caves are."

"You don't think Lambert planned it?"

This would be easier if Jeremiah were a stupider man. Tom has considered himself whether Leo Lambert might have planned the delay, not that he would blame him. He's not lying when he says the reporters will love it. The mystery of the vanishing committeemen will keep them from getting bored until the real hunt starts.

"He didn't scheme," Ed says from the other side of the coffee table. "He doesn't have it in him. If Leo says something, he means it."

"He finds waterfalls. That's the kind of guy he is," says the other man, who has some position in the mayor's office. Tom remembers that his name rhymes with Ed, but he's forgotten if it's Ned or Jed, and it seems impolite to clarify at this stage. It's possible he's a second Ed.

"I don't know what kind of guy finds waterfalls," Jeremiah says. "The kind that builds an ark or the kind that goes after a white whale?"

Tom chuckles, but the other two men seem to take it as a serious question.

"An ark," Ed says. "He could raise the money to do it, at least."

"I'd make the argument Noah was crazier than Ahab," Jeremiah says as he lays down a run of spades, Queen, King, and Ace.

"You can't play that," Ed says. "Aces are always low."

"High or low," Jeremiah counters. "Either one."

"Not in Tonk," insists Ed. "In Tonk, they're always low."

Jeremiah leans back, cards loose in his hand, elbows hanging over the chair. He's wearing an expression that means he's thought of a way to entertain himself, and Tom knows he will not like it. He wishes desperately for a knock at the door. He wishes for a bottle of something. He wishes he were in his own den, with Rachel sewing in her chair and the children rolling marbles, although Jeremiah would have to be elsewhere. Rachel can't abide sharing air with him.

"Listen," Tom says, because he is out of lollipops and all he has left is compromise. "Give it twenty minutes. If we haven't heard anything, I'll get a group of reporters together and we'll offer an interview in the lobby. They can keep you in their sights the whole time, and you'll get a change of scenery."

Jeremiah straightens. "Twenty minutes?"

"That wasn't what the committee agreed to," Ed says, although Tom can tell he won't put up much of an argument. He can't be eager to prolong this Tonk game.

"I didn't agree to lock myself in here for the length of a transatlantic crossing," Jeremiah says, drawing another card. "Who's the reporter again?"

"There're plenty of them," Tom says.

"The one who's coming with us."

Tom lays down a set of threes. "Howard Waylander. Wrote me a very smart letter, very enthusiastic. He was the only one who went to the trouble. Plenty of folks are squeamish about going underground."

"Waylander." Jeremiah runs his tongue over his teeth like he's tasting the name. "Where's he from?"

"*Chicago Times.*"

That shuts Jeremiah up. He drops his eyes back to his cards for long enough that Tom's shoulders almost relax. He doesn't mention that he feels confident the reporter will either be a very good choice or a very bad one: Based on the time and effort that went into the man's letter, odds are that he's either a true believer or a true skeptic. But skeptics can make the most passionate converts, and Tom is proof of that himself. He showed up to see Jeremiah for the first time in Mount Joy, the pig's anus of Ohio, because Rachel wanted to see the show, and when the girl in sequins picked him out of the audience for the murder trick, he would've walked out except that it would've caused too much of a fuss. Then the girl slapped the knife in his hand, and his brain shut down entirely.

In those days the sight of anything serrated took him back to the shed when he'd first seen Lanny on the ground, but he wouldn't have said anything about that, not even to Rachel. Instead, he took the knife and he made himself stomp through the hay-covered ground to play his part. Rachel grabbed his hand when he sat back down, her hands sticky from candied apple. It was all fine—it was all almost fine—until Jeremiah came onstage and announced he would find the victim and the killer. *The murderer will not escape justice,* he said, and Tom's chest caved in on itself.

He couldn't breathe. He put his head in his hands as the audience clapped, and his palms were damp against his cheeks when he heard Jeremiah say from several rows away, *Here we have the unfortunate victim,* and the room roared with approval. Tom steadied himself enough to look up and see that, yes, it was the man he'd pantomimed stabbing. He could feel as much as hear Jeremiah moving through the crowd. Not footsteps—the hay muffled those. But the crowd murmured and whispered as Jeremiah passed, and as the whispers got louder, Tom knew the mind reader was close. Then everything went silent, and he felt a hand on his head, like a blessing.

You're the murderer, Jeremiah said to him.

Yes. Tom said it aloud, and when he looked up, Jeremiah's eyes were black moss. The audience whooped and hollered—even Rachel was cheering—but Jeremiah leaned closer so that only Tom could hear.

There was nothing you could have done, Jeremiah said. *He would have died before anyone got there.*

The words sent Tom flying back through time and space to his younger body, sitting at the kitchen table and hearing his little brother call out, ignoring the yell entirely because he was stretching a good piece of rubber into a slingshot but also because Lanny was ten years old and he'd hog the bed and spit on the last cookie and once he hurled rocks at the neighbors' mutt until it ran at him and Tom jumped forward and took the bite on his own arm—the same thing happened in a Cincinnati bar with Jeremiah, only it was an Irishman instead of a dog—but the upshot was that Tom tried not to pay his brother much attention. It was an hour before he made his way to the barn and saw Lanny on the ground pale and still, pieces of cast iron scattered on the ground. The band saw was turned on its side. The flywheel had broken into three pieces, and one of those pieces had lodged deep in Lanny's side and everything that would ever happen had already happened.

His parents asked *Why did God take him?* and they asked *Why was he fiddling with that saw*? but they never asked Tom if he let his brother die. He asked it of himself every single day, though, until Jeremiah said those words. When Tom heard them, it was like something sharp and always bleeding was pulled out of his own side.

Power comes with responsibility, supposedly, and Jeremiah has power. The responsibility falls on Tom.

"We've got to get some food when we go downstairs," Jeremiah says. "I could eat a horse."

"You should have said something," says Ed, and he pushes back his chair and walks to the briefcase he propped against the wall hours ago. He totes it to the coffee table, laying it on top of all the cards, and springs the latches. He pulls out a paper bag, dangling it between finger and thumb.

"Roast beef and homemade chutney sandwiches," he says.

It's an extravagant sort of sandwich, and Tom considers that being a grocer has advantages. He can't remember the last time he had roast beef. He stops thinking about cold cuts when Jeremiah stands, his face alight, and it's clear his giddiness isn't about sandwiches.

"You brought a razor," he says, leaning toward the briefcase.

Ed, still holding his paper sack, glances down at the wooden Gillette box. "I grow a beard faster than I can light a cigarette," he says. "I thought I might need to clean up for dinner."

"I tell you what we'll do," Jeremiah says. "I'll shave you."

"Jeremiah," Tom says. "We're in the middle of a game."

But Jeremiah tosses his last three cards onto the pink-peony pattern of an empty armchair. Both chairs are empty now because the Chattanooga men are standing. The paper bag lands on the carpet with a crackle.

"Let me shave you," Jeremiah repeats, bending over the briefcase.

He pops the clasp on the box, pulling out the straight razor, and no one stops him. No one moves at all.

"It's not a pleasure I get to enjoy anymore, you know," he says, stroking a hand over his thick beard, smiling.

He's a performer by profession, and that smile can charm an auditorium full of people, but he's not trying to be charming. The Chattanooga men step back, as any sane men will do when someone waves a razor at them.

"Professor—" starts Ned or Jed, palms out.

"Let's go on downstairs," Tom says. "Get some food in you. This isn't as clever a joke as you think it is."

He knows "joke" is the wrong word, but he's never figured out the right one.

"Did you bring soap?" Jeremiah says, ignoring him.

He takes a step forward, and Ed takes one backward.

"Never mind, I've got soap," Jeremiah says. "You sit down, my good sir, and we'll lather you up and I'll see what I can do. Go on.

Have a seat. It'll be just like the barbershop. We'll work up the kind of lather you can shape into a snowball."

He's followed Ed until the grocer is pressed against the wall, and he's got the damn razor an inch from the man's throat, and finally, finally, the grocer finds his voice and loses his politeness.

"What in God's name are you talking about?" he shouts, shoving Jeremiah back with both hands, the razor slicing through the air.

Jeremiah grins even as he falls against the armchair, catching himself with the arm not holding the razor. Both Chattanooga men are looking to Tom, and they are doing it, Tom knows, because they've categorized Jeremiah as a lunatic and Tom as his keeper and neither of these assumptions are exactly correct.

"He's not going to hurt you," Tom says, even as Jeremiah pushes to his feet, holding out the razor like a bouquet of flowers.

"You're not getting anywhere near my throat," Ed says, his voice raised.

Everyone's voice is raised, and Tom is glad for it. He hopes the noise will carry.

"You need to put down that razor, Professor Hagathorn," says Ned or Jed. "We'd rather not have to call the police, but we will."

"All I want to do," Jeremiah says, still smiling, "is to help you get ready for dinner."

The bedroom door opens, as Tom has been hoping it would. Editha stands with her hand on the knob, her dress belted and buttoned, her hair down around her shoulders. She's pretty as always, but she's watching Jeremiah in the same fascinated way she watches armadillos on the roadside. Tom has never figured out whether she wants to cuddle them or run them over.

"You can't play with other people's razors," she says to her husband.

"I'm not playing," he says.

"You're always playing."

Jeremiah laughs. His wife brings out the same giddiness in him that the razor does. She lifts her hand from the doorknob and flicks a finger in his direction, her instructions clear enough. He bends at the waist and drops the razor back into its box.

"Please step away from the briefcase, Miah," she says. "Make peace. I want to get back to my crossword."

The Chattanooga men are still as far away from Jeremiah as the walls will allow. Tom catches Editha's eye and gives her a nod, appreciative. When he smiles, she does not smile back, and if he were an armadillo, he'd keep himself far away from her car.

One Day Later
1932

8:20 a.m.

Ada's relieved to spot Quinton standing near the roses at the castle. They look to be the only people here, although tables are set up along the lawn, tablecloths flapping. It's nearly an hour until the big send-off, but she expected other early arrivals.

"Where is everyone?" she asks as soon as Quinton is in range. He's in a pair of khaki work pants that look washed and pressed, and his beard is neatly trimmed.

"Running behind," he says. "They're taking photos. They were supposed to do it yesterday, but they fell off schedule."

"What happened?"

"Morris and Talmadge ran late hiding the pin. By the time they showed up at the hotel, it was too late for pictures. The magic man was pitching a fit, apparently."

The sun is lifting over the trees, and Ada holds up a hand against the glare. She was wide-awake circling the kitchen floor when the moon was still bright, and she got dressed before the birds woke. Her nervousness has boiled down now, thicker and heavier. *Twelve hours,* she reminds herself. *You can handle anything for twelve hours.*

"It doesn't worry you that a grown man threw a fit?" she asks.

Quinton steps in front of her, blocking the sun from her eyes. "We knew he'd be a nutjob before he got here, didn't we?"

Two women appear at the lobby doors carrying silver coffeepots and trays of porcelain cups. They angle themselves through the door and take careful steps down the front stairs, heading across the grass toward the tables.

"Did they tell you where they hid it?" she asks.

"Not allowed to."

She knows that, but "not allowed" is not the same as "not doing." Surely not everyone in this group is good at keeping secrets.

"It has to be in the lower caverns," Quinton is saying. "It'd be over too fast if they hid it around the falls."

"Did they say why they took so long?"

"They say they lost track of time."

She can tell he doesn't believe this any more than she does. Talmadge supposedly knows everything about these caves, and Morris Efrom doesn't lose track of anything. Over Quinton's shoulder, one of the women lets out a high-pitched sound as she catches a coffeepot right before it tips onto the white tablecloth.

In the next half hour, the lawn fills up. Leo materializes from the dimness of the lobby, ready to play host. Over these past weeks, he's seemed nothing but delighted to discover that Ada's been sneaking around his caverns. *Imagine. You as a caver. I thought Quinton was pulling my leg,* he said, and then he gave her a hug and that was all. Now he shakes hands and thumps shoulders as men arrive in their Sunday suits, with Ruby moving more quietly through the crowds, offering her own hellos. Women's hats catch the sunlight in flashes of red, yellow, and green as they stroll up the walk, and children flit like mosquitos, never staying on the footpath.

Ada wonders what they all make of her and Quinton's bulky pants and jackets. When the professor and his group arrive, they're not dressed for church, either, of course. They come clomping toward the lawn in their own heavy boots. The woman with them is dressed in caving clothes as well, which is a surprise.

"The mind reader's wife," Quinton says. "Apparently, he plans to bring her along."

There's something in his tone, and Ada nearly asks him if he's offended at the idea of a woman in the caves, but Leo's jogging across the grass to greet the new arrivals, an empty coffee cup dangling from his hand. Behind Ada, a camera flashes.

She expected to be treated like a ghost, invisible, but Leo brings the expedition members over and introduces her and Quinton by name, although he doesn't mention any other details. No one seems to notice their clothes: Maybe the others think they've come in costume for a lark. The professor and his party all shake her hand politely and likely forget her immediately. They have so many hands to shake: A line has formed, snaking around the castle. Ada sees multiple men with notebooks and cameras.

She doesn't mind being forgotten. It gives her an opportunity to watch.

She studies the slender, long-faced man standing next to the mind reader. Talmadge Cunningham is smiling easily enough, apparently feeling more sociable than when he gave her the cold shoulder on the castle steps. She can't feel much friendliness toward him. The mind reader, bearded and olive-skinned, keeps scanning the crowd, never quite keeping his attention on whoever happens to be in front of him. He's as tall as Quinton—surely around the same age, too, early fifties—but where Quinton always makes sure she doesn't have to crane her neck at him, Jeremiah Hagathorn stands too close. He's looming over one of the city council members to the point that the other man is arched backward, and he has a belly that might make some of the tighter spots tricky.

His wife is small and dark-haired, with fawn's eyes, at least a decade younger than her husband. Her heart-shaped face could be on a movie screen, and she's wearing what seem to be riding breeches. She smiles, closemouthed, at each introduction, as she did when Ada said her own *pleased to meet you.*

Ada watches her steadily for a few minutes, and she never sees her speak.

The manager is average-sized, with a square jaw and glasses. Each time he shakes hands, he clasps the other man's hand with both of his. He was the only one who used Ada's name when she was introduced to him. He turns as Morris Efrom comes hurrying down the lobby steps, catching up to the rest of them. Morris is younger looking than his sixty-something years, and he's a good friend to Leo. He invested in Ruby Falls before anyone else did, and Ada's not sure it's humanly possible to dislike the man. He wrote thank-you notes to every person who attended his wife's funeral last fall, and he's run his store so smartly that people say he hasn't let go of a single employee over these bare-bone years. People say, too, that he's stopped taking a salary himself.

It's wise, what Leo's done. She hasn't fully appreciated his strategy until this moment. People don't doubt his honesty, but they think he might be hopeful enough to imagine a miracle. He's a dreamer, Leo. Morris, though—if he says this psychic demonstration is real, people will believe him.

The newspaperman is barely a man, or at least that's her first thought. The longer she looks at him, the more she suspects he's one of those men who never does look old enough to shave. Or maybe it's only that as she gets older, everyone looks younger. Could he be in his thirties? Anyway, he's rust-haired and thin, with a too-big Mackinaw jacket and pants that nearly brush the ground. Surely Talmadge will see to it that he tucks them into his boots.

Another thing about the newspaperman: He keeps looking at the mind reader's wife, who never looks his way once. Quinton, too, watches the wife, and it's as Ada has always suspected—the ideal woman for most men is both beautiful and mute.

Leo moves the official start time to ten a.m., and Ada and Quinton have barely gotten themselves hidden in the old streambed at the entrance to the falls level when they hear the elevator descending. Soon the elevator door clangs open, metal on metal, and boots scuff against rock.

"Which way, gentlemen?" Morris asks, his voice echoing.

All the men laugh, or at least Ada assumes it's all of them, even though it's not obvious why the question is funny. She can't see anything but rock and Quinton's pants. The two of them are well-concealed, assuming no one gets a wild hair to crawl into tight spaces only fifty feet from the elevator. The hiding spot is likely unnecessary, since the group will have to come back to the elevator to access the lower caverns, but there's the small chance that the hatpin will be discovered on this level or that someone breaks a leg. Leo said to stay within shouting distance at all times, so here they are, crouched in the dark.

Sound gets swallowed up in these caves, the rock shutting out voices the same way it does heat and cold. Ada can't make out any other words until footsteps crunch closer to the opening of their hidden cranny.

"I need you to form a clear picture in your mind," says a voice. "If it's blurry, I can't make it out. You need to envision it as clearly as possible."

That must be the professor. His voice isn't as deep as she expected.

"I still don't understand your process exactly," Morris says.

"Picture the hatpin," the professor says, and there's the snapping of fingers. Three loud clicks with a pause in between, like a musician keeping time. "Picture the item itself and the place where you left it. Picture every detail you remember about its location. Picture the route there. But this next part is even more important: You need to project that image to me."

Ada isn't sure about the next sounds. The man is either slapping his thighs or stomping his foot. Maybe he's clapping with his gloves on. It's the same pattern: three slow beats.

"The stronger your mind," he says, "the stronger the image comes through. From my end, it's the difference in someone communicating with a whisper versus a shout. Mr. Efrom, I specifically asked Mr. Lambert to send a man who was unfamiliar with the caves so that your impressions would be stronger and fresher. He told me you had the sharpest mind of anyone he knew."

Ada would like to see Morris's face during this exchange, but when he speaks, he doesn't address the flattery.

"So if you fail to find the hatpin," he says, "the fault is with our minds?"

Ada can hear a smile in his voice, a tribute to his good nature, given that the psychic seems to be an utter ass. The man's whole world is a stage. The voices haven't been moving, and she imagines Jeremiah Hagathorn is intentionally holding his audience captive.

"If the scouts at Little Bighorn had given General Custer the correct number of Indians," the professor says, "the battle would have turned out differently. He could not win the battle when they offered up bad details."

"You're General Custer, I take it?" Talmadge says.

"If it helps," Hagathorn says, "the scouts got a happier ending."

A couple of the men laugh, not much more than puffs of breath, but enough to ease the tension that Ada can feel even through the rock.

"Look," Hagathorn says, "we're down here to find a hatpin. My understanding was that you all want that as much as I do."

A water droplet falls into a nearby pool of water, ringing soft and clear, before the men murmur their assents.

"We do, of course," Morris says.

"In order for me to find the pin," the professor says, "you have to do your part. Mental power is as much an art as a talent, and all I'm asking you to do is to work at it. Maybe you don't believe I can do this, but that truly doesn't matter. If you envision the hiding place clearly enough, I will absorb it. I'll recognize the spot as soon as I see it, and we can all go home."

"And if you don't believe in him, you will soon enough," says another voice. "I've known him a decade"—it must be the manager, Tom—"and I started out not believing. He saw straight through me. He told me a secret I'd never told anyone, and I've watched him do a lot more than that. You'll see."

The elevator rumbles: The soft whine that follows is a sign that it's been summoned back aboveground. Ada wonders if the reporters want to confirm that everyone entered the caves.

"No disrespect intended," Morris says when the whirring has faded. "It's more a question of working out our nerves. I'm picturing the hatpin now, exactly where we left it."

"Me, too," Talmadge says.

The cave goes quiet. Someone slides the sole of their boot back and forth, a scraping like sandpaper or stubble.

"Can you see anything yet?" Morris asks.

"It's still solidifying," the professor says. "I can see the hatpin itself. Maybe six inches long. A shiny bead—gold, maybe? silver?—or some sort of rhinestone, I think."

Ada assumes the silence that follows the statement means he's gotten it right, and the men are impressed. She is not particularly impressed, although she knows which hatpin Ruby volunteered for this demonstration, and he's described it correctly. He's also described the vast majority of hatpins.

"So do you want to lead the way, Professor Hagathorn?" Talmadge says. "Or you want me to lead? There aren't any junctions on this level. It's a straight-ahead path, and we'll retrace our route when we turn around at the falls."

"You go first," Hagathorn says. "I need to focus on my thoughts, not my footing, and it'll be easier to follow. I'll call out if I want to stop."

"And if I say stop," Talmadge warns, "you do. Without question. If I say duck, you do it. We're on our own down here, and there's no margin for error."

"Watch your head, Jeremiah," the manager says. "I've watched you run into plenty of chandeliers."

The footsteps start again, faster than Ada expects. The dangling bulbs above the pathway are glowing just as they do for the tour groups, which makes a quick pace easy, but she expected mind reading to require slowness, like small stitches. The professor does not seem to be taking his time.

"Where's the water in the waterfall come from?" asks a voice she doesn't recognize.

"No one knows for sure," Talmadge answers. "It could be surface water that comes through cracks in the mountain. But we know over the years—thousands, millions—it's flowed through the limestone of the mountain and carved out these rooms. This formation here is the Cactus and Candle. The minerals got dripped down along with the water, and the sediment piles up after a while."

It's getting harder to hear him.

"Is your ability entirely visual, or can you sense location?" Morris asks. "When we get close to the hatpin, can you feel it?"

"I only see what you show me," the professor says.

"Soda straws," Talmadge announces. "See right there? They're hollow stalactites. They grow at most a few millimeters every year."

He's doing some version of his usual tour guide routine, and his patter frustrates Ada nearly as much as the professor's posturing. It's possible that she's holding a grudge.

"I expected to sweat," says the voice she hasn't placed. The newspaperman, she assumes. "I wore the jacket because I believe in following instructions, but I admit I didn't think I'd need it. Don't they sweat all the time in coal mines?"

"It's a steady sixty degrees here, year-round," Talmadge says.

"You still growing into that coat?" the professor asks, and Ada knows who he means even before the reporter answers.

"My landlady lent it to me," the younger man says. "It was her husband's."

His tone makes it clear that Ada is not the only one irked by Jeremiah Hagathorn.

"Well, I expected bats," says, maybe, the manager.

"No animals at all on this level," Talmadge says in his louder-than-necessary guide voice, and Ada does appreciate the volume. "Other than an occasional bird or butterfly that comes down the elevator shaft. Not even gnats."

"Not quite true," Quinton mutters, his breath on Ada's cheek. He smells of orange juice. "A fair number of salamanders wash over the falls."

"No fish of any kind in these streams?" asks the newspaperman. Howard.

"The metal content is too high," Talmadge answers. "We put a couple of catfish in the pool under the falls last year, but they were dead within a week."

Ada wonders if the psychic's wife can make it through the whole trip without saying a word.

"There's still sometimes animals in the lower caverns," Talmadge says, and she misses his next sentence. "But when they closed up the old railway entrance—"

Ada doesn't hear any more as his voice fades to nothing. The silence swells and settles.

"Sealing up the railroad entrance blocked the bigger animals," Quinton whispers. "There used to be raccoons. Weasels, too. A bear now and then, they say. Everything but beavers, thank God."

"I'd love to see a beaver," she whispers back.

"Not close-up, you wouldn't. They're territorial as hell. I had one come after me like it wanted to gut me."

"You got attacked by a beaver?"

"I would say 'chased.'"

She thinks he's smiling, not that she can see him. She scoots forward slightly, getting a clearer view of the empty footpaths. "Should we head after them?"

"Let's give 'em a little more space," he says.

Ada pulls back as Quinton slides forward. His knees crack as he stands, and he holds out a hand to help her, which comes close to shocking her. She's not sure whether to be flattered or offended—she's well able to stand on her own, otherwise she'd never make it down here—but she gives him one hand, and she feels the callouses on his palms as he gives a tug.

She nods, letting go of him. His bare hands remind her that she should make sure her gloves are still in her jacket pocket. They'll need them in the lower level.

"Talmadge will have to keep a firm grip on the reins," Quinton whispers.

"I'm sure he can manage," Ada says. She kneels to tighten the laces on her boot. "He doesn't seem like the overly polite type."

"Talmadge?" Quinton answers. "Polite enough. A little timid. Better with rocks than people. Speaking of, I'd have thought the newspaperman would have more to say."

Ada doesn't know what she thinks of the newspaperman. She likes that he asks questions. She likes that he follows instructions. She, too, has always believed in following rules, although maybe not as much anymore.

Whatever the man writes, that's what the truth will be, Leo said at their last meeting.

"It seems like the smartest thing is for him to listen," she says.

"At least one of them is smart."

"How do you mean?"

Quinton turns to her, his jacket hanging open so she can see the buttons of his shirt.

She noticed his buttons, too, when he came to her front door. She noticed them when he showed her through the cave that first time and she noticed them this morning, when he did nothing other than say hello. She notices them when she's alone and he exists only in her head. She wants to undo them and slide her hands under the fabric. There it is. She tries not to think it and she tries not to feel it, but she wants to touch his bare skin and she wants to press herself full against him and it is astonishing how much she wants it.

Her annoyance with herself is almost as strong as her lust. She thought all that was finished. She thought, truly, that it never started. She remembers feeling curiosity about Gerald's body—wondering what she might lay her hands on one day—but this is not curiosity. This takes her back to whisperings with school friends, more unspoken than spoken. She'd had a sense in those days that climbing into bed with a man would unlock some great mystery, and it might be terrible or wonderful, but it would be significant.

She never found it significant. Not in all these years. She'd forgotten all about those school whispers, but now her body and mind are trying to drag her toward this man who thinks of her as a man or a sister or possibly an anthodite.

"Morris and Talmadge seem like they believe the saphead," he says. "They think they can follow along and he'll conjure up the hatpin."

If we don't believe that, why are we down here? she thinks.

"That's a strong opinion considering you've barely met the man," she says.

"Did you like him?" he asks. "Do you trust him?"

She tries to come up with something generous, but no words come to mind. Quinton nods as if she's answered.

"That's what I thought," he says.

He's grabbing the bag of supplies, slinging it over his arm and sliding it to the spot where shoulder meets neck. She would like to stop being aware of the parts of his body.

11:40 a.m.

Jeremiah

When he agreed to this whole affair, he pictured a setup like the top level of the caves, which was no more threatening than a department store. They didn't even need to put on their helmets. Only now that they've ventured into the lower level does Jeremiah realize how wrong he was to expect a cave to be a simple, long, dark tunnel, like a hallway in a house. This is nothing like a hallway. The rock is closing in on them from all sides, dripping down from the ceiling so close overhead that he can't shake the feeling that if he straightened too quickly, a shard might drive straight through his helmet into his brain.

It's too loose, his helmet. It slides over his forehead when he bends down, and he is always having to bend down. He has to crawl. No one mentioned crawling. The floor beneath him is sandy as a beach, and it is not made for humans, this place.

He's staying as close as possible to the guide and the businessman in hopes that he might get what he needs from sheer proximity: Sometimes he can pick up the answer from a few inches away. Mostly, though, he needs to get his hands on people. Everything is clearer with physical contact. This isn't normally a problem on the stage, where whatever he says becomes the rule of law. A stage has a power, at times transferrable to a podium or the head of a table.

Onstage, if he asks a man to hold out his arm, the man does it. If he asks a woman to take off her bracelet, she does it.

There are other laws at play in this place, and he doesn't control them.

On the waterfall level, Lambert's men might as well have held up a sign telling him to get moving. No, the pin is down here, and he knows it, yet he's miscalculated. The mechanics of what he needs won't be physically possible in some of these narrower passages, and that's not taking into account the social awkwardness of it.

He stops, studying the cracks running along the wall, black against gray. He tilts his head, shining his lamp toward the higher crevices where wall meets ceiling. Without looking, he can tell the businessman has stopped in front of him, turning so that he's added the power of his own light to the cracks along the ceiling.

"Are you seeing anything, Professor?" he asks.

Jeremiah starts forward again. Everyone is waiting on him, he realizes. "Only studying the walls."

"I meant in terms of visions," the businessman says. "Are you seeing anything more clearly?"

"It's still blurred. I can't make out the details."

"What sort of blur do you mean?" the businessman asks. "Do you see color? Shapes? What's the nature of the visions?"

The man owns a Woolworth's? He's spouting the lines of a scientist or a poet, two of the most unlikeable professions. He's another source of frustration, the businessman. His emotions are not nearly as close to the surface as Jeremiah would have hoped.

The ceiling drops precipitously in front of them, like a stairwell to a root cellar, and the guide ducks but does not warn the rest of them, trusting them to notice on their own, which feels like a form of malpractice.

"I don't think of it in those terms," Jeremiah says. "I don't know about colors or shapes, only clarity and lack of clarity. It's like a trickle of water compared to a river. I'm not receiving the image in the way that I'd like, and I understand that your companion is focused on the terrain, so I beg you—keep your mind focused. Have you kept the image in your head?"

The low ceiling extends for a solid ten feet, and when he's straightened fully he sees that the businessman has halted again. The man is only a body with a bright beam of light for a head until he turns and starts forward again.

"It's not possible to keep a single thought in your head every moment, Professor," he says over his shoulder. "That can't be your expectation, and if it is, it's doomed to fail."

It's a shift in tone from the man who until now has been all warmth, the host of this odd party. For the first time, Jeremiah understands how this fellow might be in charge of hiring and firing other men. He likes him better this way.

"I expect you to do your best to keep it firm in your head," Jeremiah says. "If you don't hold on to it, I can't possibly absorb it. The picture sharpens for me over time."

"When did you first realize you were able to read minds?" the reporter asks from behind him.

It's the only question he's asked in the last half hour. Jeremiah makes a point of turning and looking him in the eye, tilting down because the poor man isn't much taller than Editha. He's narrow-shouldered and long-fingered, and maybe the fingers come in handy for writing.

Howard, he said as he pulled out his chair in the hotel restaurant, tie hanging down into the bread rolls. *Just Howard is fine.*

"I've always had it," Jeremiah says. "It's like asking when I first realized I could breathe."

It's his usual answer: He doesn't revisit the past. It's one of the many ways he and Editha are alike, which he has, mostly, considered a blessing.

Her small hand lands on his elbow, and she murmurs an apology, but she's barely aware of him. His wife is drunk off this place. She practically thrums with pleasure, her eyes darting, bright and hungry. Ahead of them, he can see that the passage splits like two miniature railroad tunnels, and he's the one who'll need to throw the switch.

He suspects he's spotted the junction even before the guide. It's an undervalued currency, observation. But now the guide is slowing, and the businessman takes a visible breath, as if he's going to jump in a pool. They both turn to him.

"Which way, Professor Hagathorn?" the guide asks, and finally everyone's eyes shift back to Jeremiah instead of Talmadge.

Talmadge. That's his name.

Editha's been staring at the guide just as devotedly as everyone else—Jeremiah has paid attention to where her eyes are drifting—and that's natural both because they've all been told to obey every word out of the man's mouth and because women love power. Jeremiah has known this his entire life—he grew up watching the church ladies come up to his father after a sermon, hands fluttering against his arm, bodies leaning too close—and even if he'd been a different child and not noticed all the pressing of bodies, he'd certainly not have missed those same women coming over with their casseroles and too-tight blouses after his mother died. His father remarried within six months—a long-nosed blonde in her twenties, nice enough—and, yes, women like power.

"Bats up on our left there," Talmadge says, and he points to a cluster of tiny shapes Jeremiah would have mistaken for shadow. "If you don't startle them, they'll stay right there."

The rest of them stare at the bats as if he has pointed out a unicorn.

The truth is that everyone loves power. Women and men and children and dogs and train conductors and schoolmasters and governors: They are all moths, flapping toward the light. They want to see it and touch it. They came to watch Harry Keller levitate that girl, they packed the seats when Howard Thurston made a tiger disappear, and they wanted to believe that Mina Crandon could conjure her dead brother as ectoplasm seeped from her ears. They want to believe that Jesus fed the five thousand and that Elisha's bones brought a dead man back to life.

Jeremiah can drive blindfolded through an unfamiliar city, never putting a scratch on the car, but that's not enough. It only whets an audience's appetite. The men and women in the back seat will tumble from his car and insist they felt spirits on the seat next to them or invisible forces brushing against their heads.

People want to believe.

"Sometimes touch helps the thoughts come through clearer," he says, turning to the Woolworth's man. "It strengthens the connection. Would you hold out your arm?"

The man does as he asks.

"That's it," Jeremiah says. "Hold it steady. Yes. Exactly. And now I place my arm on top of yours, and we approach the pathways together. Picture the hatpin. Picture the route to it, and I will pull it from your mind."

Everyone is watching now, and Jeremiah has always done best with spectators. The energy sharpens him. He sinks into himself as he rests his arm on Efrom's, feeling the slight tremor of the man's fingers. It's a solid, strong arm, more muscle to it than Jeremiah would expect for a man this age. The forearm is unyielding as they step forward, and the tremor vanishes.

He lets his shoulder brush against the other man's shoulder. He slides his fingers until they're overlapping the hand below his, thumb to thumb and pinkie to pinkie.

"Excellent," he says. "Now let's take another step, slowly."

He closes his eyes, and he can still see bobbing circles of lamplight against his eyelids. He doesn't need sight for this. It's only a distraction. He needs to feel the leanings, and he does that, letting himself go—sinking and sinking—fully expecting the answer to be clear to him, as it always is. As it almost always is.

By their fourth step, he realizes he has no idea which direction to turn, and it's the first flash of real fear he's felt since he entered the mountain.

1:45 p.m.

It's impossible for Ada and Quinton to keep the group in sight without being seen themselves. She keeps thinking of Leo: *A psychic journeying hundreds of feet belowground to navigate trails that could lead to the very center of the earth?* he said. *That's a story. If we sent along nursemaids to mind him, who would cover that?*

So she and Quinton stay mostly in earshot, keeping a few hundred feet back. Hagathorn—or maybe Talmadge—has slowed the pace since their rush through the falls level. The group covered the mile to the falls and back in under two hours, but they've barely managed half a mile in that amount of time down here.

The voices spark and sputter. Back on the falls level, the group sounded like boys heading off on a fishing trip, chattering and laughing. They've gone quieter now, and Ada's not sure how much of that is mood versus the nature of the climbing. It's no easy stroll at this stage, and they haven't even hit the wild caves where they'll spend most of their time on hands and knees.

It's the mind reader's voice she hears the most.

Steady, he says. *Steady now.*

Focus.

Junction, Talmadge says occasionally, and she assumes Hagathorn answers him.

She flashes her light to the ceiling and spots the black-reddish stains of bat urine. The rock here sags and dimples like old skin, jowls and bags everywhere. J.H. CURTIS, 1812 is scarred along the wall, lettered as elegantly as a tombstone.

As much as she felt mind reading should demand a more mindful pace, she didn't consider that slowness would be numbing. When the group finally stops for food and water, she's desperate for a break from the listening and waiting. She and Quinton back far enough away that they can no longer hear voices, sidestepping into a pocket blessedly tall enough to stretch her arms over her head. When Quinton eases his bag onto the ground, it jangles despite his carefulness.

"You sure we're not too close to them?" she whispers. She feels as if she might never talk in a normal tone of voice again. "Or too far away?"

"Anything bad enough to involve us will bring on some screaming," Quinton says. "We'll hear them."

"What if they leave without us noticing?"

"I'll bet you a dime they sound like a herd of buffalo when they get up."

He toes his duffle bag closer to the wall. She doesn't envy him maneuvering it through the gaps and squeezes. She's carrying a much smaller pack across her shoulder, and she's still struggling to shove her supplies through the smaller spaces. Quinton has extra carbide cartridges, rope, bandages, three canteens of water, and all of it is likely pointless. With a little luck, they could be back aboveground by sunset.

Time and distance are deceptive here. After all these hours, she thinks she could make it back to the elevator in half an hour, if she guessed the turns right.

Quinton sinks down along a smooth swathe of limestone, taking his helmet in one hand and letting his head fall back with a groan. She sits as well, running a hand through her hair as she takes off her own helmet. It feels good to let her head breathe. She opens her canteen and takes a long drink.

"Pecans?" he says, shoving a hand in his pocket.

"Oh," she says, fishing inside her pack, and now what seemed like a good idea feels silly. Grandmotherly. "I have this. In case. For us both, if you want."

She gives up on full sentences and pulls out two folded napkins, damp with grease. She unfolds the first, holding out a block of cold macaroni and cheese. She made a pan last night when she couldn't sleep, thinking it would be a treat, and, if she's honest, some sort of testament to her value as a partner, but in this moment it feels clear that worthy people don't need to prove themselves and that this is not a picnic. The macaroni is congealed and misshapen with the bits of noodles looking more like larvae than she would like.

"Macaroni salad?" Quinton says, grinning.

She hopes her face doesn't give away her relief.

"My mother used to make it for church suppers," she says, handing over his slice. "She said she was the first person in Etowah County to do it where you cooked the noodles in the oven instead of beforehand."

She cannot remember the last time she told the story of this recipe. Gerald and Ruby and plenty of others have heard about her mother's claim to fame, but it's been a long time since she's said it aloud.

Quinton takes a bite, napkin flapping under his chin. In the strange dimness of caves, the cheese has turned the gold of sunlight. She bites into her own slice and wishes she'd added more salt.

"Do you think he can do it?" she asks.

"Seems like he would have done it by now, doesn't it?"

"Yes." She is not impressed by the mind reader. "It's not how I thought it would be."

"What did you think?"

She takes her time chewing as she considers her answer. "That he'd be more in command. That someone would be more in command. This feels like—"

"Wandering," he says, finding the right word before she can. "It might feel different, I suppose, if we could hear a full sentence every now and then."

Their two lamps illuminate a circle around them, shadows flailing every time they lift an arm or take a drink. Beyond that, the blackness has hints of planes and angles, if Ada wanted to look. Back in the beginning, she thought the darkness in a cave would gnaw at you over time, but the truth is that, like everything else outside your circle of flame, it ceases to exist. There is no darkness.

You stop seeing anything after a while, she supposes, like the peeling paint on her windows or the extra rooms in her house that used to seem empty but now don't seem anything at all.

"If he's a fraud, you'd think someone would have caught him by now," she says. "Maybe it's like he says. Maybe it's not predictable."

"Maybe."

She sets down her canteen, picking it up again when she sees a trickle of dark movement near her hip. It's a trail of ants gorging themselves on a dead salamander. Two pale millipedes and a cricket inch closer, hoping.

"You think Talmadge will show him where the pin is?" she asks.

"No. Not yet, at least."

This matches her own thinking. She assumes that if the hours stretch out, Talmadge or Morris could offer a few silent or not-so-silent hints.

"Because if it turns out Hagathorn is a fraud," she says, "I have trouble thinking we should help him out."

Quinton swipes at a strand of cheese on his beard. "May not matter. Nudging him along wouldn't be easy with the newspaperman watching."

She's not hungry, but she knows she needs to eat. She makes herself finish the last two bites of macaroni, and she tries not to look at the remains of the salamander. She's read they eat their own tails if they're starving.

"If they're going to help him," she says, "I wish they'd go on and do it. And if he has any ability, I wish he'd go on and show it."

"You're not the patient kind, are you?" he says.

It feels like a compliment.

"I don't like not knowing," she says.

He wads up his napkin, pauses, and lets it fall open again. He spreads it across one thigh, folds it carefully, and hands it back to her.

"Spoken like anyone who's ever climbed into a hole in the ground," he says. "You know they're cannibals?"

It takes her a moment to realize he's looking at the salamander.

"I thought they ate themselves," she says.

"That, too. But also each other. Everything's hungry all the time down here."

When she looks up into the beam of her own light, motes float and swirl all the way to the ceiling. Someone coughs down the passageway, a sign of life.

Quinton lights a cigarette, and as he inhales, he taps the wall behind them. Only then does she see the names: EDWARD or EDWIN SKELTON. Or SKELLON. The letters have faded enough that the signature has blurred into more than one person. The name below it could be B. GOODWIN or possibly H. GOODWIN, with ADALDE below. T.A. KIRBY is carved very clearly, as is J.L. WESLEY, PORTLAND, 1862.

"Civil War soldiers thinking this might be their last chance to leave a mark on the world," Quinton says.

Ada would like to know how long it takes before a name evaporates entirely. Sometimes she sees markings that are barely there, more like bird scratchings than letters.

"Adalde," she says, pointing. "You think that's a name or a place?"

"Place, I bet," Quinton says. "But I'd rather it be a name. I like the odd ones. Farrow Hailstone, I saw once."

"Mitty Mindwell," she counters.

"We used to do it with smoke from a carbon light when we were small," he says. "Write our own names next to the ones on the wall, long dead, nothing left of them but letters. A hundred years from now, they'll say the same thing about me."

He sounds happy enough about it. She thinks of her imaginings in the crystal room, her longing for medicine men or rumrunners to have stood in her place, a string of invisible twine connecting them.

A rustle carries through the passageways—feet and gravel and the bang of a canteen, and while they don't sound quite like buffalo, these people are not difficult to track. She and Quinton stand; she refastens her helmet and tucks the used napkins into her pack. He swings his bag over his shoulder.

The passages splinter more often as they move deeper into the mountain. Quinton knows the overlaps and intersections, and he keeps them moving in such a way that they hear voices every few minutes. Ada recognizes some rooms—a swathe of drapery, a head-high column, a certain long expanse where she flattens like a flounder—but she doesn't have a map in her head like Quinton does.

The larger group seems to be avoiding the tightest passages, but she and Quinton take advantage of the shortcuts. He steps to an opening the size of a manhole, dropping his bag through and then slipping down himself. As soon as he hits the ground, he crawls forward and she follows, too close at first, nearly getting his boot in her face. The macaroni jostles in her belly as the slabs of rock around them spread out and the ceiling lifts. They push to their feet, side by side, just as a man shouts in pain from somewhere through the walls.

A long groan follows, nearly swallowed up by a burst of agitated voices.

Ada starts forward, hunchbacked. Quinton grabs her by the shoulder, yanking her backward.

"Wait," he says.

The voices are already quieting. She hears Morris's laugh, abashed. She can make out Talmadge's tone—calm enough—but not his words. Quinton lets go of her. She hates being on the edges, only guessing at what's happening, never given a clear view. It's like watching a play from behind a pole, the kind of seat you pay half price for.

The two of them move in fits and starts, spending long minutes frozen with their backs millimeters from the ceiling. During one pause, Quinton wriggles into a shallow nook, and when he turns, he's got a bone in his hands.

"Hellbender salamander," he whispers.

Not a bone—an entire skeleton, over a foot long, the tail of the thing hanging over his hands. He slides it into her palms, and she expects it to feel like a chicken carcass pulled out of hot broth, but it's delicate and cool and light as a necklace, the best present anyone's ever given her. They both stare at the long spine with its feathered vertebrae, the stumpy legs and missing foot bones, and eventually she realizes he didn't mean it as a present. It would shatter into shards if she tried to tuck it in her satchel.

She inches past him, easing the skeleton back where he found it. When she turns, he's already moving forward, half crouched. Every time she looks at him, she hopes to discover that the flush of attraction was entirely imagined, but she keeps discovering the opposite.

At the next opening, she and Quinton wait until the path ahead of them goes dark, and then they crawl into a chamber that Ada recognizes. The walls are spires, with hundreds of packed stalagmites spiking toward the ceiling. It's like a cathedral. The ground is wetter in here, and shallow puddles line the walls. The mind reader and his gang are at the far end of the massive room, several hundred feet away, hidden by the bend of a wall. Ada hears a trickling, and she'd guess the others are looking at the skinny waterfall that only comes to life after a good rain.

That seems to be her only option: guessing. She can hear footsteps but no voices as she leans against the rock behind her. The footsteps turn wet. Eventually someone murmurs, and someone answers.

Again, she hates this. If they find the hatpin, she and Quinton likely won't even realize it.

She sinks to her bottom, and her light makes the rocks shine in the puddles, candy-like. There's one the color of caramel that she imagines popping in her mouth. She'd like to roll it over her tongue, suck it, crunch it in her teeth. The endless waiting seems to be shoving her mind in strange directions.

A rush of wordless sound echoes off the walls. A gasp. Metal clangs against rock, and, next to her, Quinton jolts.

"You idiot," Talmadge shouts, and she supposes Quinton was right. They will hear if someone screams.

Ada doesn't think she's ever heard Talmadge raise his voice. Whoever speaks next is quieter, though, and the words don't carry.

"I told you about the water," Talmadge answers, still too loud. "It'll tear through you, and you'll be stranded down here, hunched over with the runs."

"You could have said that," the professor says, "instead of—"

"I did," Talmadge says. "You don't pay attention."

"I do when someone is worth paying attention to."

Either Talmadge has calmed himself or he's hissing his insults too quietly for Ada to hear. She takes off her helmet and sets it on the ground, the light falling across her shins. She pulls out her flashlight, which is easier to direct.

"I'm going to take a quick look," she whispers.

Quinton shakes his head, but she ignores him, and when she starts forward, he doesn't follow. She keeps close to the wall, her shoulder and hip skimming along rock with every step. She keeps the flashlight pointing down. The outcropping of rock jutting in front of her blocks her view of everyone just as it blocks their view of her.

"Leave it there," a man says, and she can't tell which one.

"We don't have endless water," Talmadge says. He sounds more exhausted than angry now. "I'll get it."

"There's no way," says—maybe—Morris.

"I'll tie a rope," Talmadge says. "It's not quite a vertical climb."

Ada turns off the flashlight and presses her cheek against the edge of the outcropping. In the darkness of the room, the six people with headlamps might as well be in a spotlight. Her view is limited because of the formations rising from the ground, but she sees why Talmadge doesn't sound enthusiastic about the offer he's making.

He's looking up at spired limestone that rises at least thirty feet to the ceiling. Someone else's lamp catches the glint of something hanging from a strap on a ledge more than halfway up the wall.

A canteen, she guesses. It's baffling how it would have gotten there.

"I only need—" Talmadge starts.

"What the hell are you doing?" someone says as another voice shouts, "Careful!"

"Shit," Talmadge says, loud and clear.

Ada hears soft sounds of movement and gravel pinging into puddles, but her view is still obscured, and it's a moment before another figure comes into view. It's the wife. She's climbing the wall of the cavern, no rope or harness in sight. She's higher than the men's heads, making her way up the rock as if it's a ladder.

4:30 p.m.

Editha

She's always liked heights, and for that she can thank the fine people of Barnum & Bailey who used to winter across the field from her house on Route 124. She was small and polite, and they called her a natural when she wobbled on the tightrope. Fearless, they said, when she launched herself off the trapeze, and they were friendly people who weren't around children often and likely would have said the same thing about any six-year-old, especially one who had more bruises than she should.

They gave her sandwiches sometimes. They were responsible for her first taste of strawberry jam. *Pick my eye paint for me tonight?* the handwalker would say, and onstage her name was Anastasia but her real name was Mona. *Just leave me the banana,* Mr. Wilson would warn, holding out his bag of taffy, but if Ada picked anything but banana he would press one into her hand anyway because he knew it was her favorite. He was a bicyclist, white-haired but still able to jump a gap of twenty feet.

They are the kindest people in the world, circus people. Editha would bet on them against nuns any day. When it comes to her childhood, the people in that barn are the only part she chooses to recall.

By the time she was twelve, they gave fewer compliments and more instructions. At that stage, she was eighty pounds of pure lean muscle: If she'd been a calf, she'd have been too tough to eat. It turned out she had a real talent for the vertical rope, or the corde lisse, as she preferred to call it because everything sounded better in French. She started with the basic leg wraps and lean-outs and moved on to upside-down hangs, and she dislocated her shoulder trying to master a crucifixion. Before breasts and hips weighed her down, she could move on the rope like she was underwater, pulled to the top by the forces of nature itself. She lay on her pallet at night imagining some future winter where she would leave Peru, Indiana, and become one of the acrobats in the barn, but then the stage manager put his hands on her, which was another thing she blamed on breasts and hips until she got old enough and smart enough to blame the stage manager.

She can hear the men talking among themselves below, or maybe they're still talking to her. It doesn't matter. They don't matter. They throw canteens at walls. All that matters is the satisfaction of a solid grip and a firm foothold, the pleasant pull in her thigh as she makes a long lunge. It's been too long since she's worked her muscles like this, and she's missed the ache, although her fingers are throbbing. Her palms have lost their callouses, and she's ripped two nails below the quick.

"If you can get good footing, I can throw you a rope," Talmadge shouts, and she's always found it hard to take instructions from someone who's younger than she is.

She's a few feet from the canteen. Why would the fool think she needs a rope at this stage?

She intuits a ledge with her big toe and seizes it with the ball of her foot, triumphant. Satisfaction is a matter of inches.

After the barn lost its gloss, she settled on another escape route. The summer she turned sixteen, she climbed on a Greyhound bus with no guilt—her father had left long before her, her mother would be grateful for the extra bedroom, and her brother was barely old enough to know she existed. She stepped off the bus in Kokomo and worked for a month picking corn. She was hungry most nights, but that was nothing new, and it was a small price to pay for a revelation: She could learn anything. After Kokomo, she learned how to pluck chickens in a poultry farm outside Fowler, although she never mastered ducks. She could type fifty words a minute, which was sufficient if secretarial work was all she could find. She liked the rope, though. The circus had lodged in her mind as a safe place—the smell of sawdust—the velvet thump of elephant feet—and she was always trying to get back there. When she met Jeremiah in Cincinnati, she'd been working on a rope routine modeled after Leona Dare's iron jaw bit, and she'd been nowhere near skilled enough, but she could finagle it with a clear strap behind her head, hidden under her hair.

Jeremiah had been doing his hot-and-cold act, finding watches and handing out flowers to a respectable amount of applause, and he came up to her at the end of the night and asked her for coffee. That was twelve years ago, hard to believe.

"You'll need it to get back down," Talmadge calls, and Editha can't remember if she ever answered him about the rope.

"I'll toss it up," he says, even louder, as if maybe her hearing is the problem.

"*Shy*" is what she's always heard, like silence is a sign of insecurity. Silence is power. Silence is holding your cards tight while everyone keeps tossing more money into what will surely be your pot.

"Editha, be sensible," Howard calls. She hates the word "sensible." "Don't kill yourself out of sheer stubbornness."

"Slow down," Tom says. "Take your time."

He's got his arms in front of him as if he's ready to catch her. She finds it hard to believe he'd bother, unless he thought she'd land on Miah, in which case he'd all too gladly absorb the blow.

"Mrs. Hagathorn, you're more important than a few swallows of water," says Morris, and he is less annoying than the others. He reminds her a little of Mr. Wilson with his banana taffies.

"I won't have any trouble descending," she says, in hopes that they will all shut up.

The headlamps are blinding her: The men are staring straight up, and she might as well be onstage. Miah, at least, has pulled off his helmet, although he'd hate that his bald spot shines in the glare of her own lamp from this angle.

She leans over, snagging the strap of the canteen. She doesn't know who was more foolish, Miah for playing around with the water or the guide for hurling the canteen up here. In fairness to Talmadge, it was extremely unlikely it would get stuck up on the wall. He doesn't seem like the sort of man who throws things. He was solid and steady until three minutes ago, and she's not sure what flipped the switch.

Well, Miah flipped the switch. That much is clear, although he would never have taken a sip of that water. He had a bad bout of typhoid during the war, and it left his stomach sensitive. He doesn't touch hot peppers or raw vegetables, and he certainly wouldn't touch water with metal in it. Is he intentionally yanking their guide's chain? Does he want the man's emotions closer to the surface, thinking it will be easier to read him?

He's straight-backed and unfidgeting down there, Miah, helmet in hand, half a foot taller than the others. In character, as always.

Why hasn't he found the pin yet?

He smiles, and she knows he can feel her eyes on him. He likes eyes on him, especially hers. Everyone assumes that because of the kind of man he is, she must either worship him or hate him, although maybe people assume the same thing of all wives and husbands. She's not sure, but she neither worships Miah nor hates him. She knows him, inside and out, as he knows her. He's the only one down there not worried about her in the slightest.

"Did you get it?" he asks, not raising his voice.

She holds it up, although she wishes he hadn't asked. She wouldn't mind staying above everything longer.

The caves remind her of Lake Michigan, deep and vast. She's never liked noise and movement: She hates crowds, which people—the few who know about her skills—think is strange for a performer. But the stage is also a lake, with the spotlight blotting out the entire world, erasing every person on the planet so that nothing exists other than her body and the rope and the quiet.

"What's that Bible verse?" Miah says to the others. "'A virtuous woman is worth more than rubies'? Piss on virtue. What you want is a woman who can beat you in arm wrestling."

"For God's sake, be careful," calls Talmadge. "There's no ambulance to cart you away. It's a desert island down here."

"Editha, you're going to kill yourself," yells Howard, and he's got to stop calling her that. It's too familiar, and, anyway, a fall from here would hardly kill her. She'd likely only break her legs.

"You have no idea what she can do," Miah says.

Even from this height, Editha sees Howard draw himself up, and for a moment she thinks he might raise a hand to her husband. He doesn't, though, and she's reminded—how did she forget?—that he was always a gentle sort. Which doesn't mean anything. She has no idea what sort he might be now.

The men are spread out below her like pieces on a chessboard. Morris has turned back to the waterfall, so one less beam is blinding her. He seems very taken with it, considering it's no more impressive than rain running down a sandblasted roadside. He's uncomfortable down here, but he's trying to bluff his way through, which she respects. Howard's still standing too close to Miah, pushing his luck. Talmadge is pacing, all energy even when he's at a standstill.

She can't stay up here forever. She knows it. It's time to dive back into the posturing and panic and ego, and she will play the part that she needs to play, just as she always does.

"Do you need to toss it?" Miah asks.

"No," she says, slinging the canteen across her chest.

He's getting anxious himself, wanting her to come down because he knows she'd rather not. He does not like distance, especially when she's the one craving it, so she, mostly, keeps those cravings to herself. She can read exactly what he wants, every moment of the day, and without that trick, it would be harder to play her roles. As it is, she can perform them while another part of her—the true part—drifts in other directions, doing as she likes.

Miah says something to Howard, who gives him a nod, curt.

Her husband thinks he sees everything, but he can be remarkably blind. She could tell him that Morris is rapidly losing whatever faith he might have had and Talmadge is actively starting to hate him. Howard, who Miah most needs to win over, does not seem to enjoy dramatics as much as he used to.

She presses her belly against the rock again, flexing her sore hands one at a time. She adjusts her grip and lengthens her body to begin the climb down, stretching for the first foothold, but she can't resist taking one more look at the dark expanse around her. The caves seem bigger from up here. She can get a better feel for the scope of them, nothing but rock and darkness stretching in every direction—

She opens and closes her hand, considering. She studies how the ceiling arcs and how a jutting wall partially bisects the chamber. She studies the two lights bobbing on the far side of that wall.

For all Talmadge's talk of islands, they aren't alone down here.

5:20 p.m.

Ada's in the middle of a passage, enjoying the brief high ceilings, when she spots the bottle lying on its side. It's hidden in the shadows: whiskey, maybe, or whatever it is moonshiners pass around these days. She's the one who kneels first, but Quinton picks it up, taking a whiff from the open top. When he tips it upside down, a single drop hits the ground. She can see the flame of her headlamp reflected in the glass like a small moon. It's a clean bottle, like new.

She can't hear voices ahead of them anymore, but the group passed through this tunnel not five minutes ago.

"Whose is it, do you think?" she asks.

Quinton shakes his head, light wigwagging. "Maybe they shared it."

"Better than somebody polishing off the whole thing." As soon as she says it, she's not sure that's true. "You really think they might be making a party of it?"

Over the last few hours, she has heard nothing that sounds close to a good time. That scene at the waterfall, though—it did not feel rational.

"No," he says softly.

"Who would even consider drinking?"

One thing about conversations here: Silence is truly silent. She can read all manner of thoughts into Quinton's quiet.

"Do you drink down here?" she asks.

"Down here?" He's staring at the bottle, so she can't see his face. "No. I'm not an idiot."

She takes the bottle from him and lays it against the wall. She can't stop reading meaning into what he's not saying.

"I wasn't trying to say you couldn't or shouldn't," she says. "Drink at all. I'm no devotee of temperance." This feels too mealy-mouthed and mollifying. He thinks she's looking to castigate sinners? Maybe he does not know her at all. "But I don't have much tolerance for stupid drunkenness."

"I don't get the feeling you tolerate stupid soberness," he says.

Her annoyance floats away like a mote. He does know her.

"When I was a boy," he says, looking just over her shoulder, "I'd walk maybe a mile into the caves, and when I got to a room I knew like my own bedroom, I'd blow out my light. I'd picture where I'd come from, put my arms out in front of me, and retrace my steps in the dark. And you know what?"

She tilts her head.

"I never got it right," he says. "I never once made it to the right spot. There's no room for playing down here. Anybody who plans to make it back to the surface has to know that."

5:45 p.m.

Talmadge

He swipes at his neck with his still-wet bandana, the only good thing to come out of that disaster back at the falls. He has a notion that his frustration is seeping out of his skin like poison from a toad: A few handfuls of cold water to the face cut through it, but not for long.

If he were alone, he'd be covering ground five times this fast—ten times—and now he's a dog on a leash, ready to gnaw something. He'd like it to be the mind reader.

"Should we have stayed longer?" Mr. Efrom asks quietly from behind him.

If anyone were to overhear, they'd assume he's worried about whether the group needed a longer rest. He's smart, Morris Efrom, smarter than this quack calling himself a professor. It took forever to get to the hatpin, with Hagathorn choosing the wrong direction more often than not, and there wasn't anything Talmadge could do about it. He could only take whatever path the man chose. When they finally arrived at the falls, Talmadge made sure to walk right up to the pin. He stood at the edge of the water, his boots aimed like signposts. He could see the hatpin flash from where he had wedged it into the wall.

He could not have made it more obvious without pointing. He gave Hagathorn time to sense energy or vibrations or ghostly messages. But instead of seeing any kind of vision, the dolt started messing around with his canteen, making as if he'd unscrew the top and fill it up at the falls, as if he hadn't heard a word Talmadge said about water contamination. Even then, Talmadge thought he could manage him. He threw the canteen toward the hatpin. If Hagathorn had just looked in the right direction—no, if Talmadge's temper hadn't made him overthrow—

It is tiny, a hatpin. They were within a dozen feet of it for at least twenty minutes until Hagathorn insisted they head on. He has no more idea of where to find the hatpin than a cave spider.

Talmadge cannot say any of this to Mr. Efrom, not with the others so close behind.

"The professor was anxious to get moving," he says instead. "But if you wanted to get another look at the falls, we'll have to pass back through the same chamber when we head home."

"Good to hear," Mr. Efrom says, just as his foot catches, sole scuffing across the rock.

He's been solid this trip, no trace of panic, and it seems he knew himself after all. He's stumbling occasionally, but Talmadge hasn't had to worry about him.

He's worried about pretty much everyone else.

The ceiling rises, and Talmadge straightens. The path splits ahead, and they'll need to get on hands and knees for the next part, whichever way the mind reader chooses.

"Junction," he says for surely the fiftieth time today.

Hagathorn closes his eyes for surely the fiftieth time today. He places both hands on Talmadge's shoulders, swaying slightly. He lets out a breath through pursed lips.

"Steady," he says, as if they are carrying a piano instead of remembering a hatpin, and Talmadge does not know how many more times he can hear the word "steady" before he wraps his hands around the man's neck.

"We're plenty steady," Mr. Efrom says. "We've been steady for hours."

"Left," the mind reader announces, his hands too heavy.

The right path would be easier, and it would lead to the same place, but Talmadge goes left, relieved to slip loose.

"Keep your minds strong, friends," Hagathorn calls. "I can feel everything sharpening."

"Hands and knees again," Talmadge says. "Remember to keep a couple of feet between you."

He will never again lead people he cannot actually lead. Normally he explains about sediment and calcite, and he points out slick patches and low ceilings, and there is a beginning and end. This little show may never end. It takes a hundred years for an inch of stalactite to grow, and that's approximately the pace these people are keeping.

And the hell of it is, none of it matters anymore. They have passed the hatpin and they are headed away from it, deeper into the caverns. Every step is pointless, and all Talmadge can do is follow the madman.

He slaps his palms against the rock, one after the other, and hears a grunt behind him. He doesn't slow down. Hagathorn can hardly take a step without banging some part of himself into a wall.

Hand, knee, hand, knee. One in front of the other.

step after step after step

if you do it long enough you become all body and no brain and it is such a relief—

Talmadge pushes into an open space and waits for the others. Here's Hagathorn now, shining his headlamp on every square inch of rock, Mr. Efrom breathing loudly behind him. The others crowd closer as Talmadge settles on the balls of his feet.

"We're headed down," he says. For the past eight hours, the words in his head haven't come close to matching the ones coming out of his mouth. "The drop is about seven feet. If you fall, it won't be the end of the world, but I'd rather you not. I'll go in first, and then you each come down, belly to the wall. You'll feel a foothold for your left foot first—I'll help, if need be—and then your right foot, and after that you'll be able to step to the floor. Left foot, right foot, floor."

He watches them nod before he lies down on the ground, threading his legs through the opening into the next room. He finds the footholds and jumps to the ground—less clay and more gravel in this chamber—and for a few blissful seconds he's alone.

He breathes in the cool stillness. He really is good at his job. He knows this landscape as well as anyone, and so far as he knows, not one person on his tours has ever had anything but compliments for him. Like some people have perfect pitch, he has a feel for directions. Even before he was school age, his sister Maddie would take him outside to hunt for cattails or dewberries in the woods, and she'd get turned around, but he never did.

If you were a wolf, you'd gnaw your own paw off, she used to say to him. She understood how he needed to bolt sometimes, how he needed to get away

get away
get away
get away

and he feels that need pulsing now, but Morris Efrom is coming down the wall. His foot kicks until Talmadge guides it to an outcropping. The others follow, unavoidable, and it's another wait. Ten minutes, at least, while Hagathorn scans the room, head bobbing.

He always stands too close.

"Hold up," the mind reader says when Talmadge starts across the room.

Talmadge obeys. There's still a part of him that believes the man might lift his palms in the air and shout with a *hallelujah* that the pin is back at the waterfall. But Hagathorn's lamplight only glints off a cluster of bats, and one of them detaches from the ceiling, gliding low. Behind Talmadge, the rest of the group dodges and yelps.

He dodges, too. It's impossible not to flinch when a bat blurs toward your face. When they've all caught their breath, he meets the professor's eyes.

"Forward or back?" he asks, and it's the first time he's offered going backward as an option.

"Onward," Hagathorn says. He is no better at noticing hints than hatpins. "Always onward."

Talmadge starts toward the opening at the other side of the chamber, pulling out his pocket watch. However much he might want this man to fall into a hole and never climb out, he wants Mr. Lambert to succeed. He needs him to succeed, if these caves are going to stay open. If he failed to announce a few junctions and looped the group back around to the waterfall sooner rather than later, they might not notice. These men are more sluggish by the minute.

The wife does not seem sluggish. She seems invigorated by her climb. In different circumstances, Talmadge would be impressed, but since he has enough problems without adding someone prone to squirreling up walls without so much as a word, he is not feeling much admiration.

Over his head, inch-long stalactites are tipped with pearls of water, shining. He picks up his pace, and Hagathorn says something to him about slowing down, but Talmadge is thinking of Maddie again.

Pale eyelashes, big-toothed smile. She was seventeen when the fever took her, and they laid her out on her bed with the coffin waiting for her in the front room. The house was jammed full of aunts and cousins, but it was his father who found Talmadge inside the coffin. He'd liked the feel of it, lined with the quilt Maddie had kept on her bed, the one their mother had made that had been washed so many times the bluebirds were peeling off. He liked the rough of the pine and the soft of the blanket, and he liked how dark the box was and how safe he felt, and at first he'd been worried about how Maddie might feel stuck underground but instead he wound up jealous. After they buried her, he visited her every day, laying on the heaped-up dirt and imagining her down there in her box. He'd talk to her, but Aunt Arlene told his father he was fixated on death and they made him stop.

It wasn't death that took him there. It was love. It's love, too, that sets him apart down here. He doesn't worry that a lamp will go out. He doesn't worry about being blind. He's never blind. Every time he lays his hand against a rock, it's like that bluebird quilt against his fingers, clear as day. The candle-smoothness of flowstone or the minnowed-outline of fossil or the gust of a passageway, like a giant blowing a dandelion—they're as familiar to him as the tip of a cotton wing worn thin and the curved stitching of the round flower with insides like egg yolks. He doesn't need his eyes to see them.

He focuses on the curves of the passageway and tries to forget the faces behind him. He tries to forget about canteens and deadlines and the blister rubbing on his big toe. People who swear by resoling shoes with tire rubber don't spend their days walking through standing water, so when last Friday came and went without his paycheck, he dug these twenty-year-old boots from his father's closet. He needs them to work out some sort of compromise with his too-long toes because even when his paycheck does show up, he still owes nearly four dollars for Aunt Arlene's two nights in the hospital, and the pneumonia jacket was another dollar on top of that.

Her coughing is no better. He can hear her gurgling through the walls of the room he shares with his father, who hardly makes any noise at all these days. Everyone is always talking about how the rock closes in on you down here, but it's only aboveground that Talmadge feels a weight pressing on him.

Water seeps along the edge of the ceiling, and it must have been seeping for centuries because it's formed a bit of drapery like pointed teeth, and what does it matter, over the eons, that he lies awake at night listening to the sleep sounds of a gray-haired man and a stoop-backed woman, knowing if either of them need something, he needs to figure out how to get it?

It matters.

"It's been eight hours," he says, stopping. He makes himself look at the others. "We've got four left, and it's going to take us at least three to get back to the elevator. I'd vote we start circling back."

"You can't be suggesting we give up before the allotted time," Mrs. Hagathorn says.

He's not sure she's spoken to him before, although maybe she yelled at him about the canteen. He makes an effort to keep his voice calm as he studies the map in his head. He could get them back to the waterfall in an hour.

"We wouldn't be giving up," he says. "If we keep heading deeper, there's no way we'd be aboveground when the twelve hours is up."

"I have the full twelve hours to search," the mind reader says. "Which means I have the right to head anywhere I choose."

"You'd still be searching for the entire twelve hours," Talmadge says.

"He does have the right to choose," Mr. Efrom says, struggling to unscrew his canteen. "It's what we agreed to."

Blast it, Talmadge thinks at him, wishing desperately that at least one person down here could manage to read his mind. *Help me out.*

"It doesn't matter to me if he finds it or doesn't find it," says the newspaperman. His too-long pant leg has caught under his boot. "But the dice are still rolling, so I've got no interest in your hustling us out of here early."

"It's not negotiable," Tom says, mulish. "The timing is in the contract. You can't force us out."

For the first time, Talmadge sees the fundamental flaw in this plan. Everyone but the newspaperman has a stake in staying down here until the crazy man finds the hatpin, and even the newspaperman isn't eager to stop the demonstration. No one is going to yank the plug; they're willing to let the water get icy and keep pretending they're having a nice, warm bath. And Talmadge would bet all the money in his billfold that when the clock does strike ten, Hagathorn still won't admit he's failed. He's going to push to stay down here as long as it takes, and these people won't even argue.

They are not going to let him turn them around.

Howard has pulled the small notepad from his jacket pocket. Every time they stop, he jots down a few more notes. The manager has slumped against a wall, rubbing at the back of his neck. Everyone seems to be rubbing at something.

Talmadge tries once more.

"I'm only trying to keep on schedule," he says. "You never know what might happen down here."

"Surely you have extra supplies in case the unexpected happens," Howard says.

"Yeah," Talmadge says. "I have extras. But you don't want to push it too far and get us stranded, food and water gone, lights gone dead."

He's trying to scare them, yes. He's not sure how low they are on anything. Quinton and the woman have the emergency supplies.

"I don't understand," Howard says, stopping his scribbling. "The risk of getting lost or running behind was inherent. You should have brought sufficient emergency supplies."

The man's tone irritates Talmadge. The word "inherent" irritates him, as does "sufficient." These people pack a sandwich in their pocket and believe they're carrying their own weight.

"You've dragged yourself through a few tight spots," he says. "How many times did your canteen snag? How many times did you have to work to get your backside through? I'm carrying more than the rest of you combined, but every can of beans takes up space. I wasn't packing for a camping trip."

Hagathorn steps close enough that Talmadge has to crook his neck to look at him. Maybe this tactic works on people aboveground, but size is no advantage down here. It's a handicap.

"I know what you're doing," the mind reader says.

"Do you?" Talmadge bites out. It's difficult not to give the man a shove.

"You want to keep me from finding it," Hagathorn says.

"Mr. Hagathorn—" starts Mr. Efrom.

Talmadge holds up a hand. He stops himself from ramming that hand into the middle of the mind reader's chest, and he forces himself to laugh instead.

"I'm being paid to help you find it," he says. "It is my job. My job. I'm desperate for you to find the ever-loving hatpin."

"We could use another break," Mr. Efrom says, raising his voice. "We're on edge, is all. But I promise you, Professor, we're all working for the same thing."

"Are we?" Hagathorn says. "I don't believe that. I don't believe the two of you have upheld your end of the bargain."

If Morris Efrom has seemed dulled, this sharpens him. He is all edges when he turns to Hagathorn.

"Are you truly trying to blame this on us?" he asks.

"It's the only explanation," Hagathorn says. He is not exactly lit up with power at the moment, his beard streaked with soot and what might be mustard.

"It is not the only explanation," Talmadge says.

Behind him, the newspaperman is scrawling on his pad with his nubby pencil. Talmadge glances back to the teeth in the ceiling: The path ahead of them is a giant maw opening. The entire group has gathered around the mind reader, lamps shining, strangers all of them.

"Fine," Talmadge says. "Onward."

He makes it all of twenty steps before a hand lands on his elbow. "Stop putting your hands on me," he says, making every word clear and cold.

"I'll put my hands where necessary," Hagathorn says, even as he lets go. "You didn't announce a junction."

For all his thoughts of speeding along this process, Talmadge wasn't ignoring a turn. The gap the mind reader is eyeing doesn't lead anywhere, at least not for a human. Maybe the salamanders have built entire kingdoms back there, but no creature bigger than a breadbox will ever know.

"It's not a junction," Talmadge says.

"This won't work if I don't trust you," the professor says.

"Go on, then," Talmadge says. Trust hasn't been part of the equation for hours. "Lead the way."

It's childish, he knows. The passage requires a belly crawl for all of twenty feet before it becomes impassable, but he wouldn't mind seeing a little fear in the professor. Panic might make him more biddable.

It also might be fun to watch.

Hagathorn slides into the slot, arms and head disappearing smoothly enough. He's halfway inside before he stops. His feet kick twice, and his hips jerk against the rock. His stomach is surely the problem, although his rear end looks plenty round from this angle, too.

"Satisfied?" Talmadge says, and he can hear Mr. Efrom laughing softly and then not so softly. The reporter is grinning.

The mind reader answers, but the rock distorts the words into gobbledygook. They all watch him wriggle for, perhaps, too long.

"Miah?" says Mrs. Hagathorn, dropping to the balls of her feet. She glances at Talmadge, and he sobers.

"Come on back," he says. "It only gets tighter."

"I can't," Hagathorn calls.

Talmadge makes out those words just fine. "Suck in a breath and let it all the way out," he says. "Relax and stop moving. You'll slip right back out."

But Hagathorn isn't relaxing. His boots kick frantically, and his torso is twisting in a way that will only wedge him deeper.

"Stop," Talmadge says. "You have to just stop moving."

"Jeremiah," Tom says, nearly shouting. "You need to be still."

Hagathorn does not listen to either one of them. His breathing is filling up the entire cavern, and he's only twisting faster. No one is smiling now.

"I can't get out," Hagathorn says, panting. He's going to make himself pass out if he keeps on.

"You'll be fine," Talmadge says, kneeling. "I got you. But stop moving. You hear me?"

Hagathorn obeys to some extent: His boots slow down enough for Talmadge to grab hold, and he gives a yank, but he only feels a pop in the other man's knees. The meat of his body doesn't budge. Talmadge adjusts his grip and pulls harder, and this time Hagathorn screams, quick and loud.

Here is the fear Talmadge wanted, and it is not fun. The wife is looking at him again, and he doesn't like looking back at her.

"It's too tight," gasps Hagathorn. "Stop."

"There must be some sort of tool or something that could help get him loose," Howard says.

"Yeah," Talmadge says. "There's something."

He yanks again. Hagathorn's scream is briefer this time. Inside the rock, fabric rips, the sound like a husk being ripped loose from an ear of corn. It takes another half dozen tugs to get Hagathorn free, and when he finally slides into the open air, his chest is bleeding through his shirt. His glove has come off. He's conscious and clear-eyed, though, as he flops against the wall, and Talmadge hears the reporter's pencil, scritching and scritching.

6:40 p.m.

If they started this search in tunnels that were once rivers, these passageways would barely have qualified as creeks. Ada and Quinton have not gotten off their hands and knees in at least a quarter mile.

Everything ahead has been quiet since Hagathorn's accident. That drama played out as loud and clear as a program on the radio, so Ada wasn't shocked when—once they started moving forward again—her light picked up splotches of blood. It dripped along the trail for a few yards like breadcrumbs, but she hasn't seen a trace of red in nearly an hour, which must be a good sign.

"It's easier if you roll onto your back," Quinton says, motioning her into a downward-sloped tunnel on their right. "Feel the ledge above you, and just pull up."

She trusts him. She eases in headfirst, her back sliding against the limestone, arms over her head, almost like slipping on a dress. She wriggles until her fingers feel the lip of the rock above her, pulls herself through, then flips onto her hands and knees again. As she starts crawling, the sight of the path opening up is more beautiful than any sunrise she's ever seen. She has at least a foot of open space over her head. The giddiness of it makes her speed up, and as she rounds a bend, she sees a pair of legs not five feet in front of her.

She freezes, slapping a hand over her headlamp. Behind her, Quinton rests a hand on her ankle. When they've heard nothing for a long time, he removes his hand.

"No one looks behind them in a cave," he says. "Too busy looking ahead of them."

"There's no way they put the hatpin this far in," she says.

She hasn't recognized a single thing since they left the waterfall. She's tried to stop questioning things because that's not her job. She only needs to play follow-the-leader for a little while longer, and they will all go home. Still, she doesn't understand what's happening.

"No," Quinton says. "Surely not."

His hand lands on her ankle again, and he gives a tug. She inches backward, turning as much as she can. She can't see much of him, but she can see the wall.

More signatures. A handful of them spread over several feet, disconnected. She's still not sure why she and Quinton have wound up in this particular passage, but the men who came before them are simple enough to understand. They wanted to see how far they could go, and they wanted to leave a record of it.

"No matter how deep you go, the names keep popping up," Quinton says.

Ada sees the glint of his pocketknife before she knows what it is. When he offers it to her handle first, she's slow to take it. She's never done this before.

"We don't want to run into a pair of boots again," Quinton says, nodding down the tunnel. "Go on. Give it a try."

She shifts her grip on the hilt of the knife, studying the wall.

"Maybe just initials," he says.

She thought the entire point of carving your name was to make yourself known. She looks from Quinton to the knife and back again. He shrugs one shoulder.

“My sister got her name scraped off once or twice,” he says. “A girl’s name. A woman’s. It can be tempting for a certain kind of clown.”

“People do that?” she asks, and then wishes she could take the question back. She doesn’t know why it shocks her, not when she well remembers her father laughing, head thrown back, when she was six and said she wanted to be a doctor. And didn’t her mother tell her that women should never sit with their knees apart and didn’t her mother-in-law tell her to be careful about walking too much or she’d get mannish legs and didn’t Gerald tell her no decent man would have a wife who worked? And why, even now, long after they are all gone, does she wait and change into pants when she’s at the bottom of the elevator with no one to see?

She knows the boundaries, but she wasn’t aware they extended this deep.

“Some,” Quinton says.

She breathes in the cool damp of the rock and writes *Ada Smith* in her head, without touching the wall. Actually, she’s never liked “Smith,” so commonplace. It was an argument against marrying Gerald. Before him, she was Ada Fallon, but she hardly knows that girl anymore.

Maybe just initials. She studies the names and almost names cut into the limestone, flicking her gloved thumb over her blade.

DAVID ULLRICH

D. BROOKS BARLOW

J. KUBESCH

She often tries to picture the person behind the signature. Isn’t that what David Ullrich or D. Brooks Barlow wanted her to do when they crouched in this same spot—didn’t they hope to be summoned from the ether? And yet she's bound to get it wrong. She'll imagine white hair when he was a schoolboy or she'll see gentle hands when he beat his wife. A name is not a self. The initials, at least, concede that. They leave blanks that cannot be filled. She could be looking at Daniel Brooks Barlow or Dylan Brooks Barlow, or, apparently, Darlene Brooks Barlow. Each period is a universe.

She thinks of Ruby, whose name will be written across billboards and barns and road maps, a testament to how much her husband loves her. Ada will never have her name on a map. She will fade into oblivion, like everyone in the history of her family, farmers and coal miners and wives, entire lives lived and forgotten other than at the bite of a tomato.

She lifts the knife. Even if no one ever sees it, her name in this wall will not fade. It will not be the real her—the whole her—but she doesn't mind. She does not want to be filled in: She wants spaces that no one can conjure, no matter how many times they run their fingers over the shape of her.

Her hand takes over, carving the first lines before she decides them, boring into the rock. She twists and digs and blows away limestone dust until she is looking at herself:

A.D.A.

Ruby's name can be on every sign. Ada's is cut into the mountain. No one gifted it to her. She climbed and shoved her way here to carve her own self, and if anyone wants to scratch if off, they will have to cut deeper than she has. She does not believe they can do it.

7:10 p.m.

Howard

Eventually a certain level of familiarity takes hold if you're sharing a cup of coffee with a man, notepad in hand. Same if you're walking through his back pasture or sitting on his porch. Comfort. It's the key to a good interview. It lets a person's words slip out without too much thought, and Howard's always believed unthinking answers are the best ones.

He's spent today waiting for Jeremiah Hagathorn to get comfortable, but it's just now occurring to him that discomfort might knock loose the best answers of all. "Discomfort" isn't a strong enough word for what's happening down here: These men are seeping desperation like the walls are seeping water. Hagathorn—the most desperate of all—is humiliated and furious after being shoehorned into the mountain, and he's anxious for a way to re-inflate himself.

"I've been wondering, Professor," Howard says, pausing mid-crawl. He glances toward the man behind him. "That trick where you drive blindfolded—how do you do it?"

The steady glare of Hagathorn's helmet would seem hostile except that all light is welcome down here.

"It's not a trick," Hagathorn says. The blood on his shirt is still wet.

Howard faces forward again, trying to ignore his view of Talmadge's rump. He keeps his voice easy, not a reporter at all, only a man looking to distract himself.

"So how do you do it?" he asks.

"I use exactly the same method that I'm using now," Hagathorn says.

Howard bites back an answer so obvious—*It can't be the same because you were actually successful*—that he expects someone else to offer it up. The rest of them hold their tongues, though, and the magician cannot let silence stand for long.

"A committee steps up, as they did here," Hagathorn says. He's picking up steam. "They pick a hotel and a name from its registry. They write down that name and put it in an envelope, and all this happens, mind you, before I arrive. Once I get to town, I climb into a car and blindfold myself completely. A member of the committee joins me, and he's my window to the world. Just as you are here, Talmadge. Morris."

Until now, Howard has not been entirely sure that Hagathorn has learned the other men's names.

Talmadge gives no indication that he's listening. If Morris has any reaction, he's too far behind them for Howard to see it.

"The man stares at the road in front of me," Hagathorn goes on, "and I see it through his eyes. He pictures the route to the hotel, and I see that, too. I drive us there. He pictures the name in the registry, which I see as clearly as he does. I take the registry in hand, and I flip through until I find the right name."

"I read something about it," Howard says, veering around a puddle. The ground is getting damper. "You put a pair of gloves under your blindfold. And you wear a hood as well?"

"Made of mohair and broadcloth. It's as dark under that hood as it is down here."

Talmadge has slowed, which means they all slow. In the beginning, he'd glance back every few seconds to make sure no one lagged. He'd remind them that crowding too close could lead to a foot in the face. He no longer calls out much in the way of reminders.

"Do you know Angus Mulholland?" Howard asks. "He's a professor, too."

"I do not," Hagathorn says.

The end of the sentence is more grunt than word. The man makes all manner of sounds every time they wind up on their knees.

"I came across Dr. Mulholland after you visited Springfield," Howard says. "You had your send-off at the Strand and wound up at the Leland Hotel. Dr. Mulholland said you were a huge success."

The ceiling is finally rising, and the walls have widened. Howard couldn't have asked for a better setting, all sharp edges and blind turns. It's like walking through a house built by a drunken lunatic. He'll write that down next time he gets a chance at his notebook.

Like walking through a house built by a lunatic architect.

Like walking through a house built by a drunken architect.

Or possibly *Like walking through a house built by a drunken architect after no one could be bothered to pay the electric bill.* No. Too much.

"Dr. Mulholland actually tried to perform your same demonstration after you left town," Howard says. "Did you happen to hear about it?"

"I'm not typically aware of what happens once I leave town," Hagathorn answers, pushing to his feet.

"He copied you exactly," Howard says, standing as well. "He put gloves under his blindfold before he had the blindfold tied around his eyes. He said you repeatedly told your assistant to make the blindfold tighter, so he did that, too. He made sure to tell them to cross the optic nerve, just like you did."

Howard chances a look back toward Editha, who's watching him, and that's all he ever wanted from this whole experiment—for her to actually see him. Well, it's not all he wants, but her face is clean when the rest of them look like they've been rolling in soot, and he wonders if she still washes her face in lemon juice before bed.

"It turned out," he keeps on, "that when the blindfold was tied very tightly across the brow, Dr. Mulholland could raise his eyebrows and lift the blindfold enough that he could see absolutely everything in the room."

"He sounds like a hack," Editha says, as pleasantly as if she were at a ladies' luncheon.

They continue to shuffle forward, hunched. At the back of the line, Morris stumbles, catching himself on the wall. Howard has a theory about him but doesn't want to split his focus.

"Dr. Mulholland also made his own hood, modeled after yours, Jeremiah," Howard says. He wishes he could see the man's reaction to being called by his first name instead of his made-up title. "The inside layer was mohair, transparent as a woman's veil. The outer layer was thick broadcloth. He had no problem sewing the strings so that when he pulled them to supposedly secure the hood, the seam of the broadcloth opened like drapery, and he could see straight through the transparent layer."

Howard loves this part, the moment when a subject realizes he sees them as they truly are, for good or bad. Hagathorn stops, so Howard does as well, turning to face the other man. Talmadge takes a few moments to notice; he's a dozen feet ahead of them when he halts.

"When people get in the car with you," Howard says to Editha's husband, "you have them use their finger to trace their route in the air. You have them trace the name of the hotel and name in the register. You say it's to help focus their minds, but you're watching them through your trick hood. It's impressive to be able to translate signs made in the air, but it's not mind reading."

Hagathorn is remarkably still. The right side of his face is rubbed raw like he slid into home base on his cheekbone. He's been bristling all day long, but now that he's been insulted directly, he seems unbothered.

"When we get out of here," he says, "I'll demonstrate for you. I'll let you see the hood for yourself, and I'll drive you through downtown Chattanooga. I'm used to cynics, Howard. They don't shake me."

"If I go on a ride with you, I want to try on your hood first," Howard says.

"That's enough," Tom says from behind them both. "I've let you throw out your questions—such as they are—and Jeremiah has answered you. You don't know what you're talking about."

"I promise that I do," Howard says.

He always knows what he's talking about. He makes sure of it.

"This is why you wanted to come along," Tom says. He adjusts his glasses, sliding them down and up again. "I knew it was a possibility you were skeptical, but I hoped you'd be fair."

Water drips steadily from a spear of rock hanging behind the manager. Howard has figured out these men, one by one, but he cannot entirely fit together Tom's pieces. The manager seems intelligent, but he's blindly loyal to Hagathorn—as is Editha, apparently, although loyalty must be a trait she learned later in life. Their loyalty clearly isn't warranted.

"I've been fair, Tom," Howard says. "I had my concerns from the beginning, yes, but I was willing to be convinced if I saw the slightest hint of ability."

"I'll say this," Morris says slowly. "I'm not the biggest fan of the man, but what you're saying about the blindfold doesn't seem to apply here. He's not covering his eyes. We haven't traced anything in the air. He's failed, mind you, but I can't see any framework of a scheme."

"He has not failed," Editha says.

"He has a history of fakery, Morris," Howard says. "I'd say that's relevant."

"That's what you'll be putting in the article?" Morris asks.

He's close enough that Howard can smell the hint of whiskey on his breath. It's not the first time.

"I'll be telling my account of what happened down here," Howard says. "I can't imagine that it would be much different from your account of things."

"There is no account yet," Hagathorn says. "You can't know what you'll write when you don't know the ending."

"He knows a good bit by now, I'd say," Talmadge says.

"What do you think he knows?" Hagathorn says, and his calm is finally splintering.

They've wound up huddled together in the light. The chamber around them could be five feet wide or five hundred: Howard can't see the walls anymore. The darkness doesn't bother him, though.

He grew up in a house where the candles and coal ran out as often as the food—his childhood was excellent practice, it turns out, for both caves and a worldwide economic collapse.

Morris shifts his feet, rocking from left to right.

"We didn't have to do this," he says to the ceiling. "I told Leo we could bring the dances down into the caves. Or theme nights or, Lord, a giveaway. Leland Forrest over on Ninth Street gave every person who entered his five-and-dime a ticket for a lottery to win an upright piano, and he saw business double."

Howard has heard of Ninth Street, and if Morris Efrom is brooding about the colored section of town and upright pianos, he's more hammered than he seems.

"Then why'd you tell Mr. Lambert to invite a mind reader?" Talmadge asks.

Morris stops rocking. "I didn't. It was his idea."

"He told me he wished he'd thought of it himself," Talmadge says.

"He invited Jeremiah," Tom says, raising his voice, "because it's a big idea. It's not coupons or dressing up in cowboy hats. It's a chance to get this place in papers across the country for free. And it will work. I've known this man for ten years, and I'm telling you he has a gift."

"And I'm telling you, respectfully, that you are not objective," Howard answers.

"And neither are you," Tom says. "Even though it's your job."

They've all raised their voices.

"The night I met Jeremiah," Tom says, "I didn't believe in this business at all. My wife dragged me to a tent out in the middle of a field, and Jeremiah stood up there and told the audience—you remember what you said?"

Hagathorn smiles. "I do."

"He said, *I'll pluck your thoughts like splinters,*" Tom finishes. "And he did."

"What was the thought he plucked?" Howard asks.

"He told me I'd killed my brother, and he told me how it happened."

Howard takes a single slow breath. He's mapped out all the possible routes he thought this conversation might take, but none of them included a dead brother.

"You didn't kill him," Hagathorn says. "It was an accident, and he did it himself."

"That's what you said back then, too," Tom says.

The light around them pulses: Talmadge's headlamp is flickering. The carbide cartridge must be getting low.

"Based on what we've seen here," Howard says, "I find that story hard to believe."

"You're saying I'm lying?" Tom says.

"Maybe you believe it happened," Howards says. "People hear what they want to hear."

He believes the man is lying. Talmadge has opened his pack, and he pulls out a backup cartridge. His movements are quick and efficient, and he's no longer looking at the rest of them.

"This story you're writing," Morris says, and he seems sober enough. "It's not just about Hagathorn. Leo and Ruby have everything they've got invested in this. Dozens of people have jobs here at Ruby Falls."

"Don't put that weight on me," Howard says.

"It is on you."

"It's on the two of you," Hagathorn says, waving a hand at Talmadge and Morris. "You're the ones who failed to hold up your end of the bargain. You're sending me in different directions."

Talmadge has relit his headlamp, and he refastens the strap on his helmet. His hands fly up fast enough to make the flame dance. "You're talking gibberish," he says, cutting a quick glance at Hagathorn, "and you're trying to shift the blame because you have no idea what you're doing."

"You believe I can't find the pin?" Hagathorn presses.

"That's been obvious for hours," Talmadge says.

"So once you gave up on me, you surely stopped keeping the image in your mind?"

Talmadge sees the trap, too late. He clamps his mouth shut and drops his head, and Editha shows her white teeth.

"Your end of the bargain, I believe," she says.

"If I write a story detailing what happened down here," Howard says, "you can no more blame me than you can blame a reporter for saying that the Cubs lost a game. And if anyone loses their job, they deserve to lose it."

"What does that mean?" Talmadge asks.

"It means you're not much better than he is," Howard says, jerking his head at Hagathorn. "Yes, he's been dragging us around down here. But you're the one who's in charge."

"If I were actually in charge, we wouldn't still be down here," Talmadge says.

"You must've know that Jeremiah would get stuck in that rock," Howard says. "You didn't catch that Editha has been favoring her left hand ever since the waterfall. You haven't even noticed that this one is soused."

It takes Morris slightly too long to realize that he's being discussed.

"I am not," he says.

"You're telling me that you haven't been drinking?" Howard presses.

The man does not try to lie at least.

"I needed something for my nerves," Morris says, delivering his answer to Talmadge, not Howard. "I doled it out over six or seven hours, just enough to relax me. I am absolutely not drunk."

"You were drinking?" Talmadge says.

The man is not the sharpest tool. If he can't even smell whiskey on someone's breath, how can he lead them through a maze of rock? Everyone has done poorly on this test, and it's almost a pleasure delivering their grades.

"I'm here to tell the truth of what happens," Howard says. "He's here to find a hatpin, and you're here to help him, and none of you have done what you were supposed to."

Morris shakes his head. "You think you know the truth when you've known us for a day?"

"Yes."

"People know me here," Morris says. "I've lived a whole life with them. You cannot tell them that I'm some sort of drunk."

"I write what I know," Howard says. "If they know you so well, I guess they'll believe you and not me."

"But you don't know anything," Morris says.

Next to him, Hagathorn's legs buckle. It's a small movement, not much more than a flinch, and then Editha's husband drops to his knees with a thud of bone on rock. His palms hit the ground.

Howard steps forward automatically and feels Editha's hands on him for the first time in many years.

"This is how it happens," she says, her arm slapped across his chest.

It's not worry on her face. It's joy, even as her husband's spine curves and arches. He's frozen for a split second before he falls forward, his hands smacking the ground again. He looks like a shirt on a clothesline during a storm.

"Stop this," Howard says, pulling away from Editha. "Stop the act."

Hagathorn rips off his helmet, and it rattles against the stone. He sucks in a breath like a drowning man, his neck all tendons. It's a commanding performance, Howard has to admit. It's terrifying.

"God Almighty," Morris says.

"I saw a man at the barbershop like this once," Talmadge says softly. "Apoplexy. He was dead before the ambulance showed up."

Even as Talmadge is speaking, Hagathorn slows. His head droops, his eyes close, and the tension evaporates from his body. With one thready breath, he lifts his head. Tom is next to him in a heartbeat, although Editha hasn't taken a step toward her husband, and Howard takes some satisfaction from that.

The mind reader makes to rise to his feet but sinks immediately. His pants are ripped; both the fabric and skin around his knees are blood-soaked, shining in the dim light. The blood on his chest looks insignificant by comparison.

"Take your time," Tom says. "Get your bearings."

Talmadge kneels, angling his headlamp so he can get a look at Hagathorn's eyes, and he's wearing the mask of a professional again. Hagathorn pulls back, head whipping from Talmadge to Morris.

"Liars," he says.

Lying bloody on the floor, he looks as sane as Howard has ever seen him, but Talmadge and Morris are even more fascinating. Neither of them has much of a poker face—their eyes give away the game immediately, and Howard can see the columns of his story expanding, inch after inch.

Maybe everyone down here is a fraud in one way or another.

8:20 p.m.

"We'll take an hour," Talmadge calls from the other room, loud enough that Ada suspects the words are aimed at them. "He needs it, and so do the rest of you."

Ada lets her mouth fall close to Quinton's ear. He smells of sweat, and she imagines she does, too.

"He needs it?" she whispers.

"There's no telling," Quinton answers.

The waiting has left her jangly. The group has been in the same passage for nearly an hour already; at one stage she heard a commotion, and she hoped they'd found the hatpin, but then they quieted. She and Quinton have edged closer to them as the minutes ticked past, and now they're crouched in a niche no more than fifty feet away.

It's dark outside by now, surely. She'd look at her watch, but it hardly matters.

The quiet in the next chamber has gained texture—soft rustlings and taps, inanimate sounds. She hears a click and pop that might be a can being opened. Quinton has his eyes closed, and she wonders if he can actually fall asleep sitting up.

"So we've got an hour," she whispers. "I believe I'm going to step away for a moment."

She's pleased she doesn't sound sheepish. No one has ever explained the etiquette of going to relieve yourself in a cave, and when she excused herself earlier this afternoon, she's not sure what words came out of her.

"Ah," he says, eyes opening. "If you want to—"

"I was thinking we should move into the upper chamber," she interrupts, both because she would like to change the topic and because this is a legitimate concern. "If any of the others also want a moment of . . . privacy, they might wander in this direction."

He agrees with her. They have almost entirely agreed with each other, which has made these long hours easier than they might have been. He tells her he'll head up after she's had a few minutes to herself, and he closes his eyes again as she slings on her pack and sizes up the wall behind her for handholds. In another moment, she's hauling herself over the ledge into the upper passageway.

She stands, brushing her blackened gloves. With time, the layout of a cave is as knowable as the layout of a house. This one might be a mansion with endless hallways, but she has a solid picture of the rooms around her. Talmadge's group has made camp below on the first floor. The passage now in front of her leads to a set of second-floor rooms. It's as simple as taking a set of stairs from the sitting room to the bedrooms.

She really does need to pee.

Her light skims over the mottled rock, mostly mud colored now. The soot hasn't penetrated this far. A translucent, blind crayfish in a puddle near her feet darts away from the light. She suspects it's been raining aboveground—the walls are trickling water, and the drip of stalactites rings from the shadows. A heavy rain would be bad news—it could mean flooding down here, and even shallow water would chill them to the bone.

She moves down the passage and looks behind her twice before she pulls off her gloves and loosens her pants. This would be much easier with a skirt. She's lowering her pants with one hand and holding on to a knob of stalagmite with the other when she hears voices.

She jumps, stumbling, and she's buttoned up before she realizes that the voices are coming from the lower level. Heart pumping, she crosses the chamber and finds a split in the floor wider than her shoulders: When she tilts her headlamp, she's looking down at the first floor of the house, maybe twenty feet below her.

The voices become louder, and they puzzle her. If the people below her want privacy for the same reasons she did, it doesn't make sense that she's hearing both a male and female voice. The woman can only be Editha, but the other voice is less obvious.

"—appreciate you not mentioning," Editha's saying.

"You thought I'd announce it as I shook hands with your husband?" the man asks.

The conversation is clearer than if Ada were listening on the telephone. The two headlamps light up the sliver of canyon visible through the crevice below her.

"It crossed my mind," Editha says.

"I didn't even tell him my full name, not that he asked. He's not the curious sort."

"You'd be surprised," Editha says.

Bits of silhouettes—a forearm, a leg—wobble across the rock below. Editha and the man are almost directly underneath Ada.

"When did you realize it was me?" the man asks.

"When Tom introduced you to me before dinner!" Editha hisses. "I assume you made a point of catching me away from Miah. All I knew was that a reporter was joining us. I had no idea you'd become a writer. You could've been a lumberjack for all I knew."

Until now, Ada hasn't been entirely sure that the man below is Howard. Now that she knows, she's more confused, not less.

"You could have written," Howard says. His voice is full, bursting with a feeling Ada can't name. "Even once. You'd have known all sorts of things. You could have visited. You could have come home."

"It's not my home," Editha says, and her voice is full of nothing.

Ada wishes she could see their faces. The chamber goes silent for long enough that she starts to wonder if they've left. Then Editha speaks again.

"How did you find me?" she asks.

"I saw your name in the paper," Howard says. "Editha Hagathorn, it said, but I figured there weren't that many Edithas who'd be described as former acrobats. I looked up a photo."

Acrobat. Ada considers it. She's never known an acrobat. She puts it in the same category as a bearded lady. When Editha leapt down from the rock wall with the canteen around her neck, she only said, *I've always been good at climbing.*

"You followed me all the way to Chattanooga," Editha is saying. She does not sound flattered. "Instead of taking your own advice and writing me a letter."

"You'd shown you had no interest in keeping in touch, hadn't you? I hoped you'd feel different in person."

Someone in a more distant chamber belches, and it carries wetly.

"What do you want to happen, Howie?" Editha asks.

"I wanted to talk to you. To meet—your husband." He pauses. "And now I have, I suppose. I don't know, Editha. I wanted you to know that you're not alone. You never were. You have choices, if you want them."

"I've had nothing but choices," she says. "Endless ones. And I chose Jeremiah."

One of the shadows below jerks like a horse annoyed by flies. A headlamp veers up and away.

"Surely I know you in ways he can't," Howard says.

"You were too young to know me. We were too young."

"That's not true," he says. "Do you remember the way the cold poured through that broken—"

"I don't," Editha interrupts. "Listen to me, Howie. I do not remember. I won't. That's another choice."

The voices pause for several long seconds.

"Alright," Howard says, and now his voice, too, is full of nothing. "I'm here to do my job, Editha. First and foremost. I won't make trouble for you."

"Good. Because the last time Jeremiah had any trouble, he broke a man's wrist." She and the reporter are walking now, slow steps turning up gravel. "And you are making trouble for me, doing your job. So quick to judge. When I first saw you, I hoped our connection might make you sympathetic to him."

"That's what you thought when you first saw me?"

"He's not a fraud," Editha snaps. "Give him a chance instead of dismissing him out of spite."

"That's not why I'm dismissing him."

However Editha responds, it doesn't involve words. A pair of boots thumps rapidly across the limestone, and after a while slower footsteps follow. Once the lower cavern goes dark, Ada steps to the wall, dropping her pants again because apparently curiosity does not numb the bladder. She lets her thoughts spin as the urine hits the ground.

When she heads back around the bend toward Quinton, he's magicked two thin blankets from his pack.

"The newspaperman and the wife know each other," she says, dropping to the ground next to him.

"In what sense?" he asks.

His sack of pecans is open by his knee, and shells rustle as he shifts sideways. She explains what she heard, taking off her helmet and blowing out the flame. The light from one helmet is sufficient for now, and they might need the extra carbide later.

"So her husband doesn't know," Quinton says.

"Doesn't seem like."

He bends his knees, and a pecan tips loose from the sack and rolls across the ground. It stops against Ada's boot.

"What's happening down here?" she says.

"Damned if I know."

"Why would they stop here when they've got, what, two hours left? We should be heading back already."

"I'm hoping we'll see Talmadge and he can tell us," Quinton says.

Ada pulls out a candle, which will burn down at about an inch per hour, an interesting fact she's sure Quinton already knows. The candles are less critical than the carbide, and he nods his agreement without her voicing the thought. Mind reading.

When she pulls out the matchbox, he doesn't offer to light the candle for her. In fact, he turns his head and spits without apology, not even trying to play the gentleman, which is fine because she is not playing the lady. Her hands are steady and fast, and she surely has the wick lit faster than he could have done it.

He blows out his headlamp as she's wedging the candle into a crevice. The light it throws is flickering and fanciful, changing the cavern into something suitable for ghosts or dreams. The dim light also hides more than their headlamps, which she appreciates. Her boots and clothes look like she's been rolling in a coal bin. She suspects her face is coated, too, but she can't waste the water to clean it.

She watches the swimming shadows, and if part of her wishes for home and bed and bath, a bigger part relishes the reality: She is allowed to be here. She is supposed to be here.

"How long would it take you to get back to the elevators on your own?" she asks.

"Not sure," Quinton says. "That's part of the problem. We're off the map. At least, my map. But I imagine it'd take me a couple of hours to pick my way through."

"You don't sound worried."

He takes his time answering. "We have extra light and water. We have both of us to go fetch help. I see no reason to worry."

She reaches into her pack again, feeling blindly for the apples that have been banging around every time she bends down. "I'm guessing we shouldn't finish off the food just yet?"

"To be safe," he agrees.

It's what she expected him to say, but if she were a salamander, she'd eat her own tail right now. She's as ravenous as she is filthy: Her body's finally noticed that its tank is empty. Quinton rustles in his own pack before he stretches out, propping his jaw on his hand, legs stretching into the gravel. He sets one tin of corned beef next to her knee and another on his thigh. She hands him an apple and takes the one that's bruised for herself.

When he bites into his apple, the juice sprays through the smoke of the candle, misting her hand. She'd lick it off if she weren't so grimy.

"What else you got in there?" he asks, chewing.

Her first bite of the apple is mealy, but the sweetness cuts through the taste of cave on her tongue.

"A sack of dried apples," she says. "A few strips of fatback that Ruby insisted on sending."

He picks at a piece of peel between his front teeth. "Can't eat pork. I worked in a slaughterhouse in Cincinnati, and it put me off for good."

"Yeah? I've never been further north than Louisville. Or further south than Birmingham, except for the beach once." She leans against the wall. "They had stingrays."

"You get stung?"

"No," she says. "And they could have been some other kind of rays. But you could see them moving through the waves. Formations, like birds."

"Well, you didn't miss much in Cincinnati," he says.

She twists the stem of her apple until it snaps off, and she tosses it over her shoulder. Maybe it will bring them luck, like a pinch of salt.

"Why'd you go there?" she asks.

He's gnawed the apple so close to the core that it looks like a mushroom. His knuckles are swollen.

"I had a cousin up there," he says. "My father had died, and I thought I wanted something new. I wound up sleeping in a park. At twenty-two, you don't believe it's possible you can starve to death, but I gave it my best shot."

She tries to imagine him frail. She tries to imagine him young.

She's missed listening to stories that she hasn't heard. She and Ruby know all the layers of each other by now, and she had that with Gerald, too, of course, knew he had a pet squirrel as a child and his favorite aunt was divorced and he broke his arm when he fell off that horse in a patch of asparagus. If she had a daughter, she would tell her to marry a man whose stories were still fascinating the second or third time because marriage means hearing those stories for the rest of your life.

"I do wish you had more of that macaroni," Quinton says.

She smiles. "I'd like me another salamander skeleton, if we're placing orders."

He tips his head and tosses his apple core.

"Did you swim in the ocean?" he asks.

"I did."

"You weren't scared of being stung by rays?"

"They swam away from me every time I tried to get close," she says.

She can't remember, actually, if she was scared. She likes to think she wasn't. With him listening, she gets to build herself, bit by bit, just as he does.

The candlelight barely circles them. His toes have dropped into the darkness.

"Might as well rest a little," he says. "Seems like they're taking their time."

He flops over so he's flat on the ground, jamming one of the folded blankets under his head. Ada watches him for a moment, then slides off her boots. She strips her socks off, too, and the pleasure of bare feet makes her head fall back. She rolls her jacket into a pillow, folding up the sleeves like her father once taught her, and spreads the other blanket over herself. As soon as she's horizontal, the exhaustion hits her as strongly as the hunger did earlier. Surely there's no way they can fall asleep on solid rock.

"Your feet don't get cold?" Quinton asks.

She's kicked them out from under the blanket, as she always does. She doesn't even open her eyes.

"They're always hot," she says. "I can't stand to have them covered."

It took Gerald a year of marriage to notice this about her, and this man has discovered it within a day.

She drifts off, maybe. She has a dream or a memory of eating blackberry cobbler, her mother's hand smoothing back her hair so it doesn't get juice in it, but somehow her entire face is filthy, and then she knows she's awake—she can feel the rock beneath her—her eyes are open—but she can't see anything. The darkness has gobbled up their circle of light.

The candle's gone out, and her first thought is that it's burned all the way down and hours have passed. She can feel the shadow going down her throat as she takes a breath, like she's gone back to the beginning of time, when the earth was without form and darkness was upon the face of the deep, and if the darkness is turning solid, she is doing the opposite. She can feel her body evaporating, and maybe this is what death is like.

Quinton's knee bumps against hers, and she takes form again.

"Damn it," he says. "I think it blew out when I rolled over."

She feels him shifting and hears the strike of a match a split second before she sees the flame. She could have done that, she realizes, but she was too wrapped up in the dark.

Quinton is only disconnected angles of fingers and wrist and jaw as he reaches for the candle, still cursing softly under his breath as he lights it. The candle isn't noticeably shorter than it was when she closed her eyes, so they've lost only minutes, not hours. The room takes shape again around them, and they begin to settle back into the known world.

She's still adjusting to the light when she hears the footsteps—it takes her five or six crunches of gravel to understand that's what they are, and by that time a flashlight beam is skimming from the chamber floor to ceiling. It catches her briefly in the eyes just as Quinton pushes to his feet. Someone is climbing the wall from the lower chamber. Boots scrabble against limestone, and a lanky figure comes into view.

Talmadge.

He makes his way toward them, squatting near their feet, his flashlight now aimed at the floor. His eyes flick to her briefly before settling on Quinton, and the candlelight shifts across his face.

"I'm done," he says. "You take 'em."

He does not sound as if he's joking. Ada can actually hear Quinton's tongue slick over his teeth.

"What the hell are you talking about?" he asks.

"Just what I said," Talmadge says, rubbing his wrist. He takes his time, like a genie might pop out if he keeps up the friction long enough. "You can get them back home. Just keep on and you'll wind up back at that damn waterfall. I'm gonna head out."

He stands, turning.

"Sit your butt back down and tell me what's happened," Quinton commands.

"What hasn't happened?" Talmadge says. He isn't sitting down, but at least he's not leaving. "Hagathorn's already walked right past the hatpin, no magic vibrations at all. He got stuck in a crack and scraped himself up bad. He won't turn back. And now he's had some sort of fit and smashed his knees. I'm giving the blood a chance to clot up and hoping the break will let everybody get their heads on straighter."

Ada tries to sort through all of it.

"He had a seizure?" she asks.

Talmadge lets out a gust of breath. "He'd call it a vision."

"How bad is he bleeding?" Quinton asks.

Talmadge's fingers open and close around his flashlight. "Not too bad. I wrapped him up, not that he appreciated it. He's blaming everything on me and Morris. Says we didn't do our job properly."

"Did you do your job properly?" asks Quinton.

"Every step of the way."

"Then stop talking crazy and get back in there," Quinton says. "Get them moving. Make sure that man winds up staring straight at the hatpin and dot your i's and cross your t's and finish the thing! Because if you don't, Leo might never send you down here again."

Even though the rock eats up sound, Ada wonders how much their voices are carrying.

"The reporter says I'll lose my job anyway," Talmadge says, quietly enough. "He says I'm no better than Hagathorn. I cannot lose my job, Quint."

Since he appeared in his swirl of light, he's sounded furious in a way that promises thrown punches or broken china. It's not temper in his voice now, though, but panic.

"This isn't the way to change his mind," Quinton says.

Talmadge switches his flashlight to his other hand. "I don't think I *can* change it," he says.

"Sit down," Quinton says, and the way he says it makes Ada wonder if he has children. If he might even have a wife. He doesn't wear a wedding ring, but she's never thought to ask.

"Sit down," he says again.

Talmadge sinks to the ground, legs folding under him like a pocketknife. He is all soot and shadow except for the whites of his eyes.

"Catch your breath," Ada says. "Take a minute."

He's still squeezing that flashlight. It's the only thing he has with him—no pack, no canteen—and either he wasn't serious about leaving or he was so frantic that he wasn't thinking straight.

"What am I doing I here?" he asks, staring at the dirt.

Ada has never had patience for people who wallow. You can never solve anything if you're busy wallowing.

"You're here because Leo asked you," she says. "Because it's your job."

He looks surprised. He's looked surprised every time she's spoken. Maybe exhaustion is softening her, but her annoyance gives way to a wisp of sympathy. He's so young. At his age she still believed—

She doesn't know what she believed. She can't get close to slipping back inside that girl.

"Leo asked you because you're the best," she adds. "You're good at what you do. Everyone knows that."

"I'm not the best," Talmadge says, turning to Quinton. "He is. And he said no."

When Ada turns to Quinton, he's in profile, like a president's face on a coin. The candlelight lengthens his eyebrows.

"You're the one who was stupid enough to say yes," he says to Talmadge. "No one made you."

"You said you're not a guide," Ada says to Quinton, who's not looking at her.

"I'm not. But I know the caves."

"Leo asked you to lead Hagathorn's group?" she prompts.

"He did."

"And you said no?"

Finally Quinton turns to her, and his look says *Can you blame me?* She supposes she can't. He reaches for Talmadge, stopping short, his hand hovering over the younger man's forearm.

"What's your bunch of ducklings doing at the moment?" Quinton asks.

"Resting," Talmadge answers. He nods toward the candle. "Great minds think alike—I got them down to a candle to save our light. Gave them the last couple of cans of beans and told them to close their eyes."

"They going to wonder where you are?" Quinton asks.

"I think they all passed out before I left."

Ada believes it. She's used to these caves, but ten straight hours of them have taken a toll. There comes a point where sleep is no longer a choice.

"So you'll take a few minutes, too," Quinton says. "Then you go back and handle whatever comes next. It might still work out fine, and it might not. But I guarantee if you storm out of here now, you'll be shooting yourself in the foot."

Talmadge taps his flashlight against his heel. "You know we're not going to make it out in two hours."

"I also know," Quinton says, "that I've got an extra cartridge of carbide for everybody. We've got four hours of leeway for this to come together."

"If I go back to them."

"If you go back," Quinton agrees. "Which you are going to do. But for now, push them out of your head. Relax. If they call for you, we'll hear. I'll make sure we're up and moving in half an hour either way."

Talmadge turns off his flashlight, which Ada takes as agreement. He unfastens his helmet and watches the ground. What was it Quinton said about him? *Better with rocks than people*? It occurs to her that maybe he was so quick to spout tour guide jargon because otherwise he'd have needed to come up with his own words. He doesn't seem to have a reservoir.

She forgives him entirely for snubbing her on the staircase as she rests her head in the crook of her elbow. The candle wavers as Quinton shoves himself against the wall a few feet away.

"I heard the magic man drove a horse to death not long ago," he says into the silence. "He pushed it so hard the animal keeled over and died on the road. And Ed Lacey said he pulled a razor on them in the hotel yesterday."

"That doesn't even sound real," Ada says. "It sounds like a made-up story."

"He's real," Talmadge huffs out.

Ada closes her eyes. She wishes she could hear crickets or cicadas or bullfrogs. She's imagining train whistles when she feels a fluttering against her face like eyelashes; she slaps at the darkness and feels the soft brush of wings.

"What?" Quinton whispers.

"Moth, maybe," she says.

"The harebrained ones still find their way inside sometimes," he says, but she drifts to sleep thinking she felt the spiny wings of a bat.

9:25 p.m.

"God help me!" a man calls, so loudly that Ada thinks a stranger is in the chamber with them.

She sits up before she's fully conscious, arm over her head, ready to block a blow, absorbing the fear in the voice like it's her own. She scrambles, jamming on her boots by candlelight, and she sees Quinton already on his feet, boots on. They both grab for flashlights, which come to life faster than headlamps.

She is all movement and no thought as Quinton's flashlight goes rolling and he lunges for it. She yanks out her pocket watch, wrestling with the clasp one-handed, sacrificing a precious second to see that not half an hour has passed since she closed her eyes.

Someone down the passageway screams Talmadge's name once. Twice. Quinton spins, flashlight back in his hand, beam sweeping across the ground. Ada finally notices that Talmadge isn't in the chamber with them, and of course he's not. He could have gone back to the group while they were asleep, or even if he didn't, he's younger and faster and could be halfway down the passageway.

She scrambles toward the opening to the lower level, dropping to her knees and tucking the flashlight into her waistband so she can navigate the wall. She mostly slides down it, falling forward onto her hands when she reaches the lower chamber. She realizes she's forgotten her gloves when the gravel bites into her palms, but she's already standing before the pain sinks in.

Quinton lands next to her. They head down the corridor, the ceiling expanding in ripples as she arcs her flashlight across the path. Quinton's boot catches her heel, and they both lose a step.

They make one turn and then another, and they must be close now. Very close. Ada turns her ankle on a loose stone but barely slows down. She's not even sure why they're rushing—the voices ahead of them have gone silent. The commotion was likely a nightmare or another fit from Hagathorn, but the fear is still rushing through her, pushing her forward.

But something's wrong—something other than the scream—and she slows as she realizes that she should be seeing light by now. They must have taken a wrong turn because it's still pitch-dark, no sign of human life. Quinton is passing her, though, speeding up, more concerned instead of less. He comes to a stop in a few yards at the opening to a small chamber, and she smacks a hand against his shoulder blade to keep from running into him.

They are not in the wrong place.

Quinton's flashlight—and now hers—catches the silhouettes of two men sitting, hunchbacked. Between them, someone is still sleeping. Someone else in the room whimpers like a puppy. Ada sees a hint of movement and swings her Eveready until the beam lands on Editha, who's inching forward on her knees, loose hair falling around her shoulders.

The whimpering has stopped, and now there's only breathing, too loud. Ada tells herself that she was right—the mind reader has had another fit—but where is the candle Talmadge left burning? Why is everyone sitting in the dark? The two men sitting on the ground turn to face her, squinting at the light: It's Morris Efrom and Tom, the manager.

"We're here to help," Ada says, and only then does a second level of panic hit her. She and Quinton have given up the game.

They were supposed to stay hidden and now they are here, and she doesn't know if this was a reasonable response or a terrible mistake.

Jeremiah Hagathorn runs a hand over his head, blinking. Only the newspaperman is still lying down, showing no signs of stirring, and he must be a deep sleeper.

Ada tells herself that, even when she knows it's not true.

She remembers this same feeling when she walked into her mother's bedroom that last time, a cup filled with ice chips in her hand, and she knew even before she touched her mother's shoulder.

She knew.

Morris's face confirms it—she can see his throat working, like he might vomit. He's got a hand on Howard's sleeve. *So young* is Ada's first thought. *Maybe his heart.* And then Morris is taking hold of the newspaperman's shoulders and turning him over, and all the shadows ringing the room recoil.

"Shit," Hagathorn says.

Ada turns away, not out of emotion but because it's her flashlight that's casting the worst shadow of all, catching the spike driven into the man's neck, only, no it's not a spike. It's rock. A stalactite gone right through the Adam's apple. She touches the same spot on her own throat, feeling the thinness of the skin, just as Quinton steps in front of her, his broad back blocking her view entirely. She assumes the gesture is meant to be considerate, but she sidesteps him, annoyed because does he think she'll get an attack of the vapors? She has buried not only her mother and her father but her baby and her husband, and it is always the women who handle the bodies, arranging hair and hands and collars. She is well-acquainted with the look and feel of death.

She listens to the whisper of water through the walls. It's amazing how long people can stay quiet with a dead man between them. She looks from face to face. The mind reader is balding more than she realized, and the wife is so small, smaller than Ruby. Morris seems a decade older than he did this morning, with dirt caked in the lines of his forehead. He pushes to his feet, swaying, and Ada wonders if he's hobbled himself or if he's only exhausted.

"Who are you?" Tom asks, voice hoarse.

"Rescue crew," Quinton says immediately. "Things were running late down here, and Leo Lambert wanted to make sure everything was okay."

No one seems to question it. Morris has found his helmet and headlamp, and he fumbles with a box of matches. Tom pulls his glasses out of his jacket pocket and settles them on his ears. He grabs at a stump of a candle near his feet.

"We had this going," he says. He lifts it as if he's making a toast. "Not sure what happened."

"I closed my eyes," Morris says, still trying to strike a match. "I didn't think—"

"I didn't intend to close them," Tom says over him. "I never thought I'd sleep, but I must have. When I woke up, I thought I'd gone blind, and I was trying to get my bearings, and when I reached out, I touched him. I didn't know—I wasn't sure—I lay my hand in blood. I felt him, and it was all in the dark and I—I lost my head."

He's embarrassed about screaming, Ada realizes. The things that go through men's minds are incomprehensible.

"I woke up when you yelled," Morris says. The match in his hand flames and then dies.

"Same here," Hagathorn says. "Couldn't see a thing."

Ada can't look away from the newspaperman. It's different with a stranger: She can feel the emptiness of him, as she did that day with her mother, but at a distance. It's like a math problem she cannot quite grasp, how the shape in front of her is no longer a person but a carcass, like a plucked chicken on her counter. The carcass has a rolled-up jacket under his head, and she can picture him tucking in the sleeves and folding over the collar, trying to smooth the wrinkles out, and maybe somebody taught him—the carcass—to do that, roll a jacket up good and tight so it would make a good pillow, like her father taught her, and maybe he thought of that person as he closed his eyes and drifted to sleep and maybe he played through a thousand other memories that no one will ever know because those memories have blinked out of existence.

Without anyone appearing to move, the gap between the carcass and the others has widened. Since Morris rolled the man over, no one has touched him, although no one can look away for long.

The ceiling is smooth other than one ripple over their heads that droops down like the tongue of a dog.

"His eyes are still closed," Tom says, the unlit candle still in his hand.

"And his head still on his coat," Morris says. "It must have been fast."

The stalactite is over a foot long, thicker than a broom handle. The top is flat, snapped-off, and the point is embedded in the man's throat. When her flashlight was focused on him, Ada caught the spill of blood, but it was less than she'd expect. She thinks again of a chicken and how you can plunge in the butcher knife, but the blood only flows when you pull it out.

Someone in this room killed him.

Somehow that detail strikes her only now: The stalactite did not fall from the ceiling. It did not magically appear. One of these people broke off that spear of rock and stabbed it through the man's neck.

"So no one heard anything?" Ada says. "Footsteps? A scuffle?"

It doesn't seem possible that this happened in silence, but as if the same string is tugging at all of them, everyone shakes their head.

"He must have been asleep," Quinton says. "To not put up a fight at all."

"Wouldn't have been able to scream, I imagine," Tom says.

Editha inches forward on her hands and knees, edging around her husband's manager. Her hair blocks her face. She rests a hand on the newspaperman's ankle, tugging at a wrinkle in the hem of his pants. She holds completely still for what feels like a full minute to Ada.

Shell-shocked, she thinks. They are all shell-shocked, and they're acting aimless as sheep.

Editha sits back on her heels, pale and wild-haired.

"Where's Talmadge gone?" she asks.

When Ada looks to Quinton, he's already looking back at her. Shell-shocked. Somewhere between skittering down that wall and discovering a dead man, they forgot about Talmadge entirely.

"Y'all haven't seen him?" Ada says.

"Not since I woke up," Editha says.

Quinton gives one small shake of his head, his eyes still on Ada.

"Stay here," he says to her, and he's headed out of the chamber before she can answer.

She watches as he disappears down the passageway back the way they came, calling Talmadge's name in two quick barks. She tells herself to do something. Say something. Only as Quinton's footsteps fade does it occurs to her that she could have—should have?—gone with him, no matter what orders he gave.

His voice echoes down the passage, muted, as he calls for Talmadge again.

"We saw him not long ago," she says to the others. The room is twice as dark now that she has the only flashlight. "Talmadge. He came across us while you were resting. He can't be far."

She looks around her at the circle of white-eyed faces and realizes Quinton was right. She needed to stay here. These people need a steady hand, and she can, at least, pretend steadiness.

"Where'd he go?" Hagathorn asks.

"For help, most likely," Ada says.

It's the most comforting of answers, and these people have no reason not to believe her. But if it's true, why didn't Talmadge inform someone before he headed back to the elevator? And if he never came back to this chamber, how would he have known they needed help?

I'm done, he said, and then he agreed so easily to Quinton's request that he sit down and reconsider. She closed her eyes and likely Quinton closed his eyes and she assumed Talmadge closed his eyes, but maybe he did not. If he did not rest at all, by this stage he's had nearly an hour to head toward the elevator or anywhere else.

Morris has finally gotten his headlamp burning, and the beam brightens the center of the room. He lights the chunk of candle, too, keeping his head turned from the newspaperman the entire time.

Hagathorn stretches forward and lays his hand on his wife's shoulder. "So someone extinguished the candle and then stabbed a man in the dark," he says.

It changes the air in the room when he speaks it aloud. If the rest of them have been circling around the idea of murder, he's driven straight through the center.

"We can't know that," Tom says.

"We do, I think," the mind reader says. "And now our guide has hurried out of here, in an interesting convergence of events."

He is not wrong. Ada wonders how far Quinton has gotten and whether he's found Talmadge, and she pictures the chamber where they last saw him, their blankets and packs shoved against the wall.

The extra canteens. The carbide cartridges. They left all their extra light and water back there, free for the taking. If Talmadge did want to punish this group, she and Quinton have made it easy for him.

"You need to wait here for me," she tells the others, but she's not as fast at exiting as Quinton was.

Morris grabs at the hem of her jacket.

"You're going to leave us, too?" he asks, and if it's not panic in his voice, it's something close.

Ada does not want to acknowledge her fears about Talmadge, but she needs to hold those cartridges in her hands. She remembers the solid blackness when the candle blew out. Darkness upon the face of the deep.

She keeps her voice steady.

"I'll be five minutes," she says. "I want to get our supplies. We left our packs behind us when we heard the scream, and who knows how long we'll wait for Quinton and Talmadge to come back?"

"You truly think he'll bring him back?" Hagathorn says.

He's still sitting, she notices. Blood has seeped through the bandages wrapped around his knees, but she has no time for that now.

No, she does not think Quinton is coming back with Talmadge.

"What I think," she says, "is that I don't want us to run out of light."

"You know where you're going?" Morris asks, finally letting go of her jacket.

He speaks to her as if she's some little lady dithering at a busy intersection as opposed to a woman who has just rescued him, but she doesn't take offense at his tone. She leaves them all in the glow of his lamp, the dog tongue hanging above them, and she doesn't look back. She didn't notice the specifics when she rushed through here earlier, but it's an old streambed, newly formed enough that gravel as big as silver dollars shifts under her feet. The ground is wetter than she remembers. Overhead, a small cluster of stalactites hangs like clumps of dead leaves.

She's moving as quickly as possible over the gravel, and these rocks explain why she turned her ankle earlier. She reaches the wall to the upper chamber and only remembers her scraped hands when she tries to climb. She grits her way through it, hauling herself over the ledge, and she braces herself to find an empty room. But her pack is where she left it, and Quinton's pack, too, looks untouched. Their two blankets are strewn on the ground, as are their helmets. Her gloves are stacked on top of each other, and a full canteen is propped against the wall.

Talmadge stole nothing.

She's misjudged him, thank God. She doesn't know where he's gone or what he's doing, but he's no thief.

Her shoulders and back scream at her when she reaches for the packs. She hasn't been this sore since her first days of caving, back when she'd struggle to sit up in bed in the morning. She stuffs the blankets inside the packs and tucks her gloves in her pocket. She loops the canteen over her head and lights her headlamp before fastening her helmet and tucking away the flashlight.

She's considering the climb down when she hears water dripping nearby, a small trickle coming from a stumpy stalactite at the edge of the room. She considers her palms, caked with blood and mud, and she detours to the spill of water. She rinses her hands, front and back, and something catches hold of her so that she leans closer, sticking her head in the stream, soaking her cheeks and chin and neck. It is such a relief, the water.

It washes away everything.

Our bodies feel, where'er they be, her grandfather recited to her from Wordsworth long ago. *Against or with our will.*

She straightens, cleaner and clearerheaded. Her light has landed on a single stone, dark and speckled and silvered in the small pool at her feet. She plucks it from the water, shakes it mostly dry, and gives in to impulse—she licks it, a brief lap of mineral and cold.

Maybe she is not clearerheaded. When she turns, Quinton is there behind her. She doesn't know how he moved so silently.

"Talmadge?" she asks.

"No sign of him," he says. "Thought I'd grab our things."

"I had the same thought."

She cannot make sense of the look on his face. He's staring at the stone she's still holding between her fingers, and he must have seen her taste it.

"I'm off-kilter," she says, trying for a laugh. She tosses the stone to the ground and swipes the back of her hand across her wet mouth. "The urge just came into my head."

He's standing so still.

"I wanted to do that to you the first time I saw you," he says quietly.

"Pardon?"

"Put my mouth on you," he says.

It takes her too long to translate his words. It's not as if she doesn't understand wanting. She's wanted to put her hands and mouth on him for so long that she's stopped feeling any shame over it—her thoughts of his weight on top of her or her palms on his chest are no more relevant than her longing to hear her mother's voice one more time. She lets her thoughts of Quinton come and go unheeded, and her want hums along like a train whistle she no longer hears, because what does it matter what or who she wants?

She hears the whistle now.

It feels like she stands for hours, water plinking behind her. He comes to her and pushes back her helmet, and she puts her hands on his shoulders like she's always wanted to do. Soon they will go back to the carcass and the staring strangers and none of it makes sense but Quinton does. His fingers twist in her hair as he lowers his head. His tongue is on her neck, licking lightly from collarbone to jawline.

She hopes the water doesn't make him sick. She puts her hands to his face and pulls his mouth to hers.

9:50 p.m.

They're heading down the passageway not two minutes later. Ada knows she left a mark on his neck, but she can't see it in the shadows. She is a pot of water boiling: Everything has happened too quickly, and, instead of dissolving, her thoughts only roll and froth.

"Do you think Talmadge was only waiting until we fell asleep?" she asks.

"I didn't fall asleep," Quinton says. "But I did step away for a smoke. So it's possible."

No wonder he was moving around the chamber while she was still shrugging off her blanket. He must've already been on his feet when they heard the first scream.

"He could have gotten past without you noticing?" she asks.

"If he went back through the lower chamber. It never occurred to me the fool was still determined to leave."

"You think all he did was leave?" she asks.

Quinton swings his head toward her, light slashing across her shoulders. "I think he was desperate to get away from those people. He wanted to get out of here. Ada, that's a long way from killing someone."

She sees a bubble of light down the corridor, like a glowworm. They should pick up their pace.

"I never thought you felt like this," she says, and it's a poor moment to talk about what just happened between them, but she can't imagine she'll find a better time after they join the others.

"How do you think I feel?" he asks.

She thinks he's smiling, but she's watching the gravel.

"Like you'd enjoy me unbuttoning your shirt," she says. "Like you'd like to unbutton mine."

They were, actually, starting the unbuttoning when sanity returned. Now his mouth finds hers again, only a brief touch, but her head quiets slightly.

"Yes," he says.

"You hid it well," she tells him.

"Did I? I showed up on your porch."

She thinks back to how he filled her doorway and her rocking chair and how he talked of committees and contracts and an hourly wage. As declarations of affection go, she considers it subtle at best. But they're facing forward again, not touching, and she pushes away thoughts of him in her sitting room.

When they turn into the dimly lit chamber, once again all the dirt-streaked faces turn toward them. Only there aren't so many faces, are they? One dead. One vanished. Four still here. Ada could fit them all around her kitchen table and have leftover chairs. All four of the living ones are standing, although Hagathorn is propped against the wall, his ripped trousers flapping around his bloody knees. Someone has laid a handkerchief across the dead man's face, and she wishes she knew who. It was an act of kindness. Or a sign of guilt. She should be looking for guilt.

Hagathorn lifts his canteen to his mouth, tapping the bottom.

"We have more water," Ada says, letting the extra canteen dangle from two fingers. "But we need to go easy on it."

"You don't have Talmadge," Morris says. He takes the water from her, passing it to the mind reader without looking.

"He said he was fed up," Quinton says. "I guess he was."

"You can't believe that," Hagathorn says. "You know he killed this man. You can't think it's—what?—a coincidence that he clambered out of here right after the stabbing."

"He didn't clamber," Ada says. "He came to us before the stabbing, reasonable enough, and said he was sick of this. Sick of you, honestly."

"I just can't believe it," Morris says. "He never said a word to me."

"He came to you before we *discovered* the stabbing," Tom says to Ada. "That's different."

"It doesn't matter," Quinton says, holding up a hand. "We'll call the police as soon as we get aboveground, and they'll sort it out. It's one more reason to get out of here as soon as we can."

"It doesn't matter?" Editha echoes.

"It matters," Quinton says, tipping his head. Apologetic. "But what matters more is getting aboveground while we still have light. Ada and I can lead you out, and we'd like to do it as soon as possible."

"And him?" Morris asks, nodding toward the ground.

"We'll have to leave him," Quinton says. "Frankly, there's no way to move him with any sort of respect. We'll need to get a stretcher."

"We're leaving him lying here?" Tom says, flames glinting off his glasses.

"We don't have a choice," Quinton says. "Provided you can walk, Mr. Hagathorn. Since you're standing up, I'm guessing you can."

Hagathorn has opened the canteen and he takes a swallow, although not, Ada acknowledges, a greedy one.

"I can walk," he says. He's not looking at Quinton but at the newspaperman. "It would have been a tricky thing, wouldn't it? To stab him that cleanly in the dark. Chances are you'd miss, and he'd wake up and scream bloody murder and then where would you be? You'd have to feel very sure of yourself."

"You don't seem very upset about it," Morris says.

"I hardly knew the man," Hagathorn says, handing the canteen to his wife. "People die every day. There's no shortage of tragedy in the world."

Ada's been thinking that if she ever stood in the same room with this man, eventually his public self would fade away and she'd see the real man underneath. She's coming to believe there is no real man.

"And you, Mrs. Hagathorn?" she asks, because she cannot help it. "Are you upset?"

She's full of questions about the woman's relationship with the newspaperman, but she does not want to ask in front of the mind reader. He's volatile enough without her setting off that particular bomb. On the other hand, if he knew about the newspaperman, the bomb might have gone off already and left them with a carcass.

Editha has twisted her hair back, summoning pins from nowhere, although in these shadows everything appears as if by magic.

"I'm upset," she says quietly. "Of course I am. Someone killed a young man right next to us. You'd have to be heartless not to feel something, so quit doing that, Miah. You don't mean it."

Quinton blows out the stump of a candle and shoves it into his pack. He sidesteps to a capped canteen tipped over on the ground, gives it a shake, and tucks it away as well.

"I don't know," Quinton says. "Maybe you don't feel upset, Mr. Hagathorn. Because your life just got easier."

Ada would like to shine her light in the mind reader's face to see him more clearly, but it feels too obvious. She settles for aiming toward his torso, which makes the silhouette of his belly loom on the wall behind him.

"Professor Hagathorn," he corrects Quinton. "And I can't see how my life is remotely easier."

Ada wonders how long it's been since anyone here called this man "Professor."

"You've failed," Quinton says. "A reporter was going to record that failure for the public. Now there's no story at all, and the fellow who was going to write it is laying dead on the ground. And you're doing all you can to convince us Talmadge did it."

Hagathorn laughs. It does not even sound forced.

"You think I'd kill a man over a newspaper story?" he says. "One more naysayer wouldn't make any difference."

"He was a naysayer for the *Chicago Times*," Quinton says.

"He was a jackass," Hagathorn says. "And why do you get to ask the questions? You're as likely as anyone else, sneaking around down here."

Quinton slicks his tongue over his teeth. "That's what a rescue party does. We come along behind you. Ada and I were several hundred feet down the passage from you when this happened. You watched us come in."

"You could have come earlier while we were asleep," Hagathorn answers.

Ada can't imagine why he's making this argument, and she can't imagine why Quinton is bothering to argue back.

"How would I have known you were all asleep?" Quinton says. "And I'd met the man all of one time. I've got no stake in this."

Hagathorn shrugs. "I don't have any more reason than you have. The fault here was never mine. Talmadge and Morris don't know where the hatpin is."

As the other man speaks, Quinton has been heading toward a backpack slanted against the wall, but his headlamp dips and rises as he turns to Morris. The parabola of it catches the bloody spear of rock still jutting out of flesh. Ada wishes someone had covered it whenever they covered the newspaperman's face.

"He's been saying that since he had his fit," Morris says. "It's not true. We did exactly what we were supposed to do. We hid the hatpin and we know exactly where it is."

Editha's eyes shine wet, a sure marker of grief or sadness. Unless it's a sign of guilt. She lays a hand on her husband's arm.

"It was not a fit," she says to Morris. "It was clarity."

"And that's why I'm not headed back to the surface quite yet," Hagathorn says.

Quinton widens his stance, and Ada thinks of her brothers long ago in the schoolyard. She wonders if Quinton ever boxed.

"You cannot be serious," he says. "We're finished with that. A dead man means the hatpin does not matter anymore."

"It matters," Hagathorn says. "You think just because he can't write it, there's no story? It only means we're the ones who get to tell it."

"Jeremiah," says Tom, stretching out the word, chastening.

"We are not staying longer," Quinton says.

Hagathorn takes a step closer to him. "What I'm wondering is how you're going to force me to do anything."

Ada wonders if the man walks into a room, shakes a few hands, and immediately starts assessing how he can make himself hated by everyone. Force isn't an option. Even if Quinton knocked Hagathorn unconscious—which, granted, would be enjoyable to watch—they'd have to drag him through the caves. No, they need the professor to walk out under his own power.

"I could leave you down here alone and see how much luck you have finding anything," Quinton says. "A hatpin. An exit. Light. Water."

"I'm obviously not leaving him alone," Editha says.

"Or I," Tom says.

Ada pictures the three of them down here alone with the body, which could be exactly the scenario they want. If they're left here by themselves, they can do away with any traces of guilt that might be scattered in the shadows, or they could do away with the body altogether.

She would rather one of them did it. She would like it to be someone she does not know.

"Whose is this?" Quinton asks.

He's worked his way over to the lone pack resting against the far wall. No one answers. Morris is the only one who seems to seriously consider the question.

"Talmadge's?" he guesses. "That can't be."

Ada remembers how the guide had nothing but a flashlight when he climbed into their chamber.

Quinton kneels next to the pack, peeling open the flap and plunging a hand inside. "He left his canteen," he says. "Some water still inside. A couple of backup cartridges. He left everything he had, as far as I can tell."

"He didn't have his headlamp when we saw him," Ada says. "Only the empty helmet."

"So you people think this man kills someone," Quinton says, standing, "escapes into the caves, and leaves behind his water and light for the group to use?"

"It sounds like he was desperate," Tom says.

"It sounds like he was still taking care of you," Quinton says. "And, Mr. Hagathorn, I'm wondering why a man with his knees bashed to bits would choose—no, would insist—on staying down here longer. The more you insist you won't talk to the police, the more I wonder."

"You want it to end here?" Hagathorn says, taking a stiff step, the stained fabric of his pants flapping around his knees. "You're happy with this story as it is, a study in incompetence, not mine but everyone's? Don't you want a better ending for Mr. Lambert?"

"I just want it to end," Quinton says.

"I'll go by myself," Ada says to him, and it's such a simple solution. She might make a few wrong turns, but she can find her way. "You stay here and I'll head to the elevator. I'll tell Leo and the others what's happened."

"No," Hagathorn says before she's even finished speaking.

"What do you mean?" Quinton snaps at him. "You win. We'll stay down here and deal with your lunacy. But Ada can let the police know the situation. We owe him"—he jerks his head toward the body—"that much."

"You think she'll pop up there, announce someone is dead, and they'll sit by and let me finish up?" Hagathorn says. "It'll all be over as soon as she opens the elevator door."

"You don't seem to understand," Quinton says. "There's no option for continuing the search. We'll be out of light and water soon. You're right that I can't force you to move, so we can hunker down in this room until we get more supplies or until I have enough men to drag you out of here, but we are not roving deeper into the caves. I have no idea where the damn hatpin is, but no one put it in the center of the mountain. Use your head, *Professor.* A guide knows he's leading a bunch of people with no experience into the caverns—you think he's not nervous about an attack of claustrophobia or a flare-up of gout? There's no way Talmadge and Morris made it this difficult. You've already passed the pin."

Morris and Quinton look at each other across the professor and his wife. They stare at each other for too long. Everyone in this chamber has become prone to staring.

"You know where it is?" Hagathorn asks, hawkish.

"I just said that I don't," Quinton answers. "Because, contrary to what you think, they didn't break the rules. But I know you must have passed it because I have a functioning brain. Tell him, Morris."

"If I tell him, I'm breaking the agreement," Morris says.

"Then break it," Quinton says, nearly shouting. "This story can't be about anything but a murder now, and you think that will sell tickets?"

The older man looks thoughtful, not cowed.

"Maybe," he says.

Ada agrees, actually. She watches the play of shadow over their heads, the damp ceiling winking silver. After that family drowned out on Douglas Lake, people took picnics there and ate so they had a view of the spot where the boat sunk. Tragedy might bring more publicity than anything else would.

"Morris," Quinton says. "Please."

Morris rubs a hand over his face. He makes no effort to hide the dislike on his face when he turns to Hagathorn.

"We did pass it already," Morris says. "You looked right over it."

Hagathorn barely pauses. "Why would I trust anything you say?"

"Why in the world does it matter anymore?" Morris says. "Are you a child? You need someone to pat you on the head that badly?"

After all this, they are still standing in a loose circle. If they were playing duck-duck-goose, the carcass would be in the stewpot.

"Just tell him where it is," Quinton says. "He wants a good story so badly, we'll give it to him. Let's go grab the thing and he can add all the bells and whistles he wants and we'll all agree he's the second coming of Christ."

Ada wonders if Quinton would actually allow that to happen. She will not. She has no intention of backing up Hagathorn's claim to any sort of ability; she would not, at the moment, back up his claim to any sort of sanity.

"It doesn't work that way," Hagathorn says. "The truth will out. If you give me the answer, someone will speak of it. It'll ruin everything."

"It's all ruined anyway," Morris says. He licks his lips. They're badly chapped, cracked and bleeding in places. "Listen, I planted a weeping willow in the backyard—my wife's favorite—and it's been there for twenty years."

"I don't think—" starts Hagathorn.

"Shut up," Morris says, and, miraculously, Hagathorn does. "That tree will be there for a century after I'm gone. It's proof of something. Proof of us, me and her. Proof of more than that, is what I'm saying, and I'll tell you what this story should have been. A man found an underground waterfall that no human being had ever seen before. He loved his wife so much that he named it after her, and he carved out a mountain to show it to us all, and that's it. That's the story. It's a look at our best selves, isn't it? Or it could have been. But now it's—it's whatever this has turned into."

He waves a hand toward the body, then swings his arm around to encompass all of them. The mind reader takes a long breath, his chest inflating as if he smells something on the stove.

"That's a lovely thought," Editha says to Morris.

Hagathorn, still silent, bends toward his wife, only a tilt at the waist that brings their heads closer. Maybe it's her that he was inhaling.

"That's what you think the story is about?" Hagathorn says, still facing his wife.

"It could have been," Morris repeats. "Before you got hold of it."

Ada rolls her shoulders, which shifts her light so that it catches the edge of the ceiling. It's stained with bat urine, rust colored, and she could guess at the shape of the stain—two pickaxes, a woman's legs in high heels—like she used to guess at the shapes of clouds.

Her head swims for a moment, and she widens her feet slightly to steady herself.

"I'll leave," the professor says.

No one reacts. Shell-shocked. Then Morris blows out a breath and Quinton throws his arms up with enough force that Ada is afraid he'll jar the wiring in his flashlight.

"What the hell is the matter with you?" he asks.

Ada lays a hand on his wrist, and as soon as she does it, she remembers Editha making this same gesture to her husband and she remembers that she did it to Gerald countless times and she feels certain she's accidentally, publicly declared that she's involved with this man and she's equally certainly that he will shrug off her hand. Her head is boiling again, but no one glances at her hand other than Quinton, who does not seem bothered. He only turns and listens, as Ada hoped he would.

"He said he'll go," she says. "We should go."

"Yeah," Quinton says, and her hand is still on his arm. He takes a slow breath. "Yeah. You're right. Alright, everybody, grab your things."

It's as if someone has rung the school bell and told the class they're dismissed. In one almost coordinated movement, everyone turns to their packs and blankets, pulling on jackets and tying boots. Maybe the rest did them some good, but more likely the rush of panic has gotten their blood flowing. Ada hopes it will keep pumping until they reach the elevator.

Canteen and pack looped over his shoulder, Tom halts by the carcass. He bows his head.

"Rest in peace, Howard Waylander," he says.

It's the first time Ada has heard anyone use the man's name since he died. Tom closes his eyes for no more than a long blink and then shuffles toward the opening of the passage. Editha stops beside the newspaperman as well. She bends over his feet, low enough that it looks as if she might touch the body, but she only lifts the edge of the blanket that's twisted around his legs. Maybe she means to cover him more fully, but the cloth is trapped under the weight of his body, and she lets go with barely a tug.

Ada wonders whether the killer would be more likely to pay homage to the carcass or to ignore it.

"Another thing," Quinton says. "Who's been passing out alcohol?"

Three pairs of eyes turn to Morris, who's tucking in his shirttail on the far side of the room. He does not look up, even as Ada and Quinton shift toward him as well.

"I don't know what you mean," he says into the silence.

He's taking longer than needed to manage the buttons on his jacket. He's a terrible liar, which Ada likes about him. She wishes everyone were a terrible liar.

"As long as there's no more of it," Quinton says.

"There was never any passing it out," Hagathorn says, propping himself against the wall again. "He polished it off entirely by himself."

"Stop it," Morris says, and it feels as if they are continuing some earlier conversation.

"It's the truth," Hagathorn says, stretching out the words as if they are a punch line, but Morris doesn't laugh.

"It's a wonder you're not the one dead," he says.

It's so bitter—so unlike him—that Ada has a moment of thinking she's misheard. Hagathorn only pushes away from the wall, wincing.

"Spoken like someone who would kill a man," he says.

He limps the dozen feet to where his wife is waiting in the main passage, his helmet brushing against the ceiling even though he's bent over. Ada suspects they're all walking slumped by this stage, trained by low ceilings. Hagathorn stops in the twilight space between light and dark, and they are all ready to leave, finally.

Ada pauses, though. The strap of her pack has twisted, and she can't make her fingers work quite right. It's only the two of them left in the chamber when Quinton reaches for her, sliding two fingers between the strap and her shoulder. He gives a twist, and the strap snaps into place.

10:10 p.m.

When they finally crowd into the narrow passage to start the return trip, it's clear that no one wants to step into anything like a single-file line. They don't want to turn their backs to each other, and Ada can't blame them.

Quinton, though, wants her to turn her back on all of them.

"Ada will lead," he announces. "I'll bring up the rear."

"Why?" Tom asks, with more curiosity than belligerence.

People tend to trust him, Quinton. He has a way about him. Ada has an urge to yell out that he can undo a woman's buttons even with his gloves on, and her head is floating like she sampled some of whatever was in that bottle.

They have been down here too long.

"So I can keep my eyes on everyone," Quinton says. "No one drops behind or sneaks away. Or do any of you like that idea—the thought of somebody slipping off, hiding in one of these crevices, free to surprise us somewhere down the line?"

"We already have someone out there, free to surprise us," Hagathorn says.

"If you believe that," Quinton says, "that's even more reason for me to be back here, watching. But that man you distrust so much? He took care of you, despite yourselves. Listen."

He motions down the passageway, and Ada hears a whisper of sound after a moment.

"The waterfall," she says. "He said if we kept going, we'd be back at the waterfall."

Quinton runs a finger under the edge of his boot, and Ada sees a flash of skin. He nods. “It’s closer than I realized,” he says.

“There’s water dripping everywhere,” Editha says. “Has been for hours.”

“This isn’t a drip,” Ada says. “It’s the only waterfall on this entire level. Talmadge was looping you toward home without you even knowing.”

“We could be back to the elevator in a couple of hours,” Quinton says. “I know you’re all nervous, but we just need to get going. No one is going to try anything out here in the open.”

“That’s assuming the killer is logical,” Morris says. “If he’s unhinged, there’s no telling what he might do.”

It’s a reasonable point, Ada thinks, although she does not believe the killer is a maniac. He seems to have managed the murder in a sensible way, which doesn’t address the issue of whether it’s better to have a logical murderer or an illogical one.

She tamps down the question before it escapes into the open air.

“Morris,” she says, “the only way we get out of here is to move forward. We’re going to have to risk it, and you’re a smart man. I don’t think you believe that anyone is going to try to bash in your head in full view of the rest of us.”

She has learned this trick: If you compliment someone, they are more likely to listen to what you say. It works now, and Morris nods, taking a step toward Ada as she shifts to the front of the group. She starts down the passageway, and he falls into step behind her, with Hagathorn, Tom, and Editha coming next, keeping a healthy space between them. It’s only then that Ada spots the other problem:

The professor can't bend his knees. His stiff-legged walk keeps his steps short and his shoulders tick-tocking, and she pulls ahead by at least twenty feet before she realizes he can't keep pace.

She waits, glancing behind her, reading Quinton's thoughts. He's doing the same math that she is: This will slow their progress. If he thought they could make the elevator in two hours, it might be closer to four. Longer, maybe.

They creep along the passageway. When she looks behind her, she can barely make out Quinton—the scope of her beam doesn't reach that far. She sees, though, when Hagathorn manages to duck the lower points of the ceiling by bending low, more flexible than she would have expected.

He's not whining. She'll give him that much.

"I'm not worried about my head getting bashed in," Morris announces, squatting and then rising again. "Whoever killed him must not have a weapon."

Their boots crackle against the gravel. The whisper of water grows louder.

"I see what you mean," Tom says. "He wouldn't have used a stalactite if he had something better."

"There weren't stalactites in that room," Quinton says. "It was snapped off somewhere else. Ahead of time. For what that's worth."

"It's a good thing, is what I'm saying," Morris says. "No one has a pistol or a knife. At worst, they've got another rock."

"They might have no interest in killing someone else," Editha says, and, as always, the sound of her voice is unexpected. "Someone wanted to get rid of Howard, and they did. They achieved their purpose."

Ada reminds herself that one of these people is the killer, pretending to discuss himself.

"It was risky," Morris says. "In a room full of people. When anyone could have woken up."

"Not that risky," Ada says. Her own voice sounds like a shout to her after a full day of whispering. "When the killer blew out the candle, anyone who was awake would have said something. And once it was dark, no one would have seen anything."

"That's the strangest part to me," Tom says. "Like Jeremiah said, how could anyone hit what he was aiming for? How could Talmadge even know he was getting the right person, much less kill him with one try?"

"Don't do that," Quinton says. "Don't act as if we know it was him. We don't know anything."

They've reached a streambed that leads to the waterfall chamber: Ada remembers this stretch from a lifetime ago, when she and Quinton were following instead of leading. Everyone drops to a crawl except for Hagathorn, who eases onto his rear end, turns backward, and scoots on his palms with his legs dragging behind him. He breathes audibly, but he moves more quickly than Ada would expect.

The ground is wetter than it was only an hour ago when they first heard Tom screaming. The mud soaks through the knees of her pants, and she feels sure that there's been a deluge aboveground. They plod along, quiet for a while, focused on not banging their heads. When they stand again, Ada sweeps her light behind her, checking to make sure everyone is keeping up. Editha is nearly to her feet, reaching for the wall to get her balance, and Ada's about to swing the light away when she sees that the fingers on one glove are stained reddish brown, the color of cinnamon.

"Can I see your hands?" Ada asks.

"Why?" Editha asks, even as she offers both hands for inspection, palms down. Ada turns the other woman's hands over, running her own gloved finger over the stains that darken the left glove. It's impossible to tell whether the wetness is from the stains or from groundwater.

"This isn't mud," Ada says, and she's considering how to say the rest when Editha announces it for her.

"You think I have blood on my hands?"

The woman is the most serene human being Ada has ever met. She's smiling slightly now, as if she's some creature playing the part of a human being, reading each line of her dialogue convincingly.

No, she is not serene, exactly. She is indecipherable. Ada would like to master the skill.

"Do you have blood on your hands?" she asks.

Editha smiles wider, all lips and no teeth. "I do."

Ada can feel the men watching as Editha takes the tip of one glove in her teeth. Her black brows draw down like an ink spill.

"It's from climbing yesterday," the mind reader's wife says, after she's tugged off the glove. "No. Today. Was it only today? I took off my gloves to get a better grip, and I sheared the skin off my fingers. They bled through."

Her fingers, true enough, are scraped and scabbed. It's the kind of injury a child would get from falling on concrete, and Ada can well imagine that grabbing at rocks would do it.

"We should stop at the pool," Ada says. "Wash them off."

"You could stand to do the same," Editha says.

She's looking at Ada's hands, and while the gloves are covering the scratches on her palms, her sleeve has rucked up to show a swathe of dried blood on her wrist that she missed when she rinsed her scratches.

"Maybe we all have blood on our hands," Editha says.

Is that meant to be funny? Ada has no idea how to take the woman. She's been curious about her, watching from a distance. Over the long hours, she's thought—she's had so much time to think—that if they ever wound up next to each other in these caverns, being the only two women would either bind them or put them at odds.

She suspects she was wrong. She doesn't think they feel anything at all about each other.

After another bend, the water is as loud as rain falling outside her kitchen window. They step into the familiar waterfall chamber, so much bigger than any other space down here, with its cathedral spires rising around them. The falls are flowing heavier than they were earlier, and the headlamps cast the room in swathes of light and dark, ripples and stones.

She and Quinton rushed past this place last time, not wanting to fall too far behind the group, but now she notices how a section of the ceiling is rimmed with drapery like the trim on a Victorian porch. She catches a sparkle of what might be gypsum along the far wall. She tracks the cascade of the falls from top to bottom, and while it's not puny, it's no Ruby Falls. It's less than a foot across, and the rock behind it is the color of mud.

She can make out a mosaic of pebbles in the water, and the shine of the stones reminds her of Quinton's mouth on her throat. She makes a point of not looking at him.

Hagathorn staggers into the pool, soaking his boots.

"Jeremiah—" Tom says.

Ada wonders how much of his life the man spends just saying his client's name in that worn-out tone. She does not feel worn-out by Hagathorn. She's furious at him, at his obstinance, at the way he complicates everything, at the way he is even now bending down and cupping both hands in the water, ready to drink. Quinton snaps his name, too, and Ada envisions herself planting one foot on Hagathorn's back and toppling him forward, and maybe she would do it, except he doesn't drink the water. He only splashes it over his face, and then he does it again.

"Good God, that's nice," he says.

When he dips his hands again, he tilts slightly and comes down hard on one injured knee. The sound of his pain is both genuine and stifled. Again he does not complain.

"Editha," Ada says, "your hands?"

The other woman has been watching her husband, but now she drops to the balls of her feet. She shifts to the side, frog-like, gesturing for Ada to join her at the water's edge, and Ada has a flicker—foolish—of a schoolgirl's delight at having a spot saved for her at lunch. She settles into the space Editha has made for her, pulling off her gloves, because it can't hurt to clean her wounds again. She twists her hands through the water, cold and numbing and blissful. Their splashing sounds like the wringing of a washcloth in the bathtub, and Ada pictures the curved edges of her old wooden tub and also the cool surface of her feather pillow. She's not sure what she will do first when she gets home—sleep or bathe. No, neither. She will drink an enormous glass of water, and then she will brew a scalding-hot cup of coffee.

Next to her, Editha is staring at nothing, but Ada knows no one stares at nothing. She would like to know what this woman sees inside her head, whether she's remembering climbing this wall in front of them or picnicking with the newspaperman on some long-ago afternoon or, possibly, feeling her husband push to his feet in the quiet dark of the cave when everyone else was asleep. She might only be imagining her own cup of coffee and comfortable pillow. Her porcelain face gives away nothing.

"How did you learn to climb like that?" Ada asks.

Editha glances up at the rock spires. "I had some training as a child," she says. "Honestly, it wasn't anything to brag about. The wall's closer to eighty degrees than ninety."

Ada is not sure how arithmetic is an answer to her question. It's certainly not an answer that invites conversation. She shakes off her hands and stands, taking stock of the others. Tom has stayed on dry land, his arms wrapped around his knees. Hagathorn, wet-faced, is picking his way over the rocks toward his manager. Morris is running his bare hands through the falls. Quinton is across the chamber, bent over his multiple packs. He's got a carbide cartridge in one hand and a canteen in the other.

He doesn't turn when she approaches, but his hands stop moving.

"You think the wife was lying about the blood on her hands?" he asks, softly enough that no one else can hear.

"No," Ada answers before thinking, and she's not sure if that makes her answer more or less trustworthy.

"Maybe Howard tried to renew their acquaintance and she wasn't interested," he says, zipping up a pack. "Maybe he threatened to tell her husband. Everyone keeps calling the killer 'he,' and that might be very convenient for her. You've seen the strength in her arms."

"The fact that she's strong isn't a mark against her," Ada says.

"It could be that the magic man found out about her and Howard."

"You think Hagathorn killed him in a jealous rage?" she says.

She says it as if it's ridiculous, but hasn't she been thinking the same thing? When Editha told—threatened?—Howard that her husband had broken someone's wrist, all sorts of badness was underneath that one detail.

"Not necessarily a rage," Quinton says, putting one hand to the ground and then sitting heavily. "More measured. He'd have a double reason, wouldn't he? Professional and personal."

His mind is clearly following the same track as hers. He's hoping the killer is one of the visitors.

"You seem determined to blame it on the woman," she says. "Even when you're saying someone else did it, you're still blaming it on her."

"Men get stupid about women."

"Men get stupid for all sorts of reasons," she says.

He tugs off his gloves, then yanks off first one boot and then the other. Even in the bad light, she can tell his socks are soaking wet.

"Whoever broke off that stalactite was patient," she says. "They waited for the right time. And when no one was looking and Howard was asleep, they did it fast. It makes me think of what you said about killing pigs."

He's pulling a new pair of socks on, and she looks away from his pale feet. She does not believe in studying a man's feet too closely.

"Don't think I follow you," he says.

"Do you think it could be a kindness?" she says. "To do it quickly? Maybe someone didn't want him to suffer."

"They don't kill pigs fast because it's humane," he says. "They do it because stress makes the meat tougher. It serves a purpose, like it did here. The death was quiet enough that no one woke up. If you used a pistol, that wouldn't be the case."

Her headlamp sputters and spits, warning her. She has time to step into the circle of Quinton's light before hers dies completely. The world shrinks down to a diameter of two feet. She taps her helmet when Quinton's slower than usual to reach into his bag for a replacement.

"Depending on where we are in a couple of hours, we'll want to start thinking about whether we all need a working lamp," he says.

He says it matter-of-factly, and she doesn't absorb the message at first: He wants to ration the light.

They are not prepared for this. She's known it, but she feels the actual weight of the accumulating hours now, looking down at the near-empty packs on the ground. They gave themselves leeway when they planned this expedition—a few extra cartridges of light, spare water—but they didn't need much because in case of an emergency, one of them would go for help and bring back whatever supplies were required. They never envisioned a scenario where the two of them were leashed to this group.

"What do we have left?" she asks.

"Aside from what's on our heads, we've got eight more cartridges," he says. "Flashlights, too. More than enough if we're out in four hours. But if someone falls and breaks a leg? If the magic man stays this gimpy? We could be in trouble."

"I could go alone," she says. "It would still work. I'll go tell Leo and come back with help. Hagathorn might not even dig in his heels at this stage."

"I wouldn't put another tantrum past him," Quinton says, "but it's not just him. I do think it's better to stay together."

She is back to reading his mind, and he means "safer" when he says "better." He hands her a carbide cartridge, and his fingers hold hers longer than required before he's bending to lace up his boots.

"I don't know how your feet don't get cold," he says. "Mine turn to ice."

He stands slowly, barely an inch between them. The others will notice. She can make out the loose skin over his eyelids and a small mole at his temple. She doesn't mind but wonders what he might be noticing about her own face. The waterfall itself has evaporated into the darkness, leaving only sound behind.

He stretches one arm over his head, making the light shimmer around them.

"Everybody get your helmets and boots and gloves on," he calls out, "and be ready to move on directly."

Ada makes herself ease back from him, even though she doesn't want distance. Only a few feet away from his light, she can barely see her next step. It's a different feeling when you can't control your own view, when someone else is deciding what you will see.

She tightens her grip around the new cartridge. Her last cartridge. She's got her helmet in her hand, unhooking the headlamp, when she registers a further darkening around them, an increase of shadow.

"Damn it," one of the men hisses as Editha says her husband's name like it's a question.

"I'm out, Quinton," Morris calls.

"Coming," Quinton says. "I expect everyone will be out soon enough. We can talk about that as we get moving."

Ada pulls her flashlight from her pack as Quinton cuts a swathe through the dark. She folds her legs under her, propping the flashlight on the ground so she can see to light the carbide. Her wet legs are dropping her temperature, and it's the first time she's felt cold down here. She rubs her bare hands together.

Her flashlight shines past her to sand and stone, catching pebbles and shards and one rock bigger than her fist. She sets down her helmet and spins the flashlight in the opposite direction. Her arms are barely visible, even to her, as she reaches for the solid hunk of rock and drops it into her bag.

She goes back to warming her hands. She needs them steady before she lights the match. It's not likely that she'd burn herself, but it pays to be cautious.

September 19, 1932

12:40 a.m.

By the time an hour passes, everyone needs a replacement cartridge. By the time a second hour passes, they've finished off the water. They stop not only for carbide and water but to change Hagathorn's soaked bandages and to let Morris catch his breath after a coughing fit. Ada doles out the remaining dried apples and pecans and fatback, which only make for a couple of mouthfuls apiece, but she hopes it will add a burst of energy.

Now, as they stare at the next section of passageway, Ada doesn't have any faith that the food helped. Whatever jolt these people got from discovering a dead man, it's gone. They are noticeably slower, and they don't always hear instructions the first time.

"If you do feel yourself start to fall," Quinton is saying, "make yourself as big as possible."

His latest estimate is that they still have another two hours until they get to the elevator, although that depends on a thousand things, including how long it takes them to get across this fissure. The two-foot-wide gulch barely made an impression on Ada when she and Quinton crossed it on their way down here. It requires a body bridge, feet on one side of the gulch, hands braced against the wall of the other side. They'll make their way across by sidestepping with hands and feet, bent at the waist, and it's easy enough, really, unless you have a fear of heights, which Ada doesn't. She's glad for the task: It will take her mind off cold and thirst and blood and stalactites.

"You make yourself big by stretching your arms and legs out, like a starfish," Quinton says. "That's the way you stop yourself, okay? Grab onto something, and we'll grab onto you. But you won't fall. Just one foot after another and you'll be fine. You've done it before."

He steps onto the ledge, arms at his side, straddling the gulch. His body is an upside-down *Y* until he slaps an arm against the rock and swings himself around in one smooth arc, stretching across the gap easily, and Ada loves his competence. He shines his light back toward the rest of them.

"We all had headlamps the first time," Hagathorn says, hefting himself onto the ledge slowly. It takes him four tries to get his foot planted.

He's the only one without a light. His last cartridge was a dud, spluttering out too early, and Quinton refused to replace it. They don't all need lamps, he said, not when they have only two full cartridges left. Hagathorn took the news better than Ada expected, shrugging and crowding close enough to Editha that he could share her light.

"Better light only gives you a better view of the bottom," Quinton says.

The truth is that only an idiot looks at the bottom, lamp or no lamp. The drop to the cavern below is twenty feet or so, unlikely to kill anyone, but when you've got your feet on a shelf a few inches wide, that cavern looks like a bottomless pit. No, you don't want to look down. The real purpose of a headlamp is to help you make sure you place your foot on rock instead of air.

Ada doesn't point this out.

"We'll be through it in five minutes," she says. "A hundred steps. Done before you know it."

"I'll stay close, Miah," Editha says, climbing up behind him in one long lunge. "Just keep your feet in my light."

Once they've all got their footing, Quinton leads the way, and Ada brings up the back. The gulch curves so that the front of the line can't always see the back of it, and dark spaces are inevitable. They're moving well, though, slowly but surely. She and Quinton bolted through here yesterday—yesterday?—feet flashing like they were dancing a reel, and she has a pang of missing those two-person races that sprang up between their bouts of waiting. But this pace has its advantages. It's less likely anyone will make a mistake.

"I have to admit," the mind reader wheezes, "I thought he'd have come after us by now."

"Talmadge isn't coming after us," Quinton says.

"You have no reason to be so sure."

"He is not some monster," Quinton says, still even-voiced. "He's a normal man, more reliable than most. Has a spaniel at home. Likes cornbread in milk."

"You think because he has a dog and eats food, he can't have killed someone?" Hagathorn slows at a narrowing of the ledge. "I'm just saying what I expected. There's nothing to stop him. We could be dead before we even see him."

"You need to stop talking, Mr. Hagathorn," Quinton says. "Pay attention to your feet."

The mind reader obeys. Maybe blood loss has weakened him. If so, Ada wishes he had scraped himself up a bit more. The gap between the walls widens slightly, which the taller men have no issue with. She needs to lengthen her reach, though, so she bends lower, walking her hands down. The wall is cold even through her gloves.

She doesn't see it happen, but there's a bleat of sound and a spray of rocks on the ground below, and then Tom is splayed at their feet. He's stretched between the two walls with one leg dangling in the chasm. Morris, directly in front of Ada, partially blocks her view, but she can see the manager's hands clinging to the far ledge.

Editha and Hagathorn both call his name, or something like it. Everyone is talking at once, indecipherable.

"You're okay," Quinton says, loudly and clearly. "One second. We got you."

They do not have him. The fallen man is between Editha and Morris, and both of them reach for him, but there's no room to maneuver. Morris grabs onto Tom's trouser leg, but he doesn't have the leverage to do more; if Tom goes into the gulch, Ada suspects Morris will go with him.

Quinton squeezes past Hagathorn and Editha, hardly pausing.

"Let go, Morris," Quinton says. "Stand up and get yourself flat against the wall if you can."

As he talks, Quinton steps across the gulch, wedging one foot onto the lip of rock. With one leg straight and one bent, he's suspended above the canyon below. Morris lurches to his feet, arms flailing so that he nearly smacks Ada in the face. She drapes an arm across his chest, pushing him to the wall.

Once Morris is secure, she tries to focus the beam from her headlamp on Tom as Quinton reaches for him. The manager's arms are trembling, and the noise he lets out trembles, too. Quinton's bent leg slips down the rock—a sickening scraping sound—but he reanchors his foot quickly. He's steady as he reaches down. Ada can't see Tom's face, but his fingers have turned into claws.

"Can you grab onto me?" Quinton asks the manager, and Ada admires how he doesn't sound the least bit worried.

"No," Tom says, the word huffed out.

"That's okay," Quinton says. "I'm gonna lift you. I can't take your deadweight for long, though, so you're going to need to get your feet set, you hear me? Get them under you as soon as you can. Easy. No problem."

Ada's aware of a shuffling and shifting, but she can only see Tom and Quinton. Quinton gets a hand under the other man's armpits, and when he lifts him, the two of them are precarious as propped playing cards for a moment. Tom's feet bicycle, but his feet find the ledge, and then Quinton's easing him backward against the wall and everyone is on solid ground again, even if it's only a few inches wide.

The man was hanging in midair for at least a minute. Or possibly an hour.

"Thank God," Hagathorn says. "Tom. Thank God."

"You hurt?" Quinton asks. He's not breathing hard, and it occurs to Ada that maybe the two men were never all that precarious. Maybe the whole thing was more terrifying because she could only watch.

"Not much," Tom says, chin tucked against his chest. He's gulping in all the air that Quinton isn't. "Banged my forehead."

He unfastens his helmet, pulls it loose, and raises his head toward them all. Again everyone is making noise, indecipherable. Ada peers around Morris and gets a full view of Tom's face covered in blood, a thick spill of it from his brow to his chin, dripping onto his jacket. He's managed to slice his eyebrow underneath the edge of his helmet.

"I honestly don't think it's that bad," he says, untucking his shirt and swiping at his eyes.

"How can you see?" asks Editha.

"He can't," Quinton says.

"I'm fine," Tom says. The blood is curtained on his eyelashes. "It's not too bad."

It's a long conversation to be having over a twenty-foot drop. Ada adjusts her foot, and her ankle turns just enough to throw off her balance. Her shoulder bangs against the rock before she rights herself.

"You're not going to bleed to death, no," Quinton says. "But you can't move through here blinded, and we've used up all the bandages on your boss here."

Tom is still blotting the cut with his shirttail, but every time he lifts the cloth, blood seeps out. Ada's not sure whether the injuries on this excursion are some version of a plague—locusts and frogs and firstborn sons—or whether they're a natural result of bodies that have pushed past their limits. She's not sure which is worse. She doesn't know whether they're more likely to escape God or exhaustion.

"We can rip off part of a shirt," Morris says, shifting so he blocks Ada yet again. "Tie it on."

"Our shirts are filthy," Quinton says, "and they'd wind up more blindfold than bandage. Hold on."

Feet still spanning the gulch, he slings his pack onto the crease of his elbow, digs around, and comes out with a candle. He slides a matchbook from his pocket and seems to pull out a match and strike it in the same smooth movement.

"Lean in," he says to Tom. They are already less than a foot apart. "Tilt back your head. Ada?"

She understands immediately what he wants. She lays a hand on Morris's shoulder as she sidesteps to the far ledge, using him for leverage. She's past him in a moment, and then she's next to Tom and Quinton. She crooks her head, aiming her light on the wound and wondering about the purpose of the candle. Tom has pressed his bare hand to his forehead, and blood's still oozing through his fingers.

"Close your eyes," Quinton says. "And take away your hand."

Tom does as he's told, and Ada wonders if anyone would follow orders so quickly if she gave them.

"This will sting," Quinton says, lifting the candle. "But keep your head still, alright?"

He moves quickly enough that no one gets the chance to ask what he's doing, or maybe they are so baffled that they can't make words come. No one speaks before the first drops of wax fall on Tom's bloody skin, and he hisses in pain.

"What the hell is this?" Hagathorn asks.

"It'll seal the cut," Quinton says, his thumb and forefinger pressing at the wound, holding it closed.

"It's burning him," Editha says, her hand landing on Tom's arm.

"He's shaking, Quint," Morris says. "Look at him."

He is, but Ada suspects that's from leftover panic and dropping body temperature. Tom's pants and jacket look as soaked as hers do.

"This is nothing but snake oil," Hagathorn says, righteous and angry and loud.

"You're one to talk," Morris says.

Noise, Ada thinks. They are full of noise. She spent hours wishing she could hear these people's conversations, and now she only wants to shut them up. Through their jabbering, Quinton keeps working, fingers pressing and pushing.

"It's going to run into your eyes if you don't look up," she says to Tom.

He tilts his head, and Quinton nods, still wielding the candle. "Good," he says. "That's good. It's starting to harden."

He's entirely covered the cut in wax, a pale blob stretching the length of Tom's eyebrow. Leaning closer, Ada pulls off her gloves and slides a hand around the back of the manager's head. She blows on his skin the same way her mother used to do when the iodine blazed like fire on Ada's scraped-up knees. The air whistles slightly between her lips, and a spray of liquid wax speckles her hand.

The others are talking, but she's blocked them entirely. She breathes in through her nose and out through her mouth, and it takes seven breaths before the wax turns solid. It's soft as a blister when she presses it.

She lifts Tom's head with both hands. "All done," she says.

He taps at the wax. "Bleeding stopped?"

"Looks like," she says.

"Sorry," Tom says. "Sorry for—all of this."

He lifts his shirt again, scrubbing at his chin and cheeks as the others push close. He only smears the blood and dirt.

"You don't think it'll peel right off?" asks Morris.

"It might hurt like hell when he does peel it off," Quinton says, "but it won't come off by accident."

They're still perched on the narrow ledge with broken bones only one careless step away.

"Glasses are gone," Tom says, still blotting at his face.

That quiets them all. Ada can't believe she didn't notice earlier. She only saw the blood, but now it's obvious that the man's face looks naked without the frames propped on his nose.

"How badly do you need them?" Quinton asks.

"I'm alright," Tom says.

Ada has no idea whether to believe him. Quinton scans the ground below them with his light, and she peers down as well—she suspects her vision might be better than his—but the first thing she sees is that Tom's boots are spattered with blood. Hers have a few drops as well. Far below them, the ground is shiny with mud. There's not a glint of glass anywhere, and even if they do spot the glasses, it doesn't matter much unless someone grows a pair of wings.

"I've already slowed us down plenty, haven't I?" Tom says, tucking his hands into his armpits, likely to cover up his shakes.

"We're going to hope that you really are alright," Quinton says. "Because we've got to get off this ledge, glasses or no."

Tom nods, eyes down, and Ada assumes he's mourning his glasses until she sees that he's looking at her ungloved hand.

"That ring," he says.

For a moment, it doesn't occur to her that he's talking about jewelry—she thinks of a smoke ring—a pineapple ring—her father liked to slide pineapple rings onto his finger one at a time and nibble them into nothing—and her mind has slipped gears again. No pineapple. Tom is talking about her wedding ring. It's the only piece of jewelry she wears. Her fingers have swollen over the years, and at some stage she realized that she couldn't slip it off when it came time to wash the dishes, so now it's hardly jewelry at all—it's a part of her finger, another knuckle or nail. She twists her hand in the light, aware of Quinton looking on, and did he notice her ring when she had her hands on his body? She didn't.

She considers the glint of gold. The thin band—and most of her finger—is shellacked in wax.

"It'll come off," she says to Tom.

He catches her off guard by taking her hand, holding the tips of her fingers lightly. She half expects him to kiss them like some fancy gentleman.

"I'm sorry," he says. "We ruined a table that way once, my wife and I. Rachel thought she blew out the candles, and I thought she blew them out, too, but they burned all night and overflowed. Never did come off the wood."

Ada pulls her hand away. She wonders how badly he hit his head.

"I'm not worried about my ring," she says. "It'll be fine. And if it's not, that's okay, too."

In front of her, Hagathorn stiffly body-bridges across the chasm with Editha in front of him, mostly obscured by his bulk. Her light shines across his feet.

"We moving?" he calls.

For someone who didn't want to leave the caves, he's been eager to make good time. Quinton nods.

"Editha, looks like you're good leading?" he asks.

"I'm comfortable," she answers.

"You'll go straight another minute or two and then you'll hit a slope where you can hop down," Quinton says. "Give a shout if you feel uncertain. I'm going to stay back here next to Tom, just in case."

"Sorry," Tom says again.

Ada pats his shoulder and reaches for her gloves. The others get situated—feet shifting, arms reaching, palms pressing against rock—and Quinton slips between her and Tom, his light shining over lips and ledges.

"You should lead, Tom," Hagathorn calls back. "You don't need the headlamp. We can stick a wick on your forehead and light you up."

Although Ada can't see Tom's face, she hears him chuckle. Hagathorn is, occasionally, amusing. He hasn't slowed them down for psychic demonstrations and he hasn't complained. He glances back, checking on Tom once more before he starts forward.

She wishes he would be one thing and stick with it.

She struggles to get her second glove on, her fingers numb. She would swear that every one of these people is concerned about Tom, and it's disorienting, like standing up too fast, to remember that they are not a group of friends or even a band of strangers. The fact that they grabbed hold of a falling man does not mean they are bonded together by anything. Someone has slaughtered another human being, and unless it was Talmadge—it was probably not Talmadge?—it was someone who just now laid their hands kindly on Tom.

"How did you know about the wax?" she asks Quinton as they start forward.

He twists his head toward her.

"I didn't, not entirely," he says. "I've never done it on a person. I learned it back when I used to work on beer barrels. You could seal the staves that way."

Ada catches herself thinking of pineapple again—her father sliding a slice onto her finger—and she orders herself to think only of where her hands and feet are landing. She tells herself to think only of reaching the elevator or—better—to think only of the murderer. Shouldn't that single fact be filling her mind entirely—that someone down here might kill again? Shouldn't she be alert, every second? And yet her mind is spinning off to pineapple. After Gerald died, she got used to sorting the valid thoughts from the crazy ones—no, don't set the extra place at the table and talk to someone who isn't there like some too-old child with a tea party—yes, give away his shirts because you do not need to try them on, one after the other—and that is a significant part of life, the sorting and labeling of craziness, and surely everyone—

She looks down, watching her boots move. She sorts and labels. They have all been down here too long.

"Beer barrels," she repeats, when she finally absorbs Quinton's words. She's not sure she's ever seen a beer barrel. She has no idea what a stave is.

"I worked in a bar," Quinton says. "In Cincinnati."

"You from Cincinnati?" Tom calls over his shoulder. "I got married there."

"I was only there a couple of years," Quinton answers, then his voice lowers in a way that tells Ada he's speaking to her alone. "The fellow who owned the bar was good to me. He took me in and fed me, let me spend a few nights sleeping behind the bar when I needed a place."

The gulch has narrowed enough that Ada can drop her arms and walk with a leg on each side. They are nearing the end. She lifts a hip with each step, like those cowboys swaggering around in *The Virginian.*

"I was trying to send money home and help out," he says. "Did I tell you I was the oldest?"

"No."

He's whispering now, like they talked when they were their own sufficient group instead of part of this one.

"It didn't go like I'd hoped, but I was too stubborn to come back," he says. "Then I met the bar owner. Emory Webster. When I told him I didn't know how to do a thing, he'd teach me. And I didn't know how to do anything."

"You must have learned quick."

Ahead of them, Morris jumps clear of the gulch, a little awkward, landing with both feet on a flat expanse.

"He died," Quinton says. "After he lost the bar. A flimflam man came to town and stole it out from under him. He shot himself in the end."

She can't answer because Quinton has leapt to lower ground, slipping in front of Tom to offer a hand. Tom does not take it, managing the step down easily enough. Morris and Editha both offer an arm to the mind reader, who's been stuck on the ledge even as the others climb down. He puts his hands on their shoulders and lowers himself, heel-toe, heel-toe, straight-legged. It takes him ages. Herding a passel of grandmothers through this cave would be faster, Ada thinks.

When she jumps to lower ground, Tom glances at her hand, and she knows he's thinking about her ring again. She's still not sure whether that's a sign of kindness or delirium or both. Quinton is shining his light around the new chamber, but she aims her beam into the gulch they've just crossed. The gap to the bottom level has shallowed. The drop must be less than ten feet.

"I'm going to look for the glasses," she says.

Quinton follows her gaze. "There's no way."

"I can slip through there," she says to him, pointing. "You couldn't fit, but I can. It's a doable drop, and do you really want him to do the rest of this when he's half blind? It's worth five minutes."

"You don't need to do that," Tom says.

The wax on his forehead seems to be working beautifully, and she feels a rush of fondness for him, illogical. Sometimes the threads between people take time to form, and sometimes they pop up as quickly as spiderwebs across a doorway. She likes Tom. She can barely remember the sense of distance she felt hours ago, when the strangers in the other chamber were across an ocean.

"They're likely broken anyway," Quinton says.

"It's not worth you hurting yourself," Morris chimes in.

She leaves them there, still talking at her. She's not sure whether she's being driven by kindness or delirium or both, but it's like shrugging off her backpack—a dozen backpacks—losing the weight of the whole unwieldy group. She sidesteps a dozen feet in that many seconds, and after the miles of slowness her speed feels euphoric, like one of those dreams where running turns into flying.

She's back to the pure navigation of footholds and low crawls. She drops to her knees and rolls over so that her belly is against the ledge, stretching her feet to the opposite wall. Once she has a decent grip, she lowers one leg at a time into the crevice, walking herself down until she can't anymore, and then she's dangling, having to trust that she's judged the distance correctly. And, yes, she feels a rush of terror as she falls, but she was right: It's not much of a drop. She stays on her feet, although the impact snaps her jaws together.

Her boots stick to the mud with every step. Her thighs and belly have gotten as soaked as her knees, and she's getting colder by the second. Water seeps all over the chamber, as if a dozen leaky faucets are going at once, drip by drab. The gray ground and walls are shiny as modeling clay, and the stalactites on the ceiling are young, more like anthills than spears.

Beads of water shine like sequins when she swings her light overhead. Her sleeves are damp, she realizes. Her pants are soaked from ankles to hips.

"Everything fine?" Quinton calls, and it's amazing how close his voice sounds. As if he's only a few stairs above her on a staircase.

"Looking around," she says.

"I can manage," Tom says again, too loud. "There's really no need."

She studies the ceiling, trying to judge the point where he lost his footing. She keeps her light on the ground, thinking that the glasses might have buried themselves in the mud.

A steady drip of water has created a formation like a giant mushroom cap, slick and glistening. It's bigger than her head, and it looks as if a potter might have shaped it on a wheel.

"Anything?" Quinton calls again.

Without realizing it, she's come to a stop. She turns from the limestone mushroom, refocusing.

"Another minute!" she answers.

They need to get moving—she knows it. She's bracing herself to turn around and head back when she sees the shine of glass in the mud, reflecting her light back at her. She's got the glasses in her hand before she fully absorbs that she's found them.

It's a miracle.

She's embarrassed about the thought as soon as it's fully formed. She pictures Howard on the ground, handkerchief over his face, rock buried in his throat, and does she truly believe that the universe—God—will save a pair of glasses and not a man?

Was he wearing a wedding ring? Did anyone check? And his notepad—didn't he have a notepad? They shouldn't have left it behind. They should have checked his pockets and they should have said a real prayer over him, and how is it possible that they don't know if he has children?

"Got them," she calls, not too loudly because of the way sound carries. "They're in one piece. Dirty and a bent rim, is all."

The others murmur above her as she turns the glasses in her hands, but she doesn't try to decipher the words. *You can't listen to everyone all the time,* her friend Nellie said as she climbed the highest branches of the plum tree, so narrow that they bent like fishing poles under her feet, Nellie's mother screaming bloody murder from the kitchen window. Nellie would have loved these caves—she was fearless—but she got married and moved to Louisville and for a while she was ink on paper and then she was gone.

The glasses are covered in mud—everyone and everything is covered in mud—and Ada heads back to her impressive mushroom with its steady drip to rinse them off. She glances up, planning her climb, and at least it's easy to see her exit point. The glow from the headlamps is incandescent compared to the pitch-black around it. She can pinpoint exactly where the group is standing.

She's holding the glasses under the dripping water, feeling the faint spray on her cheeks, when she puts the pieces together.

1:15 a.m.

It's harder to get up than it was to get down: She should have learned that by now. But Ada boosts herself high enough to latch onto Quinton's hands, and he hefts her the final inches until she can scrabble over the edge. It is not graceful, but she's only interested in speed.

"Editha," she calls before she fully gets her legs under her.

The other woman is sitting against a wall, her elbow resting on her knee. She watches Ada come toward her, alert but closemouthed.

Ada stops when Tom steps in front of her, smiling and holding out his hand. His glasses. She forgot. She pulls them from her pocket and sets them in his palm. He's saying thank you, but she doesn't look away from Editha.

"Last night—" Ada pauses, doing the impossible math of the time down here. It does not feel right that she woke in her own bed yesterday morning. "After your husband fell down and busted his knees, you all stopped to rest. You were in the lower level of a chamber that looked a little like this one, and Quinton and I were camped out on the level above you."

"Yes?" Editha says.

"You know we were there," Ada says. "You knew exactly where I was."

She's close enough that their boots are nearly touching, and Editha has to tilt her head back. Her dark eyes are bloodshot, which could be exhaustion or dust or proof that she's feeling more emotion than she shows. Hagathorn, who's likely standing because it's too difficult for him to sit down, sidles closer to his wife, and Ada's glad because she'd like to keep an eye on him, too.

"I can't see why you'd think that," Editha says.

It's a less vehement denial than Ada expected. "You were right below me in the cavern," she says, "talking to Howard."

She's watching Jeremiah Hagathorn's face as she says it. If he's surprised, he hides it well. He looks, if anything, impatient.

"I couldn't see the two of you down there," Ada adds. "But I could see your headlamps, and I don't know why it didn't occur to me, but you must have seen mine, too. A pitch-black ceiling above you, and I'm up there with a light? You must have seen it."

She has everyone's attention now. Morris and Tom edge closer as Editha rubs her eye with one gloved knuckle.

"I knew you were there," she acknowledges, dropping her hand to her lap.

"But you pretended you didn't," Ada says.

"I'd known someone was behind us ever since we were at the lower falls," Editha says. "I saw you and Quinton when I was up on that wall, only obviously I didn't know it was you. I could only tell that there were two people—two lamps. So I'd been watching for you. Howard seemed oblivious."

Now Hagathorn does look surprised. "You were behind us at the waterfall? You were following us, what, from the beginning?"

Surely it doesn't matter now, Ada thinks. The entire venture has been thoroughly derailed.

"We were here in case of an emergency," she says.

"Well, I didn't know who was following us," Editha says, rubbing at her eye again. "Look, in Toledo, someone let mice loose inside the car Jeremiah was driving blindfolded, thinking it'd be interesting to see if they rattled him. He could have been killed. In an auditorium where he was performing his victim-and-murderer act, a man pulled out a real gun. He dared Miah to tell him whether there were any bullets in—"

"There were," Hagathorn says.

"And he threatened to pull the trigger if Miah guessed wrong."

"I doubt he would've," her husband interrupts again.

"What about the man who held a knife to your throat, trying to test whether you could see through your blindfold?" Editha cranes her head toward Tom, who's standing at Ada's shoulder. "There's no telling what would have happened if you hadn't grabbed him. You needed stitches."

"Just three," Tom says.

"You think you're the first ones who've doubted him?" Editha says, meeting Ada's eyes again. "Slander has always been part of it. Dirty tricks, too. I thought someone might be trying to sabotage us. It seemed possible the whole arrangement was a setup and you Ruby Falls people might move the hatpin around."

Quinton, standing next to the mind reader, takes an audible breath. "Mr. Hagathorn, you knew about her and the newspaperman?" he asks.

Hagathorn shifts his feet, wincing. "I did. After dinner that first night in the hotel, she told me she knew him."

"That's all she told you?" Ada asks. "She didn't say how she knew him?"

"She didn't need to tell me," Hagathorn says. "It didn't matter. I'm not foolish enough to think she never knew a man before she knew me."

"You did not care," Quinton says, "that the man covering you for the *Chicago Times* was someone who'd canoodled with your wife?"

"He and I did not canoodle," Editha says.

"It seemed likely that if he was still fond of her, it might be an advantage," Hagathorn says at the same time, and Ada remembers Editha saying something similar. "But, no, I didn't care. I knew the night I met her that this woman was my match and I was hers."

"You knew I could handle your ego, you mean," Editha says.

She leans her head lightly against his thigh, and there's clear affection in her voice. Ada doesn't care for seeing the romantic side of these two—she thinks of her favorite line from Yeats—*It's certain that fine women eat / A crazy salad with their meat.* It's odd that Editha told her husband about Howard yet didn't tell him that the group was being followed. Surely she had time to whisper it if she'd chosen.

It is a forgivable gap in her story, but there is a bigger one.

"You knew someone was eavesdropping on you," Ada says, "and you decided your smartest choice was to share a big secret?"

"It wasn't a secret," Editha says. "Not really. And it's not as if I planned it all out, but I had the chance to kill two birds. I needed to make Howard understand that he was wrong about Miah. When I saw the light overhead, I realized I had an audience with whoever was following us. Honestly, I wanted anyone and everyone to know that Howard was not unbiased. It seemed like that might be helpful if this excursion didn't turn out the way we hoped."

Ada has never heard the woman string together so many sentences at once.

"You thought you could discredit his account of things," Quinton says. "And witnesses might be helpful."

Editha gives the slightest tip of her head.

"And you knew she was walking off with another man?" Morris asks, jerking his head toward the professor.

"She's allowed to walk where she wants," Hagathorn says.

Editha straightens her legs, crossing them at the ankles. Her riding pants are tight around her slim calves.

"You had a lot of gears turning," Ada says to her.

"No good ever came from sitting around and waiting," Editha answers.

It's believable, her explanation, although it's convenient for her that Howard isn't here to dispute it. The two of them could have rehearsed and performed the conversation, masking some alternate purpose, but Ada can't think of what that would be. In terms of the murder, the chat with Howard made Editha more of a suspect than if she'd stayed silent.

Although it made someone else more suspicious as well, didn't it? Editha painted a picture of her husband as a man who could do violent things, and that threat of violence has been there every time Ada has looked at him, even though she's seen no evidence of it. Editha planted that seed, and maybe it was intentional or maybe it wasn't.

She's still propped against her husband, and whatever's between them, it looks very much like love. Ada takes the measure of people every day, like everyone else in the world, she assumes. She has the impression that the clerk at Garmany's hates his manager and she's almost sure that Mrs. Delano at church is going senile and she would still bet money that Gerald wished he'd kept the family farm. Years ago, she noticed how Ruby hiccupped when she laughed too hard and ate green beans with her fingers and knocked down a wasp nest with a broom, unhurried, and Ada knew they would be friends. She's watched Leo wash his own coffee cup in the sink and she's seen him come home at the end of the day and erase the exhaustion from his face before he throws Eugenia into the air, and she knows he's a good man.

She will pick a human being over a crossword any day. A person is fascinating to solve, and you can never finish one. There is always more, whether they're looking you in the face from across the table or whether they've been dead for twenty years. So here she is, taking measures even as her tongue is starting to feel too big for her mouth.

The shadows pulse, and Ada knows what to expect before she turns. A headlamp has flickered out. It's Morris.

"Maybe it's time to dole out the last two cartridges," Quinton says softly. "Mr. Hagathorn, we'll get you set up again, too."

Above them, the rock flows down in layers, like the strands of a hundred mops stretched across the ceiling. The mop strands glint in the light, either from mica or from water drops.

"And what about after those cartridges burn out?" Morris asks.

In the silence, Ada hears the *drip-drip* of the cavern below them.

"We've got a flashlight for each of us," Quinton says, "and candles, if we're desperate."

"How much longer is it going to take for us to get out of here?" Hagathorn asks.

He is the craziest of salads. He drove them to the outer edges of this place, stubborn as a mule, and now he's champing at the bit.

"As I've said, that's hard to predict," Quinton says, and his politeness has an edge to it. "We're moving slow."

"You want us to hustle up?" Tom asks.

"I want us to get back to the elevator safely," Quinton says. "We move at the fastest speed where we can still do that."

Yes is what Ada hears in his answer. *I would like you to hustle.*

2:25 a.m.

Morris and Hagathorn have the only working headlamps. The rest of them have flashlights, which are neither as bright nor as reliable as the headlamps. Ada can usually count on an Eveready to last for a couple of hours, but occasionally one will go dark after fifteen minutes, either from a bad battery or from some fault in its wiring.

They have larger malfunctions looming. Tom's blow to the head seems to have affected his balance, and he's stumbled several times. The professor's legs have stiffened further, and twice now Quinton has had to half carry him for stretches. They had their last sip of water nearly three hours ago, and they've been wet for longer than that.

Every time they round a bend, Ada thinks they'll be back to the official, well-lit trail. She's been imagining lights in the distance.

"He was so young," Morris says.

His speech has started to slur. It worries Ada, but she doesn't have room in her head for all her worries.

"It'd still be terrible no matter what his age," Tom says, and his words aren't quite as clear as they could be, either.

They haven't tried talking in a while. Maybe it will make the time go faster. Maybe it will make their feet go faster.

"When you're old, it's not really—not really"—Morris coughs—"a tragedy, is it? You reach a point where it's time to go."

The ceiling slopes, and they hunch forward. Behind Ada, someone's foot slips, and pebbles scatter, sounding like raindrops knocked loose from a branch. She has a longing to see a tree.

"When it's time to let go, huh?" Hagathorn says, low grunts between his words. "You think if someone came at you right now, you'd drop your hands and let them have you?"

Morris looks over his shoulder as he drops to his hands and knees—the passage is shrinking. The rest of them drop down, except for Hagathorn, who works to get into position for his backward scooting. They wait.

"I don't count myself as ancient," Morris says. "All I'm saying is that your body starts to fail you."

Ada flexes her fingers. She can feel her grandmother's arthritis in her left thumb, unbendable in the mornings. Her belly gets softer every day, and the soles of her feet get harder.

"You get weaker," Morris keeps on. "Shorter. Uglier. You hurt all the time. I think of my daddy in bed dying and how he didn't want me to hold up a mirror when I shaved him because he didn't want to see himself. These days I look in a mirror and think, *Who is that old man?*"

"You're not that—" starts Editha.

"No need," Morris says, and Hagathorn has gotten himself in motion, so they can all move forward. "I know what I am and what I'm not. But what I'm saying is that at sixty-three"—he does not quite manage the *x* or *t* sound in "sixty"—"I already feel like this body is barely mine. But what if that's supposed to happen? You ever think of that? What if our skin sags and our backs hump over because our soul is supposed to get less comfortable?"

Ada cannot feel her knees. Her legs are moving as they should, but she can't feel her kneecaps hit the ground.

"You took care of your father when he was dying?" she asks. She has never known a man to handle bedside chores.

"Fed him, bathed him, shaved him," Morris says. "Did whatever he needed."

Ada would like to ask him if he changed the sheets, but he's talking again. "I think you start to realize you're something separate from your body," he says. "You hate it, even. And that gets you ready to leave it."

Ada wants to ask him if he ever visits his father in the rooms inside his head. She reminds herself that she shouldn't trust anyone. She reminds herself that this is not a real conversation. It is, like everything else down here, untethered.

"You believe there's something after this?" Hagathorn asks, taking a breath after every couple of words. He lifts his weight on both palms, pushing himself backward, then doing it all over again. The motion reminds Ada of canoeing.

"I do," Morris says.

A flow of onyx spills down the slope of the wall.

"I don't feel like a separate thing from my body," Ada says.

Morris looks back at her, and the skin is loose under his jaw. His arms are solid, though, more like a farmer than a businessman.

"You're young," he says. "You have a lot of time left."

"You're hardly ancient," she says, even as she's thinking, *yes, I am. And I do.*

2:40 a.m.

Please, please, don't let us have more than half a mile, Ada thinks. She cannot shake thoughts of water, cold and fresh from the well. They've stopped at an eight-foot drop between one chamber and the next, and she's relieved that she remembers it clearly. It's the last climbing required before they hit the straightaway that leads to the marked path, and thank God for that because her hands have gone completely numb.

Quinton wedges a candle at the opening between the chambers and lights it. He turns to them, still bent in half, his match wisping smoke.

"I'll go down first," he says, dropping the match to the ground. "Hagathorn, once I've helped the others, I'll come back up for you."

"That'll take extra time," Editha says, stepping toward the drop-off.

"He can't manage the—" Quinton starts, then goes silent as Editha drops to her hands and knees. She tucks her flashlight into her belt.

"You stay here and help him down," she says, her belly sliding against rock. "I don't need help with a ten-foot wall."

It doesn't matter what Quinton might say next because Editha is already shimmying down into the darkness. She's not as smooth as she was a few hours ago, but she's surely still a better climber than any of them. She vanishes except for one hand, which flexes midair and then slips out of sight.

They hear her feet hit the ground. They watch the walls below light up as she lifts her flashlight, and then the beam swings wildly.

"Stay away from me," she says, more air than words.

The quiver in her voice grabs Ada's attention better than a scream. Even when this woman was running her hands over her—former lover's?—body, she seemed as if she could thread a needle or address an envelope without an issue. She does not seem like the sort who would panic at a spider.

"What is it?" Quinton barks, his hand braced against the wall, at the same time Hagathorn calls his wife's name.

Editha doesn't answer either of them. The chamber around them pulses in the candlelight, a room made more of shadow than rock. Quinton strides forward, crouching at the edge of the drop-off, but Ada squeezes past him, skidding down the wall before getting her grip because she's learned that the odds are at least one hand or foot will find purchase. Sure enough, her left foot finds a ridge, and she jounces from wall to ground.

It's a blessing, maybe, this lack of feeling in her hands, because she can't feel her cuts anymore.

Editha is a dozen feet away at the other side of the chamber. She's raising her flashlight like a weapon, and it spotlights the low ceiling above them. Her eyes are fixed on the edge of the room where the darkness is thickest.

"I saw a light," she says. "A man, watching me. And then he disappeared."

"Talmadge?" Ada says.

"Can you think of another option?" Editha says, and the sarcasm steadies her voice.

Ada can hear the others coming down the wall behind her, but she doesn't want to look away from Editha or the darkness in front of them. This chamber only has one exit, round as a rabbit burrow, just high enough to walk through without ducking. A man could come and go easily.

"If I hadn't turned around when I did," Editha says, "he could have had his hands around my throat before I knew he was there."

"Lower the flashlight, Editha," Hagathorn says from above, too loudly. "You look like the Statue of Liberty. Shine it where you saw him."

Editha cuts her eyes toward him and then does as he asks, although the beam isn't strong enough to pinpoint anything at such a distance. It is moonlight through clouds. Ada adds her beam as well, but it barely improves the brightness.

She doesn't believe Talmadge killed the reporter, and she doesn't believe he's lying in wait for them. But if he is, she wants to know it. She takes three long steps toward the opening. Behind her, Editha sucks in a breath.

"Don't," she says.

Ada keeps going, her light leavening the shadows until the start of the next passageway is lit clearly enough that she can make out swathes of wetness shining on the walls. Quinton catches up to her—a warmth against her back—as she steps through the opening, studying the next dozen feet of the passage.

Limestone. Nothing but limestone.

"Give me five minutes," Quinton says. "Then go on."

He starts forward with enough momentum that when Ada grabs hold of his elbow, her hand slips away. He's already into the next chamber when he turns back to her.

"What are you talking about?" she says.

"I need to know if he's here, Ada."

"I'm not hallucinating, if that's what you think," Editha says from behind them.

Quinton sidles backward, leaning close enough that Ada can feel his breath. "What if he never left the lower level?" he murmurs.

She shakes her head. "We know he—"

"No," he says. "We don't."

It takes her a moment to hear all he's not saying. She's assumed that for all these hours and miles his mind has been spinning in the same circles as hers, but it turns out he's been on a different orbit entirely. She has notched Talmadge as either a deserter or murderer, never imagining there could be a third choice.

He might be another carcass. They have no proof that he snuck off to the elevator while Quinton was smoking. He could have headed back toward the sleeping group, ready to make amends, only he ran into the wrong person. These caves are full of nooks and drop-offs where a body might never be found.

"You think we could be leaving him behind," she whispers back.

Quinton is not looking at her—he's pitched toward the next passageway. She considers that if she feels a touch of tenderness for Talmadge after seeing his desperation play out by candlelight, Quinton must feel much more than that for a man he has known for years.

"Five minutes," he says. "It'll take that long to get the magic man down here."

He's gone then. Ada stares after him. She can follow his first handful of steps, but he disappears around a bend as he calls Talmadge's name. She wonders if that's wise, and Quinton must feel the same because he doesn't call out a second time. She tells herself that he cannot be right: Talmadge is either already aboveground, putting as much distance between himself and this fiasco as possible, or he's on his way there. He can't be behind them, as cold and still as Howard. She and Quinton would have heard a struggle—someone would have heard a struggle.

No one heard Howard die, though.

"I'm not hallucinating," Editha says again.

Ada turns, her flashlight casting Editha's silhouette thin and scarecrow-ish on the wall. When Editha lifts her hand, the shadow of her finger shoots out like a yardstick.

"He was standing right there, watching me come down the wall," she says. "Waiting."

While Ada doesn't believe the woman would imagine bogeymen in the dark, this bogeyman does not have to be a hallucination. He could be an outright lie.

Five minutes, she tells herself. She has no idea which parts of her conversation with Quinton the others have heard or understood. They're all standing within a few feet of her, other than Hagathorn, who's perched at the edge of the drop between the two rooms, legs straight as a board.

"Let's just get your husband down, Editha," she says. "Quinton's checking the passageway. Making sure it's safe."

She feels a pang of guilt at casting Talmadge in the role of attacker when she's simultaneously picturing him as a corpse.

"If Talmadge stuck around down here, his flashlight would be long dead," Morris says.

"You sure he didn't have an extra?" Tom asks.

"How could anyone be sure?" Hagathorn says from on high.

They're talking quietly and quickly, all the words hissing together.

"Maybe he cooled off and came back to see if we needed help," Ada says. "Morris, can you give me a hand? You get on one side of him and I'll get on the other."

"Then he'd have spoken to us, wouldn't he?" Hagathorn says. "Instead of playing Peeping Tom? If he wanted to help, why didn't he help?"

He makes a decent point, although Ada would rather not acknowledge it. She tucks her flashlight under her chin, keeping it mostly on the professor's feet. His wet pants are sticking to his legs, and his bandaged knees are soaked, too. From the look on his face, it's obvious he'd rather not need help, and from the look on Morris's, he'd rather not be offering it. They both do as she asks, though. As soon as Morris anchors his feet, Hagathorn shifts his palms, boots clacking together, and puts one hand on Ada's shoulder and one hand on Morris. After Hagathorn is on the ground, Ada stretches up and over the wall, grabbing the candle from the higher chamber and blowing it out.

She turns to face the others, who are all watching her, except Editha, who's still pointed toward the opening into the next chamber. She has never turned away from it. Ada, too, considers the passageway. If Quinton does lay eyes on Talmadge, surely he'll call out? Or he might give chase silently, only that wouldn't really be possible. Two men running down a passage? She'd hear them, surely.

"Quinton!" she calls.

He doesn't answer, and it could be because he doesn't hear her or because he doesn't want to give away his location. Five minutes and then what? If he's not back, does she lead these people down the same passage where he disappeared?

Even with the two headlamps and three flashlights, everyone is more silhouette than real. They are still, mostly, watching her.

"Just another couple of minutes," Ada says.

Editha finally turns toward her. "He shouldn't have gone."

"He'll be fine," Ada says.

"It could be exactly what Talmadge was hoping for, you know," Hagathorn says. "For someone to follow. He was likely waiting around the bend."

"Why would you say such a thing?" Ada says. "What possible point is there to saying it?"

She can tell, though, that his words have landed with more weight than her assurances.

"We're all thinking it," Hagathorn says. "And if he's coming for us next, there's no point in burying our heads in the sand. There are five of us and one of him."

"So you think he's, what, hunting us?" Ada says. This man is the least helpful person imaginable. "You think he stabbed Howard and now he's come back to finish us off? Why would he do that? If the worst were true—if he is the killer—he'd want to get out of here. He'd head out of town as fast as he could, not waste time wandering around. Like Quinton said, he's a man. He's not some demon. He's not hiding out there in the pitch-black waiting for us."

"Then where is Quinton?" Editha says, and it sounds less like a challenge than like she's truly hoping for an answer.

Ada doesn't have one. *Safe,* she wants to say. *Nothing can hurt him,* she wants to say, but that's not true for anyone and she well knows it and also she wishes this woman would not call Quinton by his first name.

In the middle of the chamber, water drips a steady path from one point of the ceiling to an urn-shaped stone below, bigger than a watermelon.

"Ada," Tom says.

Quinton, she calls, silently this time. Inside her head, her voice is angry, not scared, and she pictures him in the darkness, mind reading. He's lost track of time, but she's reaching him now and he's hurrying back. She'll spot his light bobbing through the passageway any second.

Any second.

"Ada," Tom says again.

She makes herself focus on him. Because he's pointing his flashlight at the ground, she doesn't notice at first that the bulb has gone dark.

"Alright," she says. It's not the worst thing to have a task. "You just happened to get a dud. I'll get you another. We've got three left, I think, and that should be enough to—"

She stops, and the sound of water dripping is louder in her head. She looks back to the urn-shaped stone. The whole of it is slick like melting ice.

"He has the extras," she says, and, of course, the others don't know what she's talking about. It takes her a moment to make the words come out. "Quinton's carrying the pack with the flashlights."

"What do you have in your pack?" Morris says.

He's not grasping it. None of them have grasped it.

"Two candles," she says. "A dead flashlight and an empty canteen. He was carrying all the extra supplies."

She nearly calls Quinton's name again, but she doesn't want to hear the silence answer her. The dripping of water onto the urn-shaped stone is a slow version of *Peter Piper picked a peck of pickled peppers*. The line plays in her head, over and over.

"The candles won't be much good," she says. "Not for covering ground. No telling about the flashlights, but the two headlamps hopefully have another couple of hours."

"And then we're in the dark?" Editha says.

"We won't be in the dark," Ada says, and she mostly believes it. Quinton will be back any second, lugging the flashlights with him, and even if he isn't, she'll have everyone to the elevators in plenty of time.

"Talmadge doesn't mind the dark," Morris says. "He likes it."

He's propped against the rock, letting the wall take most of his weight. Next to him, Tom lifts his useless flashlight, whacking it against his gloved hand. He smacks it a second time, harder, and lets it clatter to the ground.

"You had to push it," he says, and it takes Ada a moment to realize he's speaking to Hagathorn. "Like you always do. And you had to drag everyone else with you, like you always do."

"This one was on you," Hagathorn says, shaking his head. "You liked Lambert's idea."

"You think I'm driving this train?" Tom says.

The mingled wax and blood have dried pink over his eye, blurring half his forehead. Blood has smeared along his left cheek and jaw like gory stubble.

"I show up where you tell me, Tom," Hagathorn says.

"No, you don't. You really don't, Jeremiah. You have never done anything you don't want to do. All the way back to Bowling Green—"

Hagathorn waves a hand, throwing himself off balance. "Bowling Green? You want to talk about that Rotary fellow after seven years—"

"I did exactly what you wanted here, Jeremiah," Tom says, voice rising. "I arranged the contracts and smoothed the way and you took over like you do and every time I try to fix it, you muck it up again. And now you've stuck us here."

Ada is mesmerized by the anger carving out the lines and veins of Tom's face. He is a new man. He is a blister burst.

"We have a way out," she says to him firmly. "We are not stuck. We've been down here a long time, and we're all wrung out."

"That's a polite way to put it," Tom says.

"You two can hash all this out when you're aboveground," Ada says, "but the sooner we get moving, the sooner you're safe."

"It's surely been more than five minutes since he left," Morris says.

He's not wrong. It's been at least ten.

"So we head to the elevator," Ada says, and she's not sure whether it sounds like an order or a question. "We'll catch up to Quinton. Maybe he turned an ankle or—I don't know. He can tell us himself."

She hooks her thumbs under the straps of her pack, lifting the weight of it and letting it fall.

"You'd have us head straight toward Talmadge?" Hagathorn says.

"We have no choice!" Ada says. "The light will run out, and if it's Talmadge that you're so concerned about, how would y'all like to sit here in the dark and wait for him to come? We either go forward or we sit here and wait for the lights to go."

With every word, she settles into herself more solidly. She will not think of Talmadge or Quinton. She will do what she needs to do. She will keep these people moving toward the elevator, and she will keep them from killing each other or her.

Hagathorn steps toward her, faster than Ada thought he could move. He lifts an arm—again, too fast—and she flinches, lifting a hand, but Morris is moving, too, shoving himself between the two of them. He gives Hagathorn a push, enough to make him stagger.

"No," Morris says, like he's ordering a dog to stay back. "Get your hands off her."

Ada isn't sure what's happening. The tension from Tom and Hagathorn is still in the air. The tension from all manner of things is still in the air. Morris has shocked the mind reader into silence—the taller man takes a deep breath that carries through the chamber as he braces his hands on his thighs.

"I was doing what you asked," Hagathorn says to Ada, looking around Morris, who's still directly in front of her. "Getting moving. Working loose a kink in my shoulder. Nothing nefarious."

Ada believes the confusion in his voice is real. He moved too suddenly, but she was too wary. Or she was the right amount of wary for these caves, but the wrong amount for responding to social graces.

"We're all jumpy," she says. "Sorry."

"It's not you who should apologize," Morris says.

Ada tries to step around him, but he lifts an arm and blocks her way.

"It's alright, Morris," she says, getting warier by the second. "No harm done."

"You don't have to say that," Morris says. "We can all see what he's doing."

This must be the voice he uses when he's sitting behind his office desk. He turns to face Ada without fully turning his back on the mind reader. Tom and Hagathorn might be tied for the bloodiest, but Morris is the palest.

"This whole trip he's been touching everybody," he says, "standing too close, always putting his hands on us."

Hagathorn holds up both hands, peacemaking for once. He lifts first one leg and then the other. He must be stiffening up.

Peter Piper picked a peck of pickled peppers, sings the dripping water.

"I was only trying—" Hagathorn starts.

"You've heard of needle men, haven't you?" Morris says, looking at the rest of them. "They inject you, just a little prick, and then you're poisoned, maybe woozy or maybe knocked out."

He's nodding his head, his headlamp flashing up and down.

"And you just kept draping your arm over me," he says, turning back to Hagathorn. "Easing up close. A hand here and a hand there. Your hands were all over Talmadge, too. I know my head's not right, you think I don't? None of us are right—that's my point. It's clear we're not thinking straight."

Yes, thinks Ada. It is clear, but Morris is not stopping.

"Maybe you gave Talmadge a nudge to push him over the edge," he says to Hagathorn. "Maybe the newspaperman was dead before the rock ever went through his throat."

Needle men. It's a bizarre notion made all the more bizarre because Morris is the one who's voicing it. Ada doesn't blame Hagathorn when he laughs.

It's not the right response. Morris shoves the larger man again, both hands straight to the chest, and with his bad knees, Hagathorn crashes into Editha behind him. She somehow keeps them both on their feet.

They are all losing their heads.

"Morris," Ada says. "Listen to me. Look at me. I don't think needles are involved."

He turns to her, blinding her for a moment. If he and Hagathorn get into a scuffle, they might smash the only two headlamps left.

"You think—you think—what?" Morris says. "He's just affectionate?"

The slur of his speech has come back: He cannot manage all the syllables of "affectionate."

"I think we've been down here a long time," Ada says. She reaches for his shoulder, but he yanks away from her. "And we're all stretched thin."

"This all goes back to him," Morris says, eyeing Hagathorn again. "You know it does."

His wife wasn't the only one who died, Ada remembers. He lost a sister a few years ago, and last month he was the one who found his neighbor's body cold on the kitchen floor. Ruby mentioned that his mother died in a bad fall when he was still a young man, and now he's stared down at the newspaperman's carcass, and he might be dehydrated or exhausted or claustrophobic or some combination, but also it could be too much death for one man to absorb.

She needs to get him aboveground. She needs to get them all aboveground.

They've gathered around Morris like witches around a cauldron. Editha extricates herself from her husband and lays her hand on Morris's arm. He does not shrug her off. It seems some thread of sympathy stretches between the two of them as well.

"Miah is not a needle man," Editha says.

"He's something," Morris says, his words running together. "Pushing. Always pushing. Always right there, not giving you any space. He's wanted—"

"To find the pin," Hagathorn says, impatient.

"And you need your hands on me for that?" Morris says.

"We're in close quarters," Tom says. "Everyone's rubbing against each other."

"There's a purpose to it," Morris says. "I'm not going anywhere with him. I'm not going anywhere near him. I'll stay right here if it comes to that."

Maybe they will not make it to the elevator.

It's the first time Ada's had the thought. Maybe they will stand in this room yelling at each other until the final light burns out, and would that be the end of the world? The dark won't kill them. Leo will send someone. Maybe she will close her eyes and wake up when someone else rounds the corner and solves all their problems.

Only they are not late enough to cause real worry—Leo will want to give the mind reader a cushion of extra time. He will want to give his star attraction every chance to succeed. And if these people are unraveling now, she does not want to see what will happen in utter darkness.

Editha still has her hand on Morris's shoulder.

"Morris," she says, and Ada would swear it's real kindness in her voice. "Miah does use his hands, but he's not a needle man."

"Don't," Hagathorn says.

"Hush, Miah," she says. "All of us need to calm the hell down."

Ada can count on one hand the number of times she has heard a woman say "hell" outside of a Sunday school class. Editha's tone is sharper with her husband than it is with Morris, and Ada decides she might be friends with the other woman after all, if she does not turn out to be a murderer.

"He's been doing a version of the hot-and-cold act," Editha says. "The touching is part of it."

"It's not an act," Hagathorn says. "Editha. Come on, now. There's no need to—"

"There are different variations," his wife says, leaning in closer to Morris. She pauses until his eyes meet hers. "Usually the performer is blindfolded and offstage, and someone in the audience is selected. They might be asked to offer up a piece of jewelry, or they might hide jewelry in someone else's pocket. When the performer comes out, he announces he can sense where the bracelet is hidden. He asks to hold on to the arm or clasp the hand of someone in the audience so that he can more clearly read their thoughts. Are you hearing me?"

Morris has twisted toward Hagathorn. When Editha squeezes his arm, he meets her eyes again. His breathing is evening out.

"The average person in the audience wants a performer to get the answer right," she says, and for someone who doesn't say much, she seems to enjoy herself once she gets started. "They'll lead him to the right person with the tension and pull of their muscles. They don't even know they're doing it, but they direct him, and then there's the audience. They help. You can hear the intake of breath as you get close, and there's always someone whispering 'That's it' a little too loud when you reach for the right pocket."

Morris nods once, slowly. Hagathorn is stone-faced, and Tom has covered his eyes with his hand. Ada wonders if his cut is opening back up.

"There's no audience here," she says.

"No," Editha says. "We knew there would be that handicap. But with two men knowing the location of the hatpin, Miah expected to be able to lay hands on them and feel where they wanted him to go. It didn't work, clearly."

"You must know this is all confidential," Hagathorn says.

Morris rubs his hands together, his gloves whispering.

"Is that sufficient?" Editha asks, loosening her hold on him. "Can we move along without fears of needles?"

Morris stills his hands, linking his gloved fingers. He straightens.

"You thought—thought—we would lead you to it?" he says to Hagathorn. "The rest of it was blather?"

"Not blather," Hagathorn says. "Think of everything Editha just explained as a contingency plan. In a rare case when I cannot pluck a thought from the air, I might—"

"You kept saying we cheated," Morris says. The aggression has gone out of him. "But you never believed that. Talmadge and I both knew where the pin was, but I could never have led you there. The tunnels make no sense to me at all."

Hagathorn gives the slightest of nods. Ada can't keep track of all his complaints and accusations, but this seems to be the root of them. He had a trick planned, but the trick didn't take the caves into account.

"I still believe you cheated," Hagathorn says. "Your signals were all mixed up. And I thought since you weren't used to the caves, your emotions would be close to the surface, but you numbed yourself pretty good, didn't you?"

"My emotions didn't matter one way or the other," Morris says. "Because I never had any idea whether you should turn left or right."

"You had other kinds of ideas," Hagathorn says.

Ada worries that the two of them will slide back into a back-and-forth about needle men or drunkenness, but Tom is the one who speaks.

"That's what you did," he says, finally lifting his head. His cut is still sealed, Ada is relieved to see. "The night we met. That's what you did."

For a moment, Ada isn't sure Hagathorn heard his manager. He stares over their heads at one dark wall, and when he does face Tom, he drops his head so Ada can't see much more than his headlamp.

"That was entirely different," Hagathorn says.

"You followed some sap to my seat," Tom says, "and you never read my mind at all."

"I swear," Hagathorn says, and if Ada fully believed anything the man said, she would believe he cared about Tom's feelings. "What happened that night—it was exactly what it seemed. The things I said to you, I couldn't have invented them."

Without a flashlight of his own, Tom nearly disappears when he takes a step into the shadows.

"I could have," he says.

"You're not making sense," Hagathorn says.

"Did you say any of it, Jeremiah?"

"Of course—"

"Or did I just want to hear it that badly?" Tom says, more voice than body. "I've told the story so many times that I'm not sure if I truly remember that night or if I only remember the way I've told it."

Peter Piper picked a peck of pickled peppers. Peter Piper picked a peck of pickled peppers.

Hagathorn takes an unsteady step forward. "You think it should be predictable," he says, "but I'm not a planet following an orbit. It's more like a comet. That night with you was real. You know what I said. You were right there with me."

His light catches Tom, who smiles, too big, big enough that Ada's afraid he'll crack the wax. He gives Editha a nod.

"I must have been very entertaining to you both," he says.

Shell-shocked, Ada thinks. She imagines she had this same look on her face when she stood up from Gerald's body at the hospital. A passing nurse told her, *They'll see you at the desk,* and she stood there until the same nurse added, *Go to the end of the hall and turn right,* and then she could move because she had specific instructions.

"Pick up your pack," she says to Tom. She waits until he looks at her. "Lace your boot. It's come untied. And then we're leaving."

Tom picks up his pack, then sets it down again, kneeling and grabbing at his laces. Ada turns: She wants to hurry them, and also she does not want to look straight at Tom's face. He is wrecked, and she cannot take on anyone else's wreckage at the moment. She expects Hagathorn to continue his apologies, to make his way over to the man who took some long-ago knife wound for him, only Hagathorn can't seem to bear the sight of Tom's face, either. He's turned to his wife, who raises her flashlight and follows Ada.

Maybe everyone has used up their words because they all follow her without comment, even Hagathorn. They make their way into the next passage slowly, no sound but dripping water and boots scuffing against rock.

Ada stares into the darkness, listening. The range of her flashlight is so slight that surely her ears will tell her more than her eyes.

Any second, she thinks. *Any second.*

"Quinton!" she calls because she cannot stand it any longer. She counts to ten and calls him a second time. She's tempted to tell him that they are headed his way, in case by some fluke he can hear her even though she can't hear him—but she doesn't want Talmadge to know where they are.

Talmadge, who is somehow dead and lurking and safe at home all at the same time.

"Can you hear me, Quinton?" she tries once more.

No answer.

"It's a long passageway," she tells the others. "And the rock eats up sound."

Both these things are true. They are the only explanations she will let herself entertain. She swings her light, confirming that everyone is lined up behind her, and only when she reaches to adjust her helmet does she realize that she can't lift her arm to her head. Her shoulder doesn't seem to be working. She rolls her neck, trying to loosen it, and the cave around her goes even darker.

Her flashlight. It's out, too.

They are losing light left and right, and maybe Quinton has batteries as well, but she has nothing. Hagathorn is the closest to her, his headlamp still bright.

"If I'm going to lead," she says, "I'll need your lamp. I can't do it blind."

He lifts his leg and lowers it, over and over, as if he's pumping an invisible pedal. She's not the only one working out aches.

"You're leading?" he says.

"Would you rather do it?" she asks. She wouldn't mind that arrangement. If she had her preference, she'd be bringing up the rear, keeping an eye on everyone.

She watches the darkness in front of her again. *Any second.*

"So Talmadge will have to go through you before he gets to us?" Hagathorn says, still pumping his pedal.

"That's the thought," she says.

"Assuming you care to stop him."

"Jeremiah," she says, "if I didn't care, I would have left you down here a long time ago."

She unbuckles her helmet, holding it out to him, but it's Morris who responds. He takes her lightless helmet and hands her his own, the carbide flame still burning.

"Take mine," he says. "And I'll take the back if you're taking the front."

"You sure?" Ada asks.

He nods, and she does not love the arrangement, but she has no better option. Morris has returned to a recognizable version of himself instead of the crazy man who raged about needles. Tom and Hagathorn are physically in worse shape than he is. And if she has to pick someone to watch her back, she can make her peace with Morris.

She buckles his helmet onto her head, and it's loose, but good enough. She keeps hold of the dead flashlight because although it might bounce off a helmet, with the right angle it could break a jaw.

She sweeps her headlamp over the edges of the cavern, and the Hagathorns are talking at her, but you cannot listen to all the people all the time. She's always thought of this stretch of the caves as boxed off and clear-cut, no more complicated than a storm cellar, but her beam has illuminated a crevice under the right wall that she's never noticed. The crack is wide enough that if she dropped to the ground, she could fit under it. It might dead-end in a couple of feet, or she might be able to crawl for a mile. It might lead to a dozen other offshoots. She thinks of her first conversation with Quinton when he showed her the dark spaces that led to underground streams, his shirt riding up.

Secret passages, he said.

She has no idea how many other crevices she might have missed or how far they might stretch. If Quinton is lying in one of these cracks, unconscious or worse, does she have any chance of spotting him? If Talmadge is here and doesn't want her to see him, will she?

She shines her beam into the crevice again, angling for a better view. She thinks of Talmadge's anxious, clenching fingers and the tremble in Editha's voice when she shouted into the dark. Did the two of them truly come face-to-face just now? It's a narrow distance between truth and lie. It is always a narrow distance—an astonishingly narrow distance—between here and gone, but the gap is somehow shrinking.

3:05 a.m.

It was easier to corral her thoughts when she was distracted by near fistfights and general lunacy. Now her flock has gone silent, and Quinton is filling up her head. They've covered a few hundred feet, and there's no sign of him—of course there isn't. It's not as if he would have settled in for a nap or decided to do a few push-ups. Ada wracks her brain for possibilities that she can bear—a sprained ankle is not beyond reason. Anyone can turn an ankle. He might have followed Talmadge further than he intended, or he might have needed to restrain Talmadge—he would not have been able to bring him back down the passage if the younger man refused to go. The thought cheers her. They'll likely come across both men in another bend or two, Quinton with an arm clamped around Talmadge, waiting for another pair of hands.

If she fully believed this, she would call out to him again.

The flashlights have all burned out. Only she and Hagathorn still have lights. She does not know how much longer the carbide will last.

She slows, jerking her head toward a movement under the wall to her left, but it must be a shadow. Her light catches a small pool ahead, and a blind crayfish, pale as the moon, darts across the surface.

As far as she knows, all the crayfish down here are blind.

With every minute that goes by, it's more likely that Talmadge is guilty of all that the Hagathorns have imagined. He is almost surely a bogeyman, unless Quinton has truly cracked a bone, in which case Talmadge could be fetching Leo right now, guilty of nothing other than getting help as quickly as possible.

She checks behind her: The passageway beyond Morris is dark and empty.

Dead. Bogeyman. Safe aboveground. She has too many pictures laid out in a row, and Talmadge is only one page in her terrible album: She sees the stalactite shoving through Howard's skin and muscle, blood spraying, and she sees his hands grabbing air and his eyes rolling white and she sees every one of these people kneeling over him. She watches each one of them kill him. The visions have the same architecture as those half dreams between sleep and consciousness, when the crow's caw outside the window becomes a dying scream and the brush of the quilt becomes the edge of a knife. There is no controlling them.

She sees Quinton, eyes open, body broken. He's not even hers, and she's lost him.

She hears Hagathorn murmuring, too low to make out the words, apologetic, maybe. When she turns, she sees that he's stopped, and Tom is shaking his head as he puts distance between them.

"It doesn't matter," the manager says over his shoulder, even as he's catching up to Ada. His boots are still blood-spattered.

"It does," Hagathorn says, starting forward again. "You know it does, Tom."

"Let's just get out of here," Tom says. "Out of the caves, out of the city, out of this mess you've made."

He reaches Ada and gives a lift of his eyebrows as if the two of them understand each other. He thinks he has her sympathy.

He does not.

"This didn't just happen to you," she says.

He shuffle-steps closer. "Pardon?"

"You chose to come here," she says. "You chose him."

"It was hardly a choice," Tom says.

"But it was," Ada says, speeding up. It's good to talk. Her mind cannot veer off when she's putting together sentences. "You could have said no. Repeatedly. You could have said the hatpin was a bad idea. You could have called it off when your professor pulled a razor on those men at the hotel. You could have agreed with Talmadge that it was time to turn around."

"We'd signed a contract."

"Life doesn't just befall you," she says. "You have a say."

Too loud. She's talking too loud. She tastes salt and metal and realizes she's bitten the inside of her lip.

She aims her light toward another crevice running along the floor, and she cannot see the bottom. She thinks of tumbling into the abyss like a child careening down a hill, shrieking. She thinks of all that might lie at the bottom of an abyss.

"Sometimes it does befall you," Tom says. "Sometimes you have no say at all."

"This is not one of those times," Ada says.

She can tell the others are struggling to keep up with her—Hagathorn is several yards behind them all—but she doesn't slow. Editha's hair has come unpinned again, falling from under her helmet and snaking around her collar.

"You think Howard had a choice?" Editha asks. "You think he got a say?"

She spits out the words, her calm cracking open, and everything and everyone is cracking open. Ada refuses to pat everything back into place. These are adults. She is tired of minding them, and is this how Talmadge felt?

"Don't be stupid," she says to the other woman. "I'm not saying that. But we have a say in what we do and what we don't. I'm not only the things that happen to me."

No one answers and Ada doesn't know if it's because she's won or because the others have lost their breath. She can see the shape of horse heads in the flowstone, muzzles pointed to the ground, and her tongue feels like it's coated with glue.

Quinton, she calls in her head again.

The thing she can't understand is the supplies. For all these hours, Quinton has been methodical, and he's been particularly aware of how much water and light they have left. Before he went haring off after Talmadge, he could have dropped his bag at her feet in a split second, and why didn't he? He would have been faster without the weight, and the group would have had the flashlights.

It slipped his mind, she tells herself, but she has never known a detail to slip his mind. That leads to the question of whether she actually knows him any better than she knows the crackpots behind her, and she steers her mind away from that particular route.

She hears dragging footsteps coming closer, and she knows these people's sounds by now. She's kept her distance from Hagathorn, but she can't avoid him when he pulls even with her.

"You believe you control your own fate," he says.

In her effort to keep space between them, her shoulder drags against the rock hard enough that she expects to hear the rip of her jacket. She does not look away from the path ahead.

"I believe we have choices," she says. "You need to get back to where you were. They need the light back there."

"I agree with you," Hagathorn says. "It's what separates us from animals, our ability to see options and choose them."

She thinks animals do this as well, but she doesn't say it. She does not want to encourage him.

"My father used to say you're only the vessel," he says. "Let God fill you up. I despised that, like I was only some shell like the husk a cicada leaves behind. Like I had no power of my own."

Ada cannot help but think of how her mother used to say *It's God's will*, and it never made sense to her that God willed her grandmother to drop dead of a heart attack or made the boy next door get hit by a train. Her mother said it was God's will when Ada lost her first baby and her second. She wasn't around for the third.

These walls are tight enough that a surprise attack cannot be part of God's will. If Talmadge has turned predator, he'd have to be on his belly, under a wall, and the most he could do without warning would be to grab a leg. Still, Ada makes sure to shine the light in a slow U shape, left and right, as she scans the path ahead.

"'His will be done,'" Hagathorn says. "He said that at my mother's funeral."

Gerald used that one about the babies, too. He never figured out that instead of comfort, it was rubbed salt.

"I was right next to Howard, did you know that?" Hagathorn says. "Not more than six inches away from him as I slept. What does that say about God's will?"

He does not seem to need her participation to have a conversation. But now that Ada's close enough to smell the sweat and hint of aftershave on him, she sees more than the arrogance she expected. She sees sadness, and she tries not to let it sway her.

"He was a preacher, my father," Hagathorn says. "Didn't figure me for a preacher's son, did you? But you never do get free of the ones who raised you, not entirely."

Ada's headlamp flickers. Only a pulse, a heartbeat, and no one else seems to notice. She thinks she sees movement ahead, but it's once again only shadow. Someone behind them trips and recovers, a quick skip and thump of sound.

"I don't want to be free of them," Ada says.

"You're lucky, then."

She understands more clearly why they've wound up here. She's thought of Hagathorn only as a bully, but she feels the pull of him now, attentive. She remembers her mother frowning at some man or another, likely a salesman. *Never trust charm,* she said, in the same tone she would use to warn against head lice.

Ada has not thought of it for a long time, her mother's views on charisma.

She stops, and although Hagathorn stops immediately as well, Tom knocks into her hard enough from behind that she has to catch herself with a hand against the wall. It's the hand she scraped on the rocks earlier, and she jerks it to her chest with a grunt.

"Apologies," Tom says, but it doesn't matter. Nothing matters except the pale glow down the passage ahead—it is not bright, but it's *not dark*. The sight of *not dark* is better, maybe, than the first sip of water will be.

"Lights," she says, pointing.

She can't see actual bulbs, but they're close. She is back in the real world, almost. In another few minutes, they'll be on the marked paths, and they will not spend the rest of their lives underground after all. She tries to make herself believe it as the others push past her, heedless, crowding together in Hagathorn's light. But her feet will not get going.

She checks behind her—only darkness and silence.

Quinton Quinton Quinton Quinton Quinton. She can barely keep his name from breaking loose.

She tries to focus on the relief she feels at the lighted path, but she feels other things, too, and her brain is not obeying her any better than her feet are. She keeps looping back to the pack of supplies. She can accept that Quinton forgot he was carrying it. The man is human, and he made a mistake. But she can start with this instead: Quinton has shown himself to be nothing if not capable, therefore he did not forget he was carrying all the flashlights. He meant to take them with him. And once her mind takes that turn, it leads her to places she would rather not go.

"Ada?" Editha calls softly.

"Coming," Ada says.

Quinton rushed down this passage saying he needed to make sure that Talmadge was alive and well, but what if his sympathy for the other man was deeper than she realized? Did he ever truly believe Talmadge might have wound up a corpse, or did he only want to help the other man escape? He'd know that taking the extra lights would buy extra time.

The idea is a cavern that deepens and darkens.

Sympathy might play no part in this. Quinton said a flimflam man ruined the bar owner who kept him from starving in Cincinnati. Ada's only met one flimflam man in her life, and he's about twenty feet ahead of her and insists on being called "Professor." It's not inconceivable. Quinton might have been biding his time, hoping for a chance at retaliation—and that notion spirals deepest and darkest of all because, as Editha said, no good ever came from sitting around and waiting. A smart man would have a plan, and—each horrible thought only leads her to the next one—Quinton refused the guide's job when Leo offered it. He instead wanted the job that kept him from being face-to-face with Hagathorn for most of these hours, letting him follow behind, unseen and unknown.

If you wanted to kill a man, it would be a good position. No one would see you coming. No one would suspect you. No one would know if, when you said you were stepping away for a smoke, you pulled a stalactite from your pack instead of a cigarette. No one would try to stop you when you slipped away for good, saying you'd be back in five minutes.

I was right next to him, Hagathorn said. *Six inches away.*

They've all agreed that a pitch-black cave doesn't lend itself to precision, and there's no guarantee that the killer got the right man. But this is where the scenario, thankfully, falls apart. Because if Quinton did set out to kill Hagathorn, he botched it, and that's the part that feels impossible. Ada believes that, if Quinton did decide to kill someone, he'd do it as competently as he does everything else.

She checks behind her again.

3:35 a.m.

In view of the first dangling bulb and the curve of the handrail, Ada catches up to the others. The electricity seems to have brought them to a standstill. She slides past Editha and Hagathorn, maneuvering herself to the front, and when Tom speaks, she thinks he's talking to her.

"So you gave up on it?" he asks.

Ada turns to see him staring at the lightbulb, glasses crooked. Before she can formulate any kind of response, Hagathorn answers.

"I did not," he says.

The hatpin, she realizes. They're talking about the hatpin. She'd nearly forgotten—it existed in a different world entirely.

"He's right," Morris says. He swallows, looking back and forth between the two other men. "You stopped all of that—that—mumbo jumbo about picturing it. You stopped giving orders."

"I say we count our blessings," Ada says. It has not occurred to her to consider Hagathorn's willingness to abandon his search as anything other than a reasonable reaction to bleeding and hurting and running low on light.

"You never were going to find it, were you?" Tom says, still focused on the bulb.

Morris strips off a glove and dabs at his mouth with the back of his hand. "Of course, he wasn't."

"You're supposed to want me to find it, you know," Hagathorn says. "All of you."

"I wanted this to work for Leo," Morris says. "It won't now, no matter—no matter what. I sure as hell don't want it to work for you.

Talmadge took you straight to it. You went right past where he hid it. Twice. And you never had an inkling."

Ada checks the passageway behind them and in front of them. No movement. She braces herself for another lecture—another tantrum—but Hagathorn nods as if he's asked for the time of the next bus and gotten a helpful answer.

"*He* hid it,'" he says. "As opposed to *we*."

"We," Morris amends. "But what does it matter now?"

"It doesn't," Hagathorn says. "Not in the least."

Ada considers Morris. He still can't manage his *d*'s and *t*'s, which makes him sound more drunk than he ever sounded when he was, apparently, actually drinking—and, speaking of drunk, something is wrong with Hagathorn. He's being gracious. He's not asking about the location of the hatpin or railing at Morris. He seems to have given up the search, yet the look of him makes Ada think of Leo. He is nearly vibrating.

Happy, but more than that. She does not have a word for what he is. She's never seen one of his fits, but she wonders if they start like this.

He does not collapse or convulse, though. He stalks through the final stretch of shadows to the marked path, stretching out a hand until electric light bathes him. He grips the railing with one gloved hand.

Morris is right: What does any of it matter now? All that matters is that they are nearly to the elevator. In a dozen steps, they're all soaking up the light of the first hanging bulb. Ada can count five more bulbs within sight, although staring at them is painful. They have made it. Almost.

Peter Piper picked a peck of pickled peppers. She can still hear it even though the drip of water is long gone.

She sets a faster pace. The others can keep up with it now that they can see the ground, although the passage is still narrow enough that they're single file. Hagathorn struggles on the spiral staircase—vibrating, he is still vibrating—but as they near the end, everything—feet, heartbeats, time itself—moves faster.

The soot-dusted walls widen as the elevator shaft comes into view: It's a solid mass of brick and cement blocks, dried mortar slathered along the edges. Ada has been dreaming of this first glimpse of the shaft for hours, but she did not dream of seeing the elevator car inside, its accordion door folded open. It's no further away than the length of her backyard, a silent rectangle with cables stretching up into infinity.

She wishes she was not seeing it.

"It's still here," she says.

"I should hope so," Editha says.

"No," Ada says. "If Talmadge beat us out of here, one way or the other, he should have taken the elevator up. Quinton, too."

"They could have sent it back down for us," Tom says.

Ada doesn't bother answering that. If Talmadge had reached the surface after having murdered a man, he would never have thoughtfully sent the elevator back down for the people left behind. And if either man had gone to find help, Leo would never have sent the elevator back down empty. The cave would be swarming with policemen and rescuers.

Ada feels someone trying to slip around her—Editha—and she extends an arm, barring the other woman's way. There is no way around it: Talmadge and Quinton are still belowground, dead or alive.

She looks behind her, and the path is empty. Silent. Editha is asking some question, but Ada faces forward, searching. Checking for ambushes is starting to be as automatic as looking both ways before crossing the street. The electric lights above them don't cut through all the shadows, and the edges of the chamber are impossibly dark. She imagines the shadows moving, turning into the shapes of men—

She is not imagining it.

A few yards beyond the elevator, two helmeted figures separate themselves from the wall, walking shoulder to shoulder. She can't see their faces, but she would recognize Quinton's shape anywhere and she does not know what to do with this rush of relief, and also terror, because it has never occurred to her that he and Talmadge might be working together but—shoulder to shoulder, unmistakable—she cannot deny what's she's seeing. This entire push through the caves hasn't been an escape—it's a trap.

"Oh, God," Tom says from behind her, or maybe it's Morris.

The sound is little more than a whisper, but it's helpful, a reminder that the others are here and when Ada was younger she could not bear the sight of a cockroach, all slick shell and spiked legs, but when she saw one on her little brother's crib she plucked it off with her bare hand and stomped it dead and that was the end of her fear of roaches.

Her thoughts are moving faster than the two men. They've only taken a couple of steps as she shifts her grip on her Eveready. She keeps the flashlight hip-level, unthreatening, remembering all those stories about women with hatpins on carriages, plucking a pin and stabbing an attacker. Men do not expect violence from a woman, and that is some small advantage.

"Ada," a woman's voice calls, and a third figure shoves past the first two.

Everything changes. The woman's dress flaps as she hurries forward, heels clicking against the rock, and it's Ruby, obviously. It's Ruby. Even as Ada absorbs this fact, the men behind Ruby come into the light more fully, and it's not Talmadge beside Quinton but Leo Lambert. He's in a suit, tie and all, and Ada can't think more about him because Ruby is flying toward her. Ada wants to warn her not to get too close—she is filthy and she stinks—but then Ruby's arms are around her, warm and tight.

She smells like Pond's cold cream, and she's laughing.

"You're a wreck," Ruby says, pulling back slightly. "Oh, God, you are a wreck, but you're here, and I didn't know. We just didn't know, Ada. Are you hurt? You don't look hurt. You must be thirsty. We didn't even bring water—Leo, we should have grabbed the water."

Ada realizes she's laughing, too, and also, possibly, crying. Ruby is in her Sunday heels, for God's sake. Her blouse is white, or it was before she hugged Ada, and everything is alright now. Everything is alright.

Over Ruby's shoulder, Leo is smiling, but it doesn't last long. Even in the nice clothes, he looks as exhausted as the soot-covered men around him.

"Thank God, you're alright," he says to Ada, but he's already looking at the other faces. "Mrs. Hagathorn. Professor. Morris." He lays a hand on the older man's shoulder, only a brief touch. "And, Tom, you need a doctor. Let's get you all out of here, and we can—"

"You really don't have water?" Tom asks.

"We didn't expect to see you," Leo says, apologetic. "It was meant to be a quick look around to try to make sense of—"

"Talmadge," Ruby says, squeezing Ada's wrist before letting go of her entirely. "We saw Talmadge."

The others all have some reaction to this, but Ada finally lets herself look Quinton in the eye. He's watching her, which she already knew. She could feel his eyes on her this whole time, but she's having trouble letting go of her fear of him, even though it was unfounded. It's fading, though, with every breath.

"—through the kitchen," Leo is saying, and Ada tries to listen to him at the same time she listens to Quinton.

"I'm sorry," he says to her. "I saw their lights and thought they were Talmadge. When I caught up with them, Leo wanted—"

But Leo is raising his voice, and Quinton cedes the floor. He inches closer to Ada, though, the edge of his boot pressing against hers. *Real,* Ada thinks. He is real. The other version of him was pure hallucination.

"The workers' entrance," Leo is saying. "Ruby and me had been biding our time, trying to keep the reporters settled, working to get them interested in a plate of sandwiches, and I looked up and there was Talmadge, still in his boots and coat, covered in muck, darting toward the kitchen. I almost thought I dreamed him. But I went after him, and, yeah, there he was, headed as fast as he could go down the dirt path."

"You didn't try to stop him?" Hagathorn asks.

"He didn't turn around when I called, and he had a head start. I had bigger concerns, Professor."

"We were lucky no one else saw him," Ruby says. "The kitchen ladies did, of course, but I mean the newspapermen. And maybe they wouldn't recognize his face, but a man covered in dirt in caving clothes, you would think—"

"They're not camped out by the elevator?" Morris asks.

"There are no chairs there," Ruby says, with a flicker of a smile. "The lobby was better for their backsides."

"We knew something had gone wrong," Leo says, "but in case we could salvage it, we didn't want to bring along the whole horde of them. So we came down, just the two of us, thinking we'd look around. See if we could avoid admitting our guide just up and left. Forgive me, but we didn't know it was an emergency. I'd hoped maybe he was just a little ahead of the rest of y'all. That he got the runs or something—like Ruby said, we didn't know. Talmadge hasn't ever been much for socializing—happier in his own head, you know—but it seemed like surely he would have said something if—if—"

"Someone had been stabbed through the throat?" Hagathorn says.

Leo plays with a button on his sleeve, fastening it even though it's already fastened. "Yeah," he says.

Ada looks to Quinton again. "Did you tell—"

"He told us everything," Leo answers. "When we took the elevator down, Ruby and I decided we'd walk a ways down the marked trail, and if we didn't run into anybody, we'd turn around and send in a full crew. We were just about to turn around when we saw Quinton coming at us."

That answers one of Ada's questions. If he didn't make it past the marked trail, it cannot have been Leo who Editha saw in the dark.

"I thought I saw Talmadge down the passage," Quinton says. "But when I caught up, it wasn't him after all. But, damn—pardon me, Mrs. Lambert—I was glad to see them."

“You didn’t come back,” Ada says.

“That was my fault,” Leo says. He waves a hand toward the dark stretch of wall where Ada first noticed him. “We have some first-aid supplies and a stretcher in that closet. I thought it made sense to grab them.”

“Howard’s the only one who needs a stretcher,” Editha says.

A train whistle blows in the distance, sounding through the rock. Tom scuffs his bloody boots against the rock.

“I’m sorry,” Morris says to Leo. “I’m so sorry it worked out like this.”

Leo lets out a loud breath. “I’m sorry the man died. I’m sorry for all of it. But all we can do now is go on up and face the music. Get everything sorted.”

He turns his back to them, a clear sign that they should head to the elevator, not that anyone could possibly have any other plan. He’s more pragmatic about this than Ada would have expected, given that there’s no way this disaster will help him sell tickets. He will likely lose his business. He hardly looks like a broken man, though. He looks like a man who wants to get home to his own bed.

Someone behind Ada catches the heel of her boot, and someone else coughs, long and wet.

“There’s not much to sort out,” Hagathorn says, slightly too loud. “You just watched the killer stroll away. He’s home now, packing up. He can head out of town and be gone before the police can stop him.”

Leo faces him, and the rest of them stop, too.

“There’s no reason to have this conversation here,” Leo says, “But I don’t believe Talmadge is a murderer. I’ve known him for too long and never seen a hint of violence.”

"We'll get you back to the hotel as soon as we can," Ruby says, hands clasped neatly in front of her. "You can clean up and get a good meal. And first thing when we get to the top, we'll get you something to quench your thirst."

She's using her hostess voice, and it's effective. The group moves forward again, even Hagathorn. He falls into steps next to Ada, leaning in.

"You don't believe he's innocent," he whispers, his shoulder tapping hers.

There's no reason she needs to believe anything. It no longer matters. She speeds up, but he doesn't let her put more than a couple of inches between them. A few yards in front of them, Leo stands at the door of the elevator, gesturing for them all to come inside. He's draped his suit jacket over his arm. Over her shoulder, Ada sees Editha whispering something to Quinton, touching him on the wrist.

Ada stops, forcing Hagathorn to either pull away or make a point of pausing with her. He sways slightly and then keeps going, lurching unevenly. She watches him go.

"Well?" a voice asks from behind her.

Quinton. As she turns to him, Editha edges past them, aiming for her husband and the elevator.

"Well what?" Ada says.

"You falling for it?" Quinton's arm brushes against hers as he nods toward the mind reader, who's saying something to Tom that goes unacknowledged.

"Are you?" Ada asks.

"The wife, you mean?"

It does not require answering. Ahead of them, Editha has caught up to Hagathorn, matching her pace to his.

"You'd rather I keep my distance?" Quinton says.

Ada will not admit to that, even though she learned with Gerald that if she does not say what she wants, she will likely not get it, but it's stupid to feel jealous of another man's wife and also there's no rule that says she has to bare her soul to Quinton at this exact moment and she'd forgotten how complicated it is to want someone who wants you back.

She can barely remember what it felt like to think him a murderer, but she can still feel the ache of thinking he was dead.

His fingers thread through hers and drift away as the two of them close the gap to the others. She wonders what will happen when they step off the elevator, after they push through the double doors of the lobby and walk past the rosebushes to their cars and homes and wake up to sun and sky. She can see Quinton pulling out a chair at her kitchen table as she fries okra or slices cornbread, and it's strange that she has no idea what he likes to eat, other than macaroni. She can see him pulling down the covers of her bed, but she doesn't know whether he'd want one pillow or two or which side he prefers.

He has a room to himself in her head now. He's moved in with everyone dead and gone.

"The man you said ruined your friend?" she asks.

"Pardon?"

"In Cincinnati. Your friend who owned the bar."

"Emory Webster."

She can hear the pleasure he feels in saying the name. She feels it, sometimes, when she says she's named after her grandmother. *Ada Emily.* Maybe it's one reason Leo wanted to name the waterfall after Ruby: It ensures his days will be full of saying her name.

"You said a flimflam man came to town," she says. "Was Jeremiah the flimflam man?"

"No," he says, his head dipping down toward her. "God, no."

"Alright," she says.

"You were thinking I might have an axe to grind?" he says, sounding nothing but amused. "I bungled it badly, then. We really do need to get you some fresh air if you're starting to think I'm the villain."

They've reached the elevator. Inside the empty car, the single bulb pulses.

It is inconceivable to think of him as a villain, but a man with a stalactite in his throat is also inconceivable and this entire twenty-four hours has been inconceivable. Ada sneaks a glance at the mud-soaked breadth of the man next to her. She has the same choice she had with Gerald, long ago, although murder was not involved. It's the same choice she has with everyone. She can add up all that Quinton says and does, and she can believe him or not. She can trust that even if she does not fully know him—and maybe she can never fully know him—he is who she wants him to be.

She believes him.

Leo's clearly impatient, still waiting with one hand on the accordion door. Quinton gestures for Ada to go first, and she's able to take a deeper breath than she has in a long time as her feet thump against metal. In a minute they'll be in the familiar rooms of Leo's castle, and they can hand over all their worries to the police, and it's surprising how easy it is to let go of thoughts of broken bodies in favor of thoughts of water and soap.

They are quiet, all of them, looking from ceiling to floor to walls. It's hypnotic, steel, after the whole world has been made of rock. The mud flakes off their clothes like sunburned skin, littering the floor.

"Do you think there's lemonade?" Editha asks.

"We can make you some," Ruby says.

Morris says something about sweet tea, and Ada doesn't know how any sane person can want anything other than water. She pictures it splashing from the pitcher to the glass as Leo pulls the door closed behind them, all of them standing closer together than they need to be. Force of habit. As Leo pushes the lever and the cable jerks, Ada gives in to her impulse to lean against Quinton.

Ruby clearly notices.

"That fruit tea that Rachel makes, Tom," Editha says. "Best tea I've ever had."

Ada doesn't remember Editha ever speaking to Tom warmly. It has the feel of a peace offering. The manager pulls off his gloves, jamming them into one pocket. He unfastens his helmet and jerks it loose. It bangs against the wall.

"You know Rachel's moved in with her mother," he says. "Kids, too."

"No, I didn't know," Editha says, looking at Hagathorn.

He's flushed, and if Editha's look is accusing, his is entirely blissful. Maybe his feverishness has only been relief at being close to the finish line.

"Are you going to invite me to dinner?" Quinton asks, close to Ada's ear.

"Yes," she says.

She is, in this moment, fond of everyone in the elevator. For all these hours, they have soaked up the same light and she can still feel the beams stretching between them. Maybe this is how mind reading starts: She's aware of Tom with his concern over spilled wax and Morris with his grief and Editha with her walls, unbreachable, and Quinton—Quinton!—and even Hagathorn, the arrogant fraud, has suffered, too, and everyone in the entire world is hurting—everyone—that seems so clear—they are all battered and filled with holes.

"They'll be waiting in the lobby," Leo says. "So brace yourselves. Reporters and photographers, too. I'll try to shepherd you through to the office, but they're going to have questions, and they'll notice we're missing Mr. Waylander."

"We stay together," Quinton says. "No one wanders off until we get the police, and we need—"

Hagathorn lunges across Leo, yanking the lever to the red slot and blocking the elevator controls with his body. He's timed it well. It takes no more than five seconds for the elevator to stop at the Ruby Falls level, faster than the rest of them can even understand what's happening.

Hagathorn shoves opens the door, and Leo gets a hand on his shoulder, but the mind reader pulls loose and hurtles out of the elevator. Quinton pushes forward, sudden enough that Ada stumbles, but she's not the only body slowing him down.

"I told you I would see it," Hagathorn says from the solid ground of the cavern.

He is vibrating at a higher speed, and the rest of them are unprepared. Ada has spent hours braced for battles of all kinds, but as soon as the elevator door closed, all that was over.

It was over.

And now the man is scuttling—as fast as he can go with those knees—down the winding path toward the falls, a pace that's only possible because of the blasted lightbulbs everywhere. He rounds the first curve and evaporates.

Quinton and Leo have moved the quickest, both of them already on solid ground. They stare down the passageway.

"Well," Ruby says, stepping lightly from the elevator.

"We can leave him be," Morris says, still propped against the metal wall. It takes him two tries to finish his sentence. "Not give him any more attention. You know he can't get out that way."

It's true. The Ruby Falls level is a dead end. Yet the idea of letting Hagathorn roam alone does not sit well with Ada: Why would he stretch this out when they are so close to home? What would he have to gain?

Secret passages, she thinks. The thought has barely taken shape when Editha slips from the elevator, landing between Quinton and Leo. She spins in the direction her husband disappeared, then forward and back again like one of the whirligigs children twist between their palms.

"He's found it," she says.

She heads down the passage, picking up speed as she goes, and Quinton calls her name once, but he doesn't go after her. None of them do.

"They've gotten stranger, the two of them," Ruby says.

Ada can't make herself leave the elevator—she has a notion that if she stays here, the Hagathorns might reappear and the elevator doors will close and all of them will be headed to ground level again. She only needs time to move backward.

"Could he have actually found it?" Leo asks, looking from Morris to Quinton.

Morris doesn't seem to be able to lift his head enough to answer.

"It's hidden on the bottom level," Quinton says. "He passed it twice already. Mrs. Lambert has it right—he's off his gourd, or maybe they both are."

"I don't need a front-row seat this time, no matter what state his gourd is in," Tom says. He hasn't moved from his spot behind Morris. "I vote to leave 'em."

"Seconded," Morris says.

"It's not a choice," Leo says, kindly enough. "I can't count on the reporters missing the elevator opening a second time. And then we step out without Hagathorn? We admit there's been a death, and we left him and his wife down here? No, thank you. It's bad enough that we've lost one man."

"In for a penny, in for a pound," Quinton says, rubbing at his elbow. He turns back to the footpath.

Ada forces herself forward, the metal floor trembling slightly under her feet, and takes her place between Quinton and Ruby. Still inside the elevator, Morris lays a hand on the lever.

"I don't want to be in for a penny or a pound," he says.

"You and I could head up on our own," Tom says. "Tell everybody what happened."

Morris straightens. "The whole city could be down here in five minutes," he says. "They'd listen to me, Leo."

Morris and Tom are so eager to push the lever. Ada can see it on their faces. Of course they're eager. They're ready to step into open spaces without rock walls to stop them, and once they get up top they could walk through those lobby doors and head in any direction at all.

Either of them could slip away for good if they chose. Like Hagathorn said, they could be gone before the police could stop them.

Ada thinks of Morris and his love for Leo and how he has kept his store running by doing whatever needs to be done and she's thought those were entirely good traits but she is no longer sure. She is not sure of anything. She runs her thumb over her ring finger, and all she really knows about Tom is that he has a wife named Rachel and a younger brother who's dead and he possibly hates Hagathorn now more than he ever loved him.

"I could go up with them," Ruby says to Leo, and she has seen plenty of loss, but she has no idea how easily a man can smash through skin and bone.

"Quinton," Ada says.

He's watching her even before she speaks, and when she turns to him she's absurdly, inappropriately joyful: She and Gerald used to meet each other's eyes like this sometimes at his mother's house on Sundays when his sister was letting her children run wild enough to rattle the dishes on the shelves. It is the look of two people who know each other's thoughts.

"We need to keep together," Quinton says. "Like Leo said. No one needs to go up."

"I can't see how it matters at this stage," Morris says, his hand still on the lever. "Aren't you tired of running around after that swindler?"

Will it be a sign, Ada wonders, *if he yanks that switch?*

"I'm telling you," Leo says, and if he's also thinking that either of these men might be a murderer, he's doing a good job of hiding it. "You set foot up there, and the newspapermen are going to make a meal of you."

Morris drops his hand to his side. He and Tom—at geologic speed—leave the elevator.

"Can we just wait here, at least?" Tom says. The blood is completely dried on his face, flaking off in spots. "While you retrieve them?"

Quinton removes his helmet, dropping it to the floor. Ada reaches for hers and remembers that her shoulder still isn't working. She switches hands, unfastening the strap on the second try, and it's some measure of relief.

"They don't want us sneaking onto the elevator once they're gone," Morris says as Ada's helmet hits the ground. "In case one of us did it."

"I'll tell you something odd," Ruby says, well-timed. "Now that the Hagathorns are gone."

She's aiming her wide, dark eyes at Tom, and he focuses on her as if Morris hadn't spoken at all.

"I went over to y'all's hotel tonight," Ruby says, "once it was clear the group was running late. I thought you'd be exhausted, all of you, and I dropped off baskets of bread and butter in your rooms, in case—I don't know—in case. I was tired of milling around here, waiting."

She inches down the pathway as she speaks, and Leo slips into position in front of her. The other men fall in behind them, but Ada can't help but take one more look at the elevator, following the path of the cables up the shaft. Up and up and up. She sends herself there, riding invisible for the length of a blink before she catches up to Quinton at the back of the group.

"I didn't mean to snoop," Ruby is saying, and it's clear to Ada that she absolutely did, "but I saw Mrs. Hagathorn's suitcase, and I couldn't help but look at all the old train tickets and flyers and playbills she's got pasted on it. She's lived a very interesting life."

"Been all over the place," chimes in Leo.

"Her name was on some of the tickets and flyers," Ruby says. "She was in the circus, apparently—but it wasn't always listed as Editha Hagathorn. In a few places, it was Editha Waylander."

As she says the name, she glances toward Tom. Leo, who usually walks at something close to a sprint, has been taking his time. He faces Tom as well, and Ada wonders if the Lamberts have choreographed this conversation.

"Same last name as the reporter," Leo says. "Howard Waylander."

"Editha's name used to be Waylander?" Tom asks.

He is the picture of bafflement. Ada hasn't gotten the sense the man is a good actor, although if he is good, she supposes she wouldn't know he'd been acting. It's possible she only believes his surprise because she shares it. It's not a common name, Waylander. It floats in her head, unhitched, until finally her mind starts turning like she's hand-cranking it in the cold. Her father used to struggle to start the tractor in winter, and once the crank kicked back and nearly broke his jaw, and that's what it's like when she makes sense of what Ruby has said.

She feels like she's been kicked in the head.

"They knew each other," she says. "Howard and Editha. I overheard them. He was hoping she would leave Hagathorn, and she made it clear that she wouldn't. I assumed he'd courted her when they were younger, but it must have been more than courting."

"They were married," Quinton says quietly.

The words hang over them all for a moment, as heavy as if they're made of limestone instead of breath.

"She wasn't married to anyone before Jeremiah," Tom says, with quick shakes of his head that look more like palsy than disagreement.

"You didn't even know her name," Ruby says. "Why would you know about an earlier marriage?"

"Hagathorn said Editha told him she knew Howard," Ada says. "But it didn't sound like he knew about a marriage."

Quinton rubs his palms along his damp pants. "We don't know that Editha divorced the man. We don't know much of anything. She had a former husband who might be a current husband. That's a real fly in the ointment, isn't it? Bound to have riled up the magic man."

"Jeremiah wouldn't have known Howard's surname," Tom says, and now he's back to defending his friend. "Not unless Editha told him. Howard only introduced himself by his first name, which I thought was odd. Not that Jeremiah even noticed."

"I knew Waylander's name," Leo says. "It landed on my desk more than once."

"I handled all the correspondence with Howard and his editors," Tom says. "Jeremiah didn't even remember that the reporter was from the *Chicago Times*. Those aren't the kind of details that interest him."

"So you're the only one who knew Howard's full name," Leo says, friendly as always, but Tom draws back, shaking his head hard enough that his glasses slip.

"She's been Editha Hagathorn as long as I've known her," he says. "I had no idea there was a connection. You think I would agree to let an old beau of Editha's write up this story? It makes sense now, doesn't it? How he treated Jeremiah."

"None of it makes sense," Ruby says.

They have barely covered any ground. Ada leans against the nearest wall before remembering that it's damp, and it's a struggle to right herself again. The Hagathorns could be halfway to the falls by now, and the addition of a secret husband does not make their destination any more logical.

"Quinton," Ada says. "Leo. Can the two of them get out? Are we sure there aren't any offshoots that lead to the outside?"

"None," Leo says immediately. "I've been down every one of the offshoots, and they all peter out. The elevator is the only way out of the mountain from here."

"I don't know if Hagathorn would be sure of that," Quinton says. "It could be he was desperate—we were about to head to the police. Maybe he thought it was worth a shot."

The rain has left its mark here, too, the water overflowing the pavement, puddling and pooling. It's seeping closer and closer to their boots. Ada thinks of Hagathorn as he danced out of the elevator; he did not look like a man out of options. He looked like a man headed to the bank to cash a big check.

"He seemed pretty happy," she says.

"So he's finally flipped," Quinton says, "and she's flipped, too. Or they're trying to outrun their sins. Take your pick. The only other choice is that his crystal ball has finally turned up the hatpin, which we know is at least three miles away through solid rock."

Ada sees something on Morris's face. She doesn't like it.

"Morris," she says. "That's right, isn't it?"

"It's hard to imagine he'd find it even if we'd hidden it up his backside," he answers, licking his chapped lips.

His wording does not comfort Ada, and Leo apparently feels the same.

"So Hagathorn isn't going to find anything?" Leo prompts.

Morris looks to the ground, where the standing water has overtaken his boot. He does not move his foot.

"There's a chance," he says.

"You're not making sense," Quinton says. He looks braced for impact. "Say it plain, whatever it is."

Morris looks to Leo. "Talmadge hid the hatpin down below. Exactly like I said."

"You said it that way earlier," Ada says. "That Talmadge hid it. As if you didn't."

"Yeah," Morris says. He's still looking only at Leo. "Talmadge hid it at the little waterfall below. I had a bad spell and couldn't go through one of the tight spots, so I sat and waited while he went and took care of it. No harm in that. It didn't change anything. He told me where he put it and told me what to picture—the water spraying, clay walls behind it—and that's what I did, and none of it"—he clears his throat—"none of it was any different than if we'd hidden the thing together. Even if I'd stuck the pin in the wall myself, I wouldn't have been able to guide Hagathorn there, not that I should've helped him along with his fakery. Leo, the man is unbearable."

"Finish it," Leo says.

"It's while I was by myself," Morris says. "I got to thinking: Why not have a backup?"

His tongue smacks against the roof of his mouth. He opens his mouth several times before he can get the rest out, and just watching him makes Ada thirstier.

"The pin could roll off," he says. "It could fall down a crack or into the water and be gone for good. Talmadge might forget where he put it—who knew what could happen? There was no need to leave everything to chance. I'd brought two pins anyway, in case we lost one. Like I said, a backup."

Quinton strips off his gloves and runs a hand over his hair. A scattering of small pebbles bounces from his shoulder to the ground.

"There are two hatpins," he says. "Lord, Morris, don't tell me."

Morris keeps flopping his tongue around his mouth. "I hid the second one at Ruby Falls. But Hagathorn already passed it once, no more sensitive than a stump."

"We never talked about that, Morris," Leo says. "There shouldn't have been two."

He does not seem angry or disappointed, though. He seems hopeful, and Ada suspects he's forgotten that finding the hatpin won't erase the dead man.

"Well, no point in talking about it now," Ruby says. "There are two."

Ada agrees completely. They have talked plenty. Quinton tosses his gloves to the ground. He paces, two steps to the right and two to the left.

"Blast it," he says.

He and Leo exchange the quickest of glances and then they're moving immediately. It takes the rest of them a few seconds longer to get their legs operating.

"For God's sake," Quinton mutters as they make their way down the footpath. "Y'all must have stared straight at the thing not half an hour after you got off the elevator!"

"You'd have to get the right angle," Morris says. He's at the back, struggling to keep up. "It's not visible from the main path. I didn't want him to find it then. It would have been too soon, no drama at all, and I did want Talmadge's plan to work. This one up here was only in case—in case things went poorly."

Ada steps over a flattened cigarette butt, another sign of the real world. She's not sure whether its closeness makes her feel better or worse. Worse, she thinks. She's colder now, after standing still for so long.

"He said the two of you were pulling him in different directions," Tom says. "And you were."

"Don't start that," Quinton says. "He's still a fraud."

"Is he?" asks Leo, who's looking less exhausted by the minute.

"Yes," Ada and Morris say at the same time.

She expects Tom to argue, but he's looking straight ahead as if he can't hear them.

"Did Talmadge know?" Quinton asks. "About the second pin?"

Morris has finally managed to get his gloves off, and they're dangling from his pocket. He's focused on the ground in front of him.

"No," he says. "He was dead set on putting it further into the caverns, and I didn't want him to think I didn't trust him. I did. He did a fine job of planning it all, too"—he says this to Leo—"and I didn't want to take away from that. So I came down in the morning before we had the big send-off, and I stuck it behind the falls."

"You weren't afraid you'd have another spell?" Tom asks, not particularly kindly.

"It's only when it shrinks down to gopher holes that I have trouble breathing," Morris says. "I've more than kept up with you, haven't I? It made so much sense. We had everything invested in this—time, money, thought, hope—and I wanted insurance."

They're crossing a footpath, and their boots sound like a train juddering over rails.

"When things did go poorly," Quinton says, "you didn't steer Hagathorn here."

"No," Morris says. "I didn't."

"But he's found his way here anyway," Tom says, eyes still straight ahead.

"Still raises the question of why he didn't find it yesterday morning," Quinton says. "With all his mystic power."

Overhead, delicate spikes drip from the ceiling in a shimmer of silver, and Ada doubts she'll ever see another stalactite without thinking of blood. Ruby's heels are clicking along; she has bad footwear but well-rested legs. She's easily keeping up with Quinton and Leo on the wide, well-lit path. Ada is hypnotized by the clack-clack of the other woman's shining feet, which seem to barely be touching the ground. Her own feet have disconnected from her entirely, and she decides to trust them. They carry her along, sufficient.

She expected to have the Hagathorns in sight by now, but she's lost track of time. There's no telling how much of a head start the couple had—two minutes? fifteen? She's not sure how quickly they were moving, and she's not sure whether the mind reader was heading to the waterfall or some other destination entirely.

Has he done it? Has he plucked the answer from thin air?

Peter Piper picked a pluck.

Peter Pepper piped a pick.

If Peter Pepper plucked a pick of pickled pipers, how many pickled pipers did Peter Pepper pluck?

It's all twisting, incoherent. She believes nothing and everything. She sees the mind reader at the waterfall, holding a dripping hatpin, and he's also tucked away in a hidey-hole with a jagged rock in his hand, waiting for them, and if there's one thing Ada's learned, it's that you have no idea about the crooks and crevices inside a person. If the professor and his wife plotted together to kill Howard, it could be pragmatic to lure the rest of them down this corridor. They could get rid of every witness to the murder in one fell swoop.

They're passing through the Hall of Dreams, with gaps above and below the footpath that are large enough to conceal a person, but the Hagathorns wouldn't know that, would they? They wouldn't have had a chance to learn the hiding places along this passage, not unless they paid unusually close attention on that first day, and even if they did, Jeremiah Hagathorn is in no condition to clamber up a slope.

Picked a pluck.

Piped a pickle.

Not unless his strategy has been more complicated than any of them have guessed. The man has been moving like an old arthritic, and his pants are covered in blood, but Ada has no proof his pain is real.

"He's moving faster than I would expect," she says. She doesn't recognize her own voice, cracking and hoarse. "For someone hurt bad."

"You asking if he could be faking?" Quinton says. "He bloodied his knees, for sure. But everyone could be lying. That's the truth. Everyone could be lying about everything."

Ada hums her agreement even as she decides he's not entirely right. It has limits, the lying. There should be logic behind it. An ambush wouldn't be of much benefit, really. The Hagathorns would step off the elevator and have to explain all the dead bodies.

She stares at the soda straws overhead, which are more delicate than she remembers—slender tubes that look like they would fall and shatter if you blew on them hard enough. There are hundreds of them, and she imagines them dropping, one by one, slicing through fabric and skin.

"You alright back there?" Ruby calls, turning toward Ada, eyebrows winging down.

"Good," Ada says.

Still, if anyone could come up with a good story, it's the Hagathorns. There is Talmadge, after all, who's been their story all along. They've written the beginning and only need an end.

Drip, drip, drip, go her thoughts, sediment piling up, a shape forming.

Quinton is taking in the walls and ceilings of the cavern, just as she is. He keeps his eyes on every curve as they approach. Leo has pulled Ruby to his side, one arm hovering at her back, and he's not sure what's waiting for them, either. Morris and Tom are muttering back and forth, and Ada leaves the talking to them. Thinking is easier and safer—thoughts aren't binding. They don't become real unless someone else hears them.

She steps in a puddle deep enough that it reaches the laces of her boots. The wall to her left is split by a seam of sandstone.

Talmadge still makes a certain amount of sense as a killer. He snuck out of the castle without a word to Leo, never mind the murdered man at the bottom of the caves. She can't figure out why he'd kill a man, though. If he wanted to save his job, he must have known that a dead body wouldn't be the way to salvage the expedition or Ruby Falls. The murder only made a bigger mess of things.

Howard, Howard, Howard, soaking the limestone red.

The mind reader saves his career—and keeps his wife—by killing him. Tom saves his own career, and he saves Jeremiah, which—at least until recently—he was eager to do. Editha protects her husband—her second one—and gets rid of a man who didn't want to take no for an answer. Morris protects Leo and Ruby Falls.

Peter Pecker pricked a puck of peckled paupers. Above them, helictites curl like pigs' tails from the ceiling. A broom of flowstone hangs over the path.

Ada gets nothing out of Howard's death, and neither does Quinton.

I bungled it badly, then, Quinton said at the elevator when she asked whether Hagathorn had been the con man in Cincinnati, and, yes, if he set out to kill a person, he would surely accomplish the task. They are two completely different failings, violence and incompetence.

She thinks of Quinton's sympathy for pigs and his grace in a rocking chair and the way he recites minerals and the breadth of his chest. She lets herself consider that if Jeremiah Hagathorn did cheat that bar owner in Cincinnati, someone might unearth the connection to Quinton if the mind reader was murdered. But Quinton had no connection at all to the newspaperman. It's Hagathorn who has his career at stake and who's volatile enough to pull a razor on a man. If Talmadge hadn't disappeared, Hagathorn would be the most likely person to be arrested, and the electric chair would be a very competent sort of revenge.

White calcium spills down the wall, and the sound of the falls grows louder. Maybe her ears have altered by geology or pressure, because the water is deafening, so loud it makes Ada's shoulders draw up.

"Where's Morris?" Leo asks.

Leo, who knows these passages as well as anyone. Who mapped them and can come and go down here anytime he likes.

"Not sure," Tom answers, barely audible over the falls. "I figured he took a rest."

It takes Ada a moment to make the world outside of her head come into focus as clearly as the one inside it. She's sped up at some point, overtaking Leo and Ruby at the front of the group. She turns to face the others, and, sure enough, Morris is nowhere in sight. She's lost track of everyone for dozens of steps—an up-and-down of limestone—and anything could have happened behind her back.

"Took a rest?" Quinton asks, sidestepping back down the path to join Tom at the back of the group.

The air is wetter here, although Ada might be hallucinating the dampness. She might be hallucinating everything.

"He was here until a minute ago," Tom says, as if minutes still exist.

"You noticed he was gone and you just kept walking?" Ruby asks.

Tom smiles. It's strange that anyone would smile now. It's strange that he would leave Morris back there without a word. It's strange that Quinton wouldn't notice.

"All of you kept on walking, too," Tom says.

His jacket is ripped from his shoulder to his elbow. Maybe it's been ripped for hours. They are no more than a hundred feet from the falls. The Hagathorns must be there. It feels as if answers must be there.

"I'll check," Quinton says, his eyes on Ada.

His eyes are often on her, and she loves that, normally, if normally can apply to anything down here, but she hopes his attention hasn't been too focused. She can tell he's reluctant to leave her, and she'd rather it be because he's worried about killers than because he's guessed what's been circling through her head.

"Go on," she says to him.

As he turns his back on them all, Ruby shuffles closer to Ada, watching her feet on the slick pavement. She, too, looks worried, her hand landing briefly on Ada's shoulder, and Ada wonders what the others are seeing when they look at her face.

Leo drifts next to her, too, and he's gotten rid of his suit jacket somewhere along the way. He puts a hand under Ada's elbow as they all step into Solomon's Temple, the ceiling soaring over their heads. It's different without the crowds. With Leo next to her—she gently pulls loose from his hand—she can believe she's standing by him years ago when he entered this place for the first time. The ground is soaked, and her boots slip and she's had a lifetime of one shrinking space dead-ending into another shrinking space—cattle chutes—and now she's staring at this immense expanse, so tall that the top of the cavern is cloud height, but it's solid. She inhales the freedom of it.

She will float up. She will take it all.

The water is so loud. It makes her head throb, but if you did hear the voice of God, it would be painful, wouldn't it? It couldn't only be beautiful.

She outdistances the others: The waterfall is straight in front of her, rushing and pouring and splattering. She'd forgotten how tall it is, and the sound of it makes it larger. Ruby deserves this beautiful thing, unearthly, but the water doesn't move Ada. It is not the picture but the frame. The walls rise on either side of the falls, incalculable. Even when she cranes her neck, she cannot see the top. The great gaping spaces turn the falls into something holy.

It's an architecture, unfathomable.

Somehow Quinton is next to her again. She hopes no one else is dead. She still cannot feel her feet, and as she lifts an arm to steady herself, her shoulder doesn't cooperate, but it doesn't matter.

It is so big. All of it is so big.

She's unsurprised to see Hagathorn several yards in front of her, getting drenched by the spray from the falls. He's beyond the sign that says VISITORS NOT ALLOWED, and he's lucky he made it across the wet rocks without falling into the water. Editha is standing at the railing on the near side of the falls, her back to Ada.

As Ada watches, the other woman extends her right leg, waist-high, dropping her small, booted foot onto the handrail. She leans toward it, stretching, her body one smooth curve until she lowers her foot back to the ground. In all of human history, Ada thinks, surely no one has ever performed that particular motion at that particular spot.

She's light-headed, so she widens her feet. You can stay conscious if you want it badly enough. She sees the arc of Editha's arm and at the same time she sees Quinton spanning the canyon hours ago, his hands clasping Tom, pulling him up. She's traveled back to look down on them as they stood on that ledge, precarious, and she thinks of how easily they bleed and how their eyes shine in the light. She thinks of their feet that keep plodding along and she thinks of their accumulated dead—wives, parents, brothers, husbands, babies—and one of them has killed a man, sure, but every person in the world is more astonishing than this waterfall. She sees that. They are, each one of them, a mountain with a thousand rooms inside, some unmappable, and they are not all pleasant, but, God, what creations they are.

She thinks she might be hearing a voice, but, no, she is seeing, not hearing. Does the voice of God not have words? Because what she sees now is Hagathorn in a different room. He's standing above Howard with a stalactite in his hand.

He killed him.

She knows it with the suddenness of a plunge off a ledge, not the accumulated steps of a climb. It is something beyond logic. She can paper over her conviction with reasons, but those reasons are more the measure of the man than anything a policeman—or a newspaperman—might write in a notebook: Hagathorn believes in not God's will but his own. He will bloody his own body for the sake of headlines. He cares for himself above all others.

If a voice were actually speaking to her, this is what it would say: Sometimes people are exactly who they seem to be. Sometimes the sum of their actions and words captures them exactly.

She's not dizzy anymore. She heads for the waterfall, Quinton next to her, and when she looks over her shoulder, Tom, Ruby, and Leo are following. Morris is slumped on the ground of Solomon's Temple, head resting against the wall. He's not attempting to stand.

"Come on, then," Hagathorn calls, giddy. "You took longer than I thought. Mr. and Mrs. Lambert! I'm delighted you could join us!"

His voice is barely carrying over the water, and his bare fingers are playing through the falls. His arm is buffeted up and down by the pressure as Ada, Quinton, and Tom reach the closest railing.

They stop next to Editha, who doesn't acknowledge them. Her eyes are on her husband. Near his head, two bright bulbs dangle low, spotlighting the water. The rise and fall of his arm is like a conductor keeping time.

"You wouldn't have had a ladder," he's saying, as if all this were planned. As if they are entirely on schedule and have bought tickets to the show. "So it couldn't be more than head-high, unless you're a climber."

He's looking past them, focusing on Morris.

"You're not a climber," Hagathorn finishes. He waits, but not for long. "But you know what sort of image appeals, don't you? I'll give you that. You wanted a love story. The sugar and spice and everything niceness of it. It came to me when you were telling us about your willow tree, floated right in front of me like a dandelion seed. By the time we got to the elevator, I was terrified, frankly, that you'd give it away and steal the moment from me."

Ada studies Morris propped against the wall. He's too far away for her to tell anything from his expression, and his arms are wrapped tight around himself. If it weren't for the rise and fall of his chest, she'd worry.

"People are suckers for love stories," Hagathorn says. "You're not wrong. It'll play in the papers."

He reaches further, his entire arm disappearing into the falls. He pulls back and adjusts one leg on the rock. He lunges.

The force of the water batters his helmet, sheering off in every direction. He is covered by the water for ten, twenty, thirty seconds, long enough that Leo starts forward, but then Hagathorn is backing up, running a forearm across his eyes. He sways a moment, blinking, and staggers to dryer ground.

He lifts his bare hand, and the hatpin is in it. The shining silver stick catches the light as he twists his wrist.

"See now?" Hagathorn says. "Didn't I tell you? I blame the delay on strain and exhaustion, and the fact that you and the murderer broke the terms of the arrangement, Morris. I assume you didn't outright lie to me. Talmadge did hide a pin down below?"

He's talking as if he hasn't noticed that the other man is barely conscious. Morris doesn't answer.

"You can't hold two images in your head at once," Hagathorn says. "It's like trying to turn to two radio stations."

"You walked past the other pin twice," Quinton says.

"Morris wanted me to find this one," the mind reader says, vibrating still. "Ask him. I could feel it."

"Thank you for explaining the science," Quinton says. "When we get aboveground, we'll confirm that it's the same hatpin."

Hagathorn laughs, stepping onto a higher rock. His knees don't seem to be bothering him anymore.

"You still think I'm a swindler?" he asks. "That I'd bring an extra hatpin?"

"Of course it's the right pin," Editha says.

She lifts her left leg onto the railing, arching toward it. Hagathorn is still talking. He may never stop.

"I've told you," he says. "It's not a trick. It's a gift. And it's all the sweeter, isn't it? After the delay?"

"After the dead man," Quinton says, shaking his head. "Let's go, Mr. Hagathorn. You've got your pin."

"It's past time to go," agrees Leo.

Now that he's staring at Hagathorn with the pin in his hand—which is all he ever wanted out of this disaster—Leo's not vibrating at all. Ada can see no trace of happiness or excitement in him. She might see revulsion.

Hagathorn steps from one rock to another, making no effort to come closer. He is disappointed by their reaction.

"Don't you want to get aboveground where everyone will hoot and holler?" Quinton calls.

How many people in the room hate this man? Is his wife one of them? Has she been watching so closely because she wants him to offer up the hatpin or because she wants him to bash his brains on a rock?

"It is a gift," Ada says. "No question."

Hagathorn advances one more step, dawdling. He's on a stretch of uneven rock that slopes down to the dark water under the falls, and he sways before he finds his footing. He nods at her, accepting his due.

"It's a shame there isn't anyone to record it," she says.

"There'll be people happy to write it all down," Hagathorn says, inching toward them. The rocks are shining with water, and the pool is higher than usual after the rain.

"It's still a shame, though," Ada says. "Howard could have captured the whole thing. It would have been better."

Hagathorn only navigates another rock. He has at least a dozen more to cross before he makes it onto the footpath.

"To have his account of nearly a full day down here," Ada goes on. "Our supplies used up, down to our final flashlight—it would have been national news. International, like Shackleton surviving the Antarctic."

Hagathorn looks from her to the rocks and back again. She's confusing him. He's not used to her talking so much. He's not used to anyone but him talking so much, maybe.

"I imagine you're sorry," she says.

"Pardon?" he says.

"That you killed him."

That stops him. He's still holding the hatpin in his wet fingers. If he were as smart as he thinks, he'd put the pin in his pocket and use both hands for balance.

"I didn't touch the man," he says.

"You did."

"And why do you think that?"

"I plucked it out of the air," she says, and what a joy it is to say it, like hitting the perfect note in a harmony.

"You're crazy."

She smiles wide because she enjoys the uncertainty on his face. She watches only him, although she's aware that Quinton has moved to the gap between footpath and rocks. He's within a few yards of Hagathorn, who's stretched between two slick boulders, close enough that Ada can see his wet pants sticking to his skin.

"Ada," Leo is whispering, caution in his voice. Ruby, next to him, only listens.

"You said you slept a few inches away from him," Ada says. "You'd have felt him jerk or shudder, surely."

"I was asleep," Hagathorn answers.

"You didn't have any reaction at all when we found him," she says. "You weren't surprised. You weren't horrified. I don't think you felt much at all."

Hagathorn shakes his head, and his foot slips slightly. "You're still talking crazy."

"You don't care," she says. "You want a thing, you take it."

"I care," he says, and he's looking at his wife.

"I wonder," Ada says.

He has made them listen to him for all these hours. He has kept talking and pushing and it has worked. They are still down here, still catering to him. But now she will make him listen. She will keep pushing, and is that all life is? A contest of who can push the hardest?

It's stayed sharp in her head, the picture of Hagathorn standing over Howard in the darkness, not that the lack of light made any difference to him. Even if he'd been looking straight into the man's eyes when he killed him, he wouldn't have felt a thing.

She lingers over the thought of Howard, the stillness and emptiness of him. She thinks of her baby in her arms and Gerald on that hospital cot and her mother tucked under the bedsheets. Her father and grandfather, too. Death—there is always death—and it would be nice to believe that it followed rules. It would be nice to impose some tidiness on it, to untangle it and know it and take it in hand and shackle it and push it back.

Her ears are filled by the rushing of water, the sound winding through her.

She can take this death in hand.

No.

She can't.

Death is a voice in her head and a sky made of rock and it's grief—not an emptiness but a vastness—and of course she cannot shackle it. A man, though, is a different story.

"You killed him," she says again.

Hagathorn shakes his head, trying a laugh. He hasn't moved since she accused him, and he's still suspended between the two rocks. She has not moved, either, and it comes to her that all she has to do is never move. She will stand here in front of him and she will give no ground and she will keep talking.

He cannot make her stop.

"I know it," she says. "Do you understand? I know."

She can hear the certainty in her own voice. She is not the only one.

"Jeremiah," Editha says, and at the sound of her voice Hagathorn looks rattled for the first time.

"You were jealous of him, I assume," Ada says. She will wear him down. "We know your wife and Howard used to be married. Were they still married? Was that it? Regardless, he still loved her, didn't he, and from that angle, why wouldn't you have killed him? He was going to end your career and maybe take back his wife. Did you think one would lead to the other? He'd ruin you, and then—"

"Wait," Editha interrupts. "No. You think Howard was my husband?"

"We saw the name on those old flyers on your luggage," Ruby says, unapologetic. "Editha Waylander. Howard Waylander. We know."

While Editha looks stunned, Hagathorn gives no reaction to the information. Ada has no doubt that he knew.

"He was my brother," Editha says.

The entire room goes silent other than the rush of the falls. Even the water seems to exhale, long and sad.

"He was four when I left home," she says, matter-of-factly. "I hadn't seen him since. And you thought that, too, Jeremiah? You thought I'd been married to him? I told you he was essentially a stranger."

"And I believed you," Hagathorn says. "I had no notion of any relationship between the two of you. But why would you not tell me who he was?"

He does a fine job of sounding aggrieved. Editha runs a hand over her dusty forehead.

"Why does it matter?" she says.

"If there was nothing to hide—"

"Don't," Editha says, and she doesn't sound matter-of-fact at all. "Don't. You needed to concentrate, Jeremiah. I thought, at first, that it might be a boon that my brother was the reporter. I thought he'd be eager to please. I was going to give you the twelve damn hours, and then I'd have told you about Howard when it wouldn't have distracted you from your job, and why would I have thought that, I wonder? That he might distract you? That he might throw you off course? How was I to know you'd think I'd married him? Married him! Why would you think it? And if you thought it, why would *you* have kept it from *me*? God, Miah."

She is rocking back and forth slightly.

"You don't know your wife's family?" Ruby asks Hagathorn.

"No," Editha answers for him.

"We don't have family," he says. "Either of us."

Ruby exchanges a look with her husband, and Editha clearly notices. She lifts one shoulder as she threads her fingers together. Her bare hands are pale.

"That part of life was done," she says. "The way I grew up. Those people. I left that house behind me, and it's no part of me anymore."

Ruby frowns. "Howard was four, you said, when you left," she says gently. "He can't have been part of any unpleasantness."

"'Unpleasantness,'" repeats Editha. "That's a polite word, Mrs. Lambert. I don't know how else to say it: If I let him in, I'd get all the rest of it, too. And you know that, Miah. You know I shut the door on everything and you know what you are to me and you thought I was married?"

It doesn't work the way you think, Ada wants to say. She doesn't believe it's possible to shut the door on ghosts—they always find a way. They will show up in a hotel with a notebook in hand if necessary.

"I didn't," Hagathorn says, emphatic. "I didn't think anything at all about him. I'd have had no way of knowing. I never heard the man's last name. You must know that."

"I mentioned his name," Tom says.

"You didn't," snaps Hagathorn.

"Back at the hotel during that game of Tonk," Tom says. "I've been trying to convince myself I didn't, but I remember your expression, Jeremiah. You recognized the last name."

Ada keeps all her attention on Hagathorn. He takes a breath or maybe two before he looks at his wife. Whatever she sees does not reassure her.

"No," Editha says, pushing away from the railing. She's a blur of movement from the corner of Ada's eye. "No."

"This is insane," Hagathorn says. "Editha, it's crazy, what this woman is saying. You know it is."

"It can be crazy and still be true," Editha says.

"It isn't," he says, and his giddiness has evaporated. He is all desperation.

Ada spares a glance at Editha, who's gone still again, hands clasped. Her heels are touching each other, like a ballet pose.

"You think I can't tell when you're lying, Miah?" she says.

"I'm not," he says.

It does not take mind reading to tell that he is. Ada has no idea whether the others see it as clearly as she does, but he is not a good actor in this moment. He's worried about Editha, though, not about Ada or Leo or the police who are somewhere above them.

He was not lying, Ada supposes, when he said he cared about something other than himself.

"You are a liar," Ada says. Her voice is calm and her feet are steady. "You killed him and we all know it. We know it, do you hear me?"

"Shut your mouth," Hagathorn says. "Just shut your goddamn mouth."

He's looking at Ada like he hates her, and she's not sure anyone has ever hated her before. Or maybe it's fear, not hate. She does not think anyone has ever been afraid of her, either.

"Did you think I'd leave, Miah?" Editha says. "Are we back to that?"

If a person is full of nooks and caverns, what tunnels are under the surface of a marriage? Ada has a feeling she will never have any idea what's between these two people.

"Listen to me," Hagathorn starts, holding a hand over the water.

Ada hopes he will confess. She hopes he will explain everything, but instead his foot slips, and he slides toward the water. He grabs at the rock behind him, but it's as slick as everything else, and he picks up momentum, leaving the ground for a moment before he lands in the middle of the pool. It is slow and fast, and they have all the time in the world to reach for him and none at all.

For a moment, only Hagathorn's helmet shows. He bobs up, arms flailing, and he doesn't call for help, but it's clear he needs it. He makes sounds, not entirely human, likely the best he can do with his mouth full of water.

Editha or Tom could duck under the railing. He's not within easy reach, but—maybe—if they tried.

"He can't swim," Editha says, unmoving.

Talmadge would have a rope in his backpack, Ada thinks. Quinton surely has one, too, but he's only standing there, as is Leo.

Ada takes a single step toward him, not rushing, although she doesn't want this man to die. She would like his head to go under again. She would like him to swallow another throatful of water, and she would like to see the fear on his face one more time. She wants him to realize that they are real enough to save him—real enough to kill him—which one counts more?—and she wants him to know what it feels like to have someone else decide that you are going to die.

He's underwater again, only his fingers sticking up. Well-shaped, those fingers that killed a person. His wedding ring is silver.

"Stand up," Leo says, and then louder: "Stand up."

Ada doesn't understand at first.

"It's not quite six feet," Quinton says. "He just needs to tilt his head back."

Hagathorn is up—an inhale and a gargle—the sound of Listerine—and he's under again. His helmet must be buckled well.

Maybe he can't stand up. Maybe his knees are shattered after all or maybe he doesn't think he's worth saving or maybe he thinks it's all finished, but he's wrong, Ada knows, because it's never finished, not entirely. You kick and you flail. You choke on water and you don't know if you can touch and maybe you've done this to yourself or maybe it's God's will—maybe—maybe—

"Stand up, you fool," Leo says, and he's leaning toward the pool as if he might jump in wearing his Sunday clothes.

Hagathorn gets his feet under him. His head bobs up and he sucks in air and then goes under again. He comes up for another breath, pushing forward. He sinks once more, but he's found some forward momentum, and he gets to the edge of the pool. He slaps a hand onto the stone rim, his head above water.

He grips the rock tightly enough that his fingers will likely bleed, twisting his head one way and then the other. He seems more frantic, not less.

He's looking for Editha, Ada realizes, and he can't find her.

Ada can't, either. Not at first. His wife isn't at the railing. She's nowhere near the water. She has not stayed to see whether her husband lives or dies.

Ada only spots her when she turns toward the exit. The overhead bulbs highlight the mind reader's wife kneeling next to Morris, and he's nodding slowly. Editha stands, offering him her hand, and when he lurches to his feet, she steers him toward the footpath. She doesn't look back.

September 23, 1932

Quinton knocks on the front door, and Ada makes herself hold still instead of rushing toward him. She has been watching from the window while trying not to watch from the window. His collar is buttoned. He's holding something, although he sticks his hand behind his back quick enough that she can't get a look at it.

Flowers, *she thinks.* Small ones, maybe violets.

She has spaghetti cooking. He said he likes mushrooms, and he doesn't mind that there's no meat and she's made tea cakes for dessert and it has been so long since she has done this.

She has never done this. The last time a man showed up with flowers, she lived with her parents. Her waist was twenty-eight inches, and she planned to name her first son after her grandfather.

She's found herself watching out the window plenty these past days. They are, all of them, readjusting to life aboveground. Talmadge and Leo hunkered down for more than one talk, according to Ruby. Editha didn't lie—Talmadge had been waiting for them as they neared the elevator, making sure all was well, and that softened how Leo viewed his desertion. He'll likely be allowed to go back to guiding tours, just the normal in-and-outs. Hagathorn will go to trial, and there's no way to know how that will turn out, since it's not as if the voice of God is admissible in a courtroom. If he denies everything, he may convince a jury.

Ada doesn't think about him much.

She thinks of Editha. It's not easy to expect one life and get another. She hopes the other woman can see how the choices are still unfolding in front of her, so many decades to come, all manner of angles. She supposes, too, that Editha knows plenty about moving forward. Even her brother's death did not soften her toward him. She did not stay to handle his arrangements, and Ada has also been thinking of Howard and how it was only this morning that a gray-haired woman arrived on the train to collect his body. His landlady, according to Ruby, which made Ada remember that Howard said a landlady loaned him the jacket he was wearing. From across the street, Ada watched the woman come out of the hotel in a perfectly ironed skirt, and now she keeps picturing that old woman hunched over an ironing board, focused on pleats, getting all dressed up to bring home a dead man who didn't have anyone else and maybe she didn't have anyone else, either.

Maybe it never happened. Maybe the woman pays someone to do her ironing. Ada's always been good at seeing what's not there—she knows this about herself, but she's getting better at seeing what's in front of her.

A spill of iron oxide. A blind crayfish. A collared shirt on a man who never wears a collar.

She's smoothing her dress when Quinton knocks again. She opens the door, and she smiles not because she intends to but because she can't help it. He's clean-shaven—she's not sure how she feels about that—and he's pulling his hand from behind his back.

He has not brought flowers. He has bones in his hands. The tiny skeleton of a frog, intricate and whole. She catches her breath because he has somehow managed to carry this here unbroken. She has a vision of her windowsill someday filled with bones, skulls and spines of countless small creatures, a testament to love and watchfulness.

"Come in," she says, and when he slides the frog into her palm, the bones are still warm from the heat of his hand.

Acknowledgments

From the first time I visited Ruby Falls, I've wanted to set a novel there. The play of light and shadow, the vastness of the rock and the shine of the water—it's a universe completely, magically separate from life aboveground. I also had a lot of fun crawling and twisting through the caves around Lookout Mountain, and Ada's joy in the caverns is absolutely anchored by my own. The world of this novel—aboveground and below—would never have come to life without the help of all the experts at Ruby Falls. I'm very grateful to Lara Caughman, Hollie Baranick, Bob White, and Drew Thackston. Aside from these living, breathing experts, H. J. Burlingame's *How to Read People's Minds* got me in the head of a con artist—plus gave me some party tricks—and both Ed Brinkley's *The History of Ruby Falls* and the Ruby Falls volume of Images of Modern America helped paint a clearer, deeper picture of the caves.

An important note: While I've tried to be faithful to the real-life story of Leo and Ruby Lambert and the history of Ruby Falls, no psychic ever launched himself after a hatpin in these particular caverns. No newspaperman was ever murdered. I came up with the idea for Jeremiah Hagathorn when I was reading the memoirs of Katie Stabler, the first woman to give tours in South Dakota's Wind Cave. While Stabler was working in the caves in 1893, she played a part in an attempt by a "clairvoyant" and "professor" named Paul Alexander Johnstone to locate a golden scarf pin in ninety miles of caverns—while blindfolded. He and his party disappeared for three days, and when he finally made it out, he was delirious, bleeding from the head . . . and holding the pin. According to Stabler, she was following the party the whole time, keeping the men supplied even as they pretended they were lost and abandoned. (You can find her memoirs online through the National Park Service website, and you can read all about Johnstone's expedition in "A Mind Reader, a Pin Head, and a Fool: The Story of 'Professor' Johnstone's Visit to Wind Cave" by Tom Farrell.)

The falls level of the caverns in these pages mirrors the real-life passage still open to tourists today at Ruby Falls. I've only added a single cave flower. Any other unintentional differences are my fault and no one else's. I did, however, take liberties with the lower level of Lookout Mountain caves, which were closed to the public in 1998. Although they do include six miles of mapped passages, those passages are tighter and damper than the passages Ada and the others explore in their hunt for the hatpin. Ada's room of crystals, for instance, does not exist in real life. But if you want to have a great time—and if you aren't claustrophobic—you can explore caves very much like the ones in this story on one of the excellent tours at Raccoon Mountain in Chattanooga.

Thank you to Joe Brosnan, who loved Ada from the beginning and made the novel better with every step. I so appreciate everyone at Grove Atlantic and Atlantic Crime for launching *Ruby Falls* into the world. Thanks to my agent, Kim Witherspoon. Thanks to Walter Smith for getting the ball rolling, Toni Burns Busot for a sharp-eyed read-through, and Rebecca Waylander, whose last name I've used both because I like it and because she's a teacher who deserves to have her name carved somewhere. Thank you to Fisher Humphries, who teaches one hell of a Sunday school class. His thoughts on God and humans have surely seeped into these pages, particularly during Ada's epiphany at the falls. Thank you to Ariel Lawhon, whose *The Frozen River* helped me to see Ada even more clearly. Thank you to Fred, as always. If you want to make a go of this whole novelist thing, I highly suggest you find your smartest, most thoughtful, most appreciative reader and marry him.